DEADLY
ATTRACTION

A SCVC Taskforce novel

MISTY EVANS

ROMANTIC SUSPENSE AND MYSTERIES BY MISTY EVANS

The Super Agent Series
Operation Sheba
Operation Paris
Operation Proof of Life
The Blood Code
The Perfect Hostage, A Super Agent Novella

The Deadly Series
Deadly Pursuit
Deadly Deception
Deadly Force
Deadly Intent
Deadly Affair, A SCVC Taskforce novella
Deadly Attraction

Shadow Force International Series
Fatal Truth
Fatal Honor
Fatal Courage
Fatal Love

The Justice Team Series (with Adrienne Giordano)
Stealing Justice
Cheating Justice
Holiday Justice
Exposing Justice

Undercover Justice
Protecting Justice
Missing Justice

The Secret Ingredient Culinary Mystery Series
The Secret Ingredient, A Culinary Romantic Mystery with Bonus Recipes
The Secret Life of Cranberry Sauce, A Secret Ingredient Holiday Novella

ACKNOWLEDGMENTS

This story came to me a while ago, I just didn't have time to write it. Mitch and Emma needed time to percolate in my imagination, both of them working through their respective grief.

Grief is a funny thing, as Emma tells Mitch in the story. Like many of you, I've rubbed shoulders with it, and it still rears its ugly head at times out of the blue. Writing this story was very cathartic and I thank my fictional characters for allowing me to explore loss and its aftermath with them.

As always, my Facebook fans picked the heroine's name, so a big shout out to all of you who are regulars on my author page and always willing to lend a hand.

If I hadn't been a writer, I might have been a psychologist. Like Emma, I find the brain, and the way we process life, fascinating. I read many resources, first-hand accounts, and watched hours of videos to understand what a real forensic psychologist does in his or her job. I'm grateful for all of the people on both sides of the proverbial therapist couch who shared stories with me.

I also share Emma's passion for rescuing animals. A portion of the proceeds from this book will go to two different dog rescue groups to help them provide care and medical support to abused and abandoned dogs. Please check out my Facebook author page for more details (or sign up for my newsletter!) and to keep up with the amount of money readers raise for this great cause!

DEDICATION

To Mark,

who understands my brand of crazy.

When we ride a horse, we borrow freedom.

~ Helen Thompson

CHAPTER ONE

Dusk in the cemetery was gray, flat. Dry winter grass stood unbending, endless gravestones stretched toward the east. The warmth of the earth bled into the cooling air, sending mist rising.

Mitch Holden raised the bottle of single malt scotch he'd brought with him to his lips and took a swig. The liquid burned on the back of his tongue, down his throat.

Mac loved foggy evenings.

Red and green grave decorations sprinkled throughout the cemetery signified the time of year. Did the dead really care about a crass holiday filled with things and people that would all fade in the end? Did they regret all the petty stuff, like Christmas decorations, they'd focused on when they were alive?

A sign at the entrance to the cemetery read, "One decoration per grave marker. All others will be removed." It appeared, by the overdone ornamentation on some of the cold marble and granite stones, that people either didn't give a shit about following the rules, or the rules weren't enforced.

Most likely both.

One sad bouquet of fake red flowers with a gold bow had been stuffed into the vase receptacle on Mac's headstone, a simple American flag stuck in amongst the glitter. Their mother had been by to visit her favorite son's grave.

Momma always follows the rules.

Mitch sipped again and poured some of the scotch on his

twin brother's grave. The 21-year-old single malt had been in Mac's locker on base when Mitch had cleaned it out five years ago. "Merry Christmas, you son-of-a-bitch. I can't believe you left me here alone."

You've got Mom, he could hear his brother say. *Stop being a dick and go see her.*

"Yeah, you'd like that, wouldn't you?" Mitch mumbled out loud.

The gates closed at sundown. There was only one other visitor in the cemetery and luckily they were too far away to hear him talking to himself.

The squeak of lousy brakes made Mitch turn his head. An old, brown pickup truck with peeling paint and gardening tools in the back pulled up at the gates. A man with white hair and overalls slid out and called to Mitch and the other visitor. "Gotta close up, folks."

Mitch propped the bottle of scotch next to the vase of Christmas flowers. Five years. Five goddamn years without his twin.

Should have been me. I should have been the one to die in Yemen.

That refrain was like a bad song stuck in his head. One he couldn't ever get rid of. He had shrapnel embedded in his chest and his brother was six feet under. *Because of me.*

Why did you have to listen to me, Mac?

Mitch kissed his fingers and laid them on Mac's headstone. "I miss you, big brother." Mac had been older by a minute. He had never let Mitch forget it. "I'd give anything to hear your smartass mouth and see your stupid face. Wherever you are, heaven or hell, I hope you're getting your money's worth."

It was an old joke between them. *Give 'em hell and get your money's worth.*

Mitch's phone buzzed as he walked toward the gates, the grass crunching under his boots. He blinked away the moisture in his eyes and glanced at the caller ID. *The Beast.* Falling into step behind the other visitor, also leaving, he hit the concrete walkway and tapped the talk button even though he didn't want to. "Yo."

Cooper Harris, head of the SCVC Taskforce, barked in his ear. "Where are you, Holden?"

Mitch squeezed his eyes shut for a second. "What's up?"

Harris didn't miss that Mitch hadn't answered his question. "You see your mother yet?"

Something like that. "Sure. Merry Christmas and all that."

"Good. Got an assignment for you and it's urgent."

"I'm on vacation."

"Taskforce members don't get vacations."

"Director Dupé told me I had three days before I needed to report to you."

"He gave you three days to see your mother. You saw her, right? Vacation's over."

Mitch didn't need more time off anyway. He was definitely not visiting his mother. "Is this about the wildfires? Dupé already briefed me."

"That's on your list too, but finding the prick who started 'em temporarily comes second."

California was no stranger to wildfires. Less than twenty miles west of where he was, a nasty one had been eating up acres of forest, homes, and businesses. Origination appeared to be in the state park that spanned thousands of acres, and initial reports suggested a lightning strike on the west side of the mountain as the trigger.

In the past twenty-four hours, a new theory had come to light. A homegrown terrorist named Sean Gordon had been caught on security footage entering the forest. The guy had a rap sheet filled with fire-related crimes.

Clearing the gate, Mitch gave the old man a nod and walked to his black Ford truck. "I can be back in San Diego in a couple hours."

"The assignment's in northern San Diego County, near the state park. That's why I'm calling you."

3

Mitch slid behind the wheel. As the sun gave up its fight with the approaching night, shadows stole over the graveyard, the perimeter lights flicking on one by one. "What's involved?"

"Not what, *who*. A woman named Emma Collins. Dr. Collins. She's in danger."

The elite SCVC team handled violent crimes stemming from drug running, gangs, terrorists, and the like. Mitch started the truck. "From whom?"

"Chris Goodsman."

It took a second for Mitch's brain to recognize the name. "That actor kid who murdered his fiancée a couple of years ago?"

"That's the one. He escaped from a transport van that was evacuating prisoners from Aleta Hills today because of the fires. The van was run off the road by a pair of hijackers in a truck and the driver of the van was killed. A second security guard was severely injured and Goodsman escaped with the two in the truck."

The Hills—a federal prison for the rich and famous who couldn't be put into a regular prison population without the risk of being killed. "What's Goodsman got to do with this Dr. Collins?"

"Collins was the forensic psychologist who testified against him during his well-publicized trial. While several experts said the kid had a psychotic break and agreed with the insanity defense, Collins claimed Goodsman was a..." There was a pause and Mitch figured Coop was reading from his notes. "Yeah, here it is, Goodsman is a 'narcissistic sociopath.' Collins said he was trying to fool the world into believing he had a temporary schizo break so he wouldn't be sent to federal prison. She believed he should remain incarcerated for life."

"But he ended up at the Hills, cushy pillows and all."

"Over the past two years, his doctors say he was making progress. Showing no signs of delusional episodes or breaks with reality. No violent outbursts or anything else they could label as dangerous, so he was up for parole in three days. Collins strongly advised against his release. She even petitioned the governor."

Mitch drove out of the cemetery, making a left. Goodsman had been America's favorite child actor who grew up playing the lead on a cable show spinoff of a popular sci-fi movie franchise. It had earned him a shelf full of awards, but when the series ended, the guy was 21 and had never done another thing. He'd spent several years as a party boy, being fired from one role after another.

With the money he'd made during the ten years the show had run, he probably never needed to work again. Unless, of course, he'd blown all of that money on drugs and other stupidass shit.

"Collins owns a ranch along the valley border of the park. Since you're heading that way, I need you to check on her. Sending you the coordinates. We believe Goodsman is dangerous and he may be looking for revenge."

Goodsman's murder trial had been headline news for months. Each year on the anniversary of the guilty verdict, fans all over the world held vigils and crap. "Guy's been in for a couple of years, right? Seems like the first thing he'd want to do is grab a bacon cheeseburger, a pack of smokes, and get laid on his way to the border."

"I'm standing in his cell at the Hills," Cooper said. "Sending you a picture of what I found under his bed."

Mitch stopped at a light, waited for the picture to come through his messages. Pulling it up, hair rose on the back of his neck. "Did you call the sheriff? They can get to Collins faster than I can."

"Cops are busy manning the holiday parade and helping folks north of where she lives with the wildfires. Dupé asked for you to personally haul ass over to Collins' ranch and get her to a safe house."

Dupé. The director of the West Coast FBI and the man

who'd created the taskforce. A man Holden respected almost as much as he did Cooper Harris.

Mitch slapped his blue light onto the hood of his truck and jetted through the red light. "What's Dupé's interest in this?"

"Personal. I'll fill you in later. Dupé himself is on his way, but it'll take him two to three hours from L.A."

He'd be at the address in under thirty minutes. "I'm on it."

They disconnected and Mitch glanced down at the picture still on his phone.

In a cheery holiday red paint, Chris Goodsman had made his Christmas intentions for the doctor quite clear.

Her fate is death. Her destiny is death.

The Resistance knows.

Collins dies bloody.

Birth was a miracle.

Even when it was a horse.

Second Chance whinnied, shifting her weight as yet another contraction faded away. Emma stroked her left rear flank, mentally willing the foal inside her to help its mother out.

Sweat ran down the back of Emma's neck. The barn was stuffy, the natural light long faded. An overhead light and extra lanterns illuminated her job.

"Where is that vet?" Will Longram said. "She should have been here by now."

Emma's farmhand had done three tours in Iraq, more in other places he didn't speak about. PTSD seemed to make him especially sensitive to Second Chance's current situation. The pregnant mare had been neglected and eventually abandoned by her former owners, coming to Emma through the local horse rescue group. In the past two weeks, she and Will had managed to bond with the horse while getting her back into shape. Her coat now glistened, her eyes were clear. The open sores on her neck were nearly healed.

But now, her foal was breach.

As a fresh contraction gripped Second Chance, Emma grabbed the two skinny legs of the foal and pulled. The resistance strained her muscles, made her lower back ache. Digging in her heels, she leaned back and tried to stifle the yell that pushed against her vocal chords. Second Chance was skittish of loud noises and new people. Emma didn't want to scare the poor girl by cutting loose with her own inner primal animal.

Suddenly, the foal shifted. The buttocks popped out.

"Progress!" Emma said, breathing hard and wiping her forehead with her sleeve. She was covered in dust, blood, and sweat, her muscles screaming for relief.

But the adrenaline rush was incredible. The foal's life was in her hands. Second Chance's too. Her exhaustion was nothing compared to the mare's, and she would not let the new mother down. "Will, help me."

The man looked left and right, his own skittishness apparent. "I shouldn't touch her."

Second Chance wasn't the only rescue at the ranch. Will believed he was bad luck.

He'd long ago convinced himself it was his fault his unit had been wiped out during a village raid, while he had lived. His imaginary bad luck extended to everything he did; if something went wrong at the ranch, he blamed himself, even though it had nothing to do with him. He'd tried to end his life more than once.

Emma hadn't yet convinced him of the opposite; that he had lived because he had a larger purpose in this world. A purpose for good. He simply needed to channel his past experiences into something that would help others the way he was helping her.

"Get in here and help me pull, Will. Second Chance needs you. *I* need you."

At his feet sat Emma's first rescue—a dog named Lady. The part Lab, part pit bull terrier, was nearly ten years old and didn't get excited about too many things. She had taken a liking to Will from the start and now followed him everywhere. Emma suspected the dog even slept in his bed.

Will's forty-something face screwed into a ball of lines and crow's feet, but he did as he was asked, climbing over the fence into the stall. He moved slowly, carefully, as Second Chance eyed him and took a step away. Lady watched, completely unruffled.

"It's okay, girl," Will said to the horse, stopping and giving her a moment to adjust to his presence. Once she glanced away, bobbing her head as if giving him permission, he took a step toward Emma.

She gave him the foal's scrawny legs and grabbed hold of it just above the buttocks, using the hips for leverage. "Next contraction, we're getting her out."

God, she was tired, but this birth was exactly what she needed. Seeing new life come into the world at this time of year would take her mind off the young life that had ended two years ago. A foal would keep her busy over the next few days, give her something to concentrate on so the Christmas depression didn't swallow her and leave her like a fish out of water, desperately clinging to life until the worst of it passed.

The next contraction hit and she and Will pulled with all their combined weights. A slippery, sucking noise sounded and the foal popped free, taking both of them down with it as it tumbled to the stall floor.

Warm, sticky fluid covered Emma, the weight of the body on top of her making her laugh. "We did it!"

Second Chance turned around and huffed breath through her nose, nudging Emma and the foal. Emma slid the newborn off her and came up onto her hands and knees.

"It's not breathing," Will said, backing up. The fear in his eyes was real. "I killed it."

Emma backed up, too, giving Second Chance space to get to her baby. "Go to work, *mamacita*. It's up to you now."

Instinct took over and Second Chance began cleaning the foal, licking off the birth sac and stimulating the foal's body. A second later, Emma saw a hoof twitch, saw the foal's lungs expand.

"You didn't kill her," Emma said, leaning back on the stall fence. She shook from head to toe. Using her shirt sleeve, she brushed hair from her eyes. "You saved her."

Running footsteps sounded outside the barn. "I'm here!"

Jane Sheppard ran in, her black vet bag in hand. She pulled up at the sight of the foal, wobbling its way to a standing position. "Well, will you look at that."

At the arrival of the veterinarian, Will's gaze went to the ground. He climbed over the fence, wiping his hands on his overalls. "I'll get some fresh straw."

They watched as he hustled out, Lady slowly getting off her haunches and following.

"He always leaves when I show up," Dr. Jane murmured to Emma, coming into the stall. Her straight, black hair was pinned back, her face devoid of makeup except for some bright red lipstick. "Did you tell him I bite or something?"

"He likes you." Emma watched Second Chance continue to clean the foal. "It scares him. He won't let himself get close to anyone for fear his bad luck will rub off on them."

"He's close to you."

Depends on your definition of close. "I don't believe in luck, and I certainly don't believe a person can bring bad luck. We create bad luck because of poor choices. I don't let him get away with hiding behind his perceived unworthiness."

Dr. Jane watched the foal do a wobbly dance around Second Chance. The mother horse stood protectively blocking her baby from Emma and Jane. "You did good tonight, Em. I'm sorry I couldn't get here faster. My waiting room is swamped with people fleeing the fires with their pets. Many of them can't take their pets with them, and they're dropping them off at my place. We're maxed out."

"I have extra dog kennels behind the barn. You're welcome to use them if you need to."

"Thanks. I'll do that. No telling how long it will be before people are able to come back for some of them."

Emma stayed while Jane did a quick check of Second Chance and the foal, keeping Second Chance calm. The mare delivered the placenta a few minutes later and Dr. Jane gave Emma the all-clear.

"Everything looks good," she declared, closing up her black bag. "What are you going to name her?"

The foal danced and kicked, enjoying her new legs. The adrenaline was wearing off, but Emma's happiness wasn't. A new life to celebrate. Maybe this Christmas would be different. "Hope, I think."

"I like it." Dr. Jane smiled as the two of them left the enclosure. "Fits the season and the horse."

Emma walked the vet to her SUV and waved her off. Dr. Jane still had a long night ahead of her. Emma's wasn't over yet either.

Will returned and the two of them finished in the barn and said goodnight. Will headed for the tiny cabin on the far side of the 21-acre farm that he rented from Emma.

As the two wandered off, Emma heard Will talking to Lady about Hope. She hoped the successful birth of the foal would change Will's mind about his bad luck.

The farmhouse was dark, Salt and Pepper, her other two dogs, waiting for her on the porch. She scratched their heads, apologized for making them wait for their dinner, and all three entered through the mudroom. Emma chucked off her dirty boots and stripped down to her underwear.

Flipping on the kitchen light, she heated water to make a cup of tea. A chill swept over her skin, but she didn't want to put on her robe or any other clothes while she still smelled like blood, hay, and sweat.

Her first client appointment tomorrow wasn't until ten. She'd have plenty of time for her morning chores as well as time to prep for their session. The young girl incarcerated for starting a house fire that had killed her mother had been granted Emma's special brand of therapy by the state. Horse therapy and psychiatry went hand in hand with many kids, especially juvenile delinquents. Emma couldn't wait for Danika to see the new foal. The girl had a good heart, she'd just made a poor choice—one that would affect her for the rest of her life.

While the water heated, Emma fed the Labs and threw her clothes into the washing machine. She'd just put her tea bag in a cup of hot water and started up the stairs to the bathroom when she saw headlights coming through the gate and around the bend in the long lane leading up to her house.

Dr. Jane must have forgotten something. She couldn't possibly have gotten to the clinic and returned that fast.

Emma hustled up the stairs and grabbed her robe, slipping it on, then peeking out the upstairs window that overlooked the drive below.

It wasn't Dr. Jane's vehicle. Emma didn't recognize the truck or the dark-haired man who unfolded himself from the front seat and scanned the area as if looking for someone.

For half a second, she wished she'd had Will close the gate at the bottom of the drive.

Closed and padlocked it, in fact.

But she didn't do that anymore since Will worked for her. They never had trouble of any kind and if someone wanted onto her property, there were plenty of unfenced areas along the tree lines and by the creek on the far side to access it.

The man beside the truck was tall, his long legs filling out faded blue jeans under the outside light. The black shirt he'd thrown over his T-shirt and left unbuttoned did little to hide his muscled arms, broad chest, and tapered waist.

What she did recognize was the blue police strobe on top of the truck and the way he carried himself across the open ground to her front porch.

Downstairs, the Labs set off a ruckus.

The memory of *that* night flashed through her head. Police, federal agents...blood everywhere. She closed her eyes for a moment and forced it away. *Not now.*

But there was no denying it. The man walking up her front stairs meant only one thing...

Bad luck might just exist, and if it did, it was coming for her.

CHAPTER TWO

The woman who answered the door wasn't at all what Mitch expected.

Her brown hair was forced into a clip on top of her head, a couple pieces of hay sticking out of it and random strands stuck to her neck. Her face was devoid of makeup and sporting a healthy smear of dirt on her cheek. She clutched the edges of a worn plaid robe close to her neck, her short fingernails showing traces of caked mud. Beneath the hem of the robe stretched sexy bare legs, slender ankles, and Barbie-pink toenails.

Mitch fought to take his eyes off her shapely calves and bring them back up to her face. "Is Dr. Collins home?"

The porch light gave her face a subtle yellow glow. He couldn't be sure about the color of her eyes. They looked brown one moment, then flashed a hint of green the next when she glanced behind him as if she expected the boogeyman to be in the shadows.

Maybe she did.

"I'm Dr. Collins. What is this about?"

"*You're* Emma Collins?"

Those eyes of hers flashed again, but she replied evenly. "Dr. Emma Collins, yes. And you are?"

Damn. Definitely not what he expected a forensic psychologist to look like. Shouldn't she be...older? More buttoned-up with a bun and glasses?

13

Maybe that was just his librarian fantasy getting in the way.

Mitch flashed his ID and she examined it. "Agent Mitch Holden. National Intelligence. Currently on loan to the Southern California Violent Crimes Taskforce. May I come in?"

She was a good six inches shorter than him, and her focus swung upward to his face. "I'm not in the habit of letting strange men into my house, Agent Holden, so no, you may not. Not until you tell me what this is about."

Brown. Her eyes were definitely brown with specks of green in them. The specks caught the light like a cat's eyes.

Get it together, Holden. Quit analyzing the woman's eyes and get down to business. "Chris Goodsman escaped a transport out of the Hills today."

Her face blanched. "What?"

She obviously hadn't heard the news yet. "Victor Dupé asked me to get you to a safe house. He's been trying to reach you, but with the wildfires and all, landlines have been overloaded and some of the local cell towers aren't working."

The mention of Dupé seemed to wipe away her hesitation about letting a strange man into her house. She stepped back and motioned him in, her pretty eyes once more scanning the shadows over his shoulder.

Two Labs, one black and one white, rushed Mitch, sniffing and wagging their tails.

"Hope you're not allergic," Collins said, closing the door behind her.

"Nah." Cold noses met his fingers. They, too, had dirt on their faces and hay in their short coats. "My brother and I always had dogs growing up."

Collins snapped her fingers and the Labs retreated, heads down, tails still wagging. They flanked her, one on each side like bodyguards. She absently petted their heads, the V of her robe falling open enough for him to see tan skin and freckles dancing across her collarbone. "How did Chris escape?"

Chris. Sounded funny for the doctor to refer to the actor—a man she'd labeled a sociopath—by his first name. "The transport van was run off the road. Goodsman escaped, the driver was killed, another guard's in serious condition. I don't know all the details, but I'm sure Dupé can fill you in when he meets us at the safe house."

Her nose wrinkled. "Have you been drinking?"

Shit. "Not enough to affect my reasoning or judgment skills, Dr. Collins. I assure you, I can keep you safe."

Pushing off the door, she headed for the kitchen, a brightly lit room off to his left. "I'll make you some coffee."

Coffee sounded good. The tone in her voice—like she was reprimanding a kid about skipping school or not washing behind his ears—didn't. "I had two sips of whiskey, that's all, before I got the call to come protect you."

He found himself following her into the kitchen, his gaze drawn to her ass as she reached up to grab a bag of coffee from a rough pine cabinet. "The holidays are hard on all of us," she said.

So now she was presuming to know he hated Christmas and the emotional shitstorm it brought on? Yeah, maybe he did feel that way, but it was still annoying that within two minutes, she seemed to see right through him.

One of the Labs nuzzled his fingertips. Gritting his teeth, Mitch did his usual trick when someone probed into his personal life—turned the tables on them. "How is it hard on you? Your boyfriend dump you right before Christmas or something?"

She paused in pouring water into the coffee maker, but her face was serene when she glanced over at him. "Touchy subject, I take it?"

Guilt clawed its way into his chest. Jesus, what was wrong with him, lashing out like that? He was here to get her to a safe house, nothing more. Then it was back to a few last hours of vacation filled with moping and a 12-pack. Mac could keep his scotch. "Yes, actually, it is."

She nodded and finished pouring the water, hit the switch. "Sorry. I'm sure this isn't what you had planned for your Saturday night."

It wasn't what she'd planned either. Once more, he chastised himself for being so defensive over nothing. For being rude. "Look, I appreciate the coffee and the chitchat, but you need to pack a bag so we can get out of here."

"I'm going to shower and get dressed." She walked by him toward the living room and the stairs. "Help yourself to the cookies in the Snoopy jar on the counter."

She was halfway up the stairs when she turned back and caught him ogling her ass. That same serene look crossed her features before she motioned at the door. "There's a shotgun above the door, locked and loaded. Just in case."

Huh. Interesting. A handsome Remington rested on hooks over the front door exactly like she claimed. He also noticed for the first time that there wasn't a Christmas decoration of any kind inside the house.

No menorah or kinara either.

Was she atheist or some other religion? Did she simply hate the holidays as much as he did?

He tipped his head at her. "Good to know."

"FYI, I also have a couple of weapons upstairs."

Was she warning him or letting him know she didn't need his protection? Either way, he found it cute. "Do you know how to use them?"

One of her dainty eyebrows arched. "Better help yourself to that coffee, Agent Holden. I'll be back shortly."

"We really need to get on the road."

"If Chris is coming after me, I'd rather not smell like a barn when I have to confront him."

She did smell. "You have livestock?"

"Horses. My practice involves therapy animals. You ride?"

"Just motorcycles, ma'am."

She glanced at his black boots. "A similar type of therapy I'm told. No motorcycle tonight, though, huh?"

He hadn't trusted himself on his bike. Too tempting to flee town, just him and his demons, and ride like hell. "Not tonight."

"Too bad."

She disappeared up the stairs, the Labs on her heels, before he could ask why.

Agent Holden hadn't been far off with the boyfriend comment.

Emma left Salt and Pepper in her bedroom and turned on the water in the shower. She dropped her robe, and touched her flat stomach, feeling the steam envelope her.

Roland, Emma's fiancé and college sweetheart, had been ecstatic when he'd found out she was pregnant. They'd been together a total of ten years. Their careers were both going great. They'd dreamed of starting a family and he'd proposed at Thanksgiving. They'd been so happy, so ready for this.

But along with his proposal came an ultimatum.

Since her first psychology class in college, she'd known she wanted to be a therapist. Roland had talked her into taking a law class with him and she'd felt the call of the judicial system as well. Combining the two, her path became clear. While Roland changed his degree as fast as he changed his socks, for her, clinical psychology had always been her chosen path with her sights set on being an evaluator and expert witness for criminal trials.

As a forensic psychologist, she helped the courts evaluate the competency of certain individuals to stand trial, as well as their mental state at the time of the offense.

Because of her work and the in-depth evaluations she provided, she was asked to sit on teams made up of psychologists, nurses, and care workers to evaluate past offenders being released and deciding on their potential for future criminal activities.

Eventually, she'd ended up contracting her services to the State of California, evaluating prisoners who were up for parole.

Chris Goodsman's trial should have been her defining moment. She knew he was manipulating the jury, the judge, and her fellow psychologist who were all too happy to get in front of the media. It was their defining career moment, too, and no one wanted to be the bad guy who said Chris Goodsman, a world-renowned, beloved actor, was a murderer.

She'd done it anyway, and her job had gone from being moderately risky to all out dangerous.

Her previous trial work had often put her in the crosshairs of gang members, drug runners, and even a homegrown terrorist who'd pleaded not guilty by reason of insanity. Emma had easily invalidated that argument and received death threats from the man's group for months afterward.

Upon their engagement, Roland had insisted she find a new line of work, to get out of the prison and judicial system and go into private practice. She'd agreed, but insisted on testifying against Chris. She'd already spent six weeks that year evaluating him before Thanksgiving and she'd known without a doubt he'd duped the others. She was the only person standing between him and a light sentence.

More recently, she'd been the one person standing between him and his early release.

When she'd testified against him the first time, she'd created a storm of publicity that put her in the spotlight. Goodsman, a media whore like most actors, rallied his fans. He was on Twitter, Instagram, Facebook, Snapchat. People all over the world believed he'd been wrongly accused to begin with, and some openly stated that the woman he'd killed—a woman he supposedly loved—deserved it.

Chris was found guilty by temporary insanity and had been sent to Aleta Hills for evaluation and treatment. Still, a dozen of his so-called fans had made ugly, vicious threats against Emma. One of them went farther than threats.

The attack happened in her and Roland's home in L.A. when Roland was out Christmas shopping for her. She survived, thanks to their security alarm and a Smith & Wesson 38 Special Lite. The baby had survived too.

But two days later, on Christmas Eve, she'd miscarried.

The doctors had told her it was a chromosomal abnormality. Roland, however, was sure she'd miscarried due to stress after the attack. He mourned the loss of their child, and every time he looked at Emma, she saw the accusation in his eyes. He blamed her and her job.

Staring in the foggy mirror, Emma felt the old crater of sorrow opening. It was expected this time of year, but Agent Holden's words had ripped the scab off, exposing the painful, unhealed wound all over again.

It took self-restraint to not lash out at his unsolicited comments, but that was her job. She couldn't—shouldn't—blame the agent Victor Dupé had sent to help her.

Two years. Two Christmases past.

Physician, heal thyself. It was time to move on.

Goodsman's parole hearing was scheduled for Christmas Eve. She'd contacted the parole board, insisting parole should be denied, but knowing it wouldn't be. She'd sent a letter and a packet of her findings from the trial to the governor, in hopes he might overrule them.

It's your own fault you're back in this.

She couldn't let Chris Goodsman walk free. Two years in a low-security, country-club jail was hardly recompense for a woman's life.

Unwilling to sink further into the muck of her mind, she

grabbed a fresh bar of soap from the shelf, unwrapped it, and stepped into the shower, focusing on making quick work of the barn odors and dirt. The light scent of rosemary and orange filled her nostrils as she scrubbed. At least she could wash this mess away.

The upstairs windows were closed, the blinds drawn. As she dried off and got dressed, the old paranoia snuck up on her. She stopped a couple of times to make sure window locks were secure and there was no movement in the yard, near the barns, or down the lane.

Everything appeared normal, but the unsettling sense that Chris was out there, free, made her fingers shake. He was without a doubt the most charming monster she'd ever met. What she didn't understand was why he would make an escape when his parole hearing, and possible freedom, were so close.

Sociopaths. Understanding one was never easy.

She'd learned long ago that privacy came at a cost, but it had been worth her sanity. The ranch was her personal oasis. She'd started over after Roland left, bringing her work home. The horses, her patients, men like Will who needed someone to believe in them again, even the dogs...it all added up to her life's mission. If she couldn't heal herself, she damn well would help others. Especially those who might have made some life-altering mistakes.

Her tangled hair took a minute of work to comb out, then she wrapped it in a high bun and secured it. Agent Holden needed healing, she could see it in his guarded eyes, hear it in his sharp tongue. He had the bearing of a military man, so maybe he'd experienced something like Will that made him irascible. Maybe it was his family or a girlfriend. Whatever it was, it wasn't her business. He hadn't come to her as a patient; he was here to protect her.

I can damn well protect myself.

She'd proven that once already.

Still, Agent Holden was a fine looking man and she hadn't

had anyone like him inside her home in a long time. Simple compassion and understanding could do wonders for some people and maybe that's all he needed. Kindness cost nothing. She could handle that.

She found herself digging out her makeup bag and putting on mascara. A swipe of lipstick too. Makeup was normally reserved for client meetings though lately she didn't even bother for her clients who were too wrapped up in their own sad worlds to care. And these days she did zero socializing, so a bare face was her norm.

Oh, my. A handsome, testy man shows up at my door and I'm suddenly a fifteen-year-old girl again.

What the hell. Lipstick and compassion never hurt anyone. It wasn't much, but it was all she had.

Adding earrings, she gave the mirror one last glance. Took the clip from her hair—too business-y—and shook out the bun. She looked good, smelled better, and had her armor in place.

Time for a cookie and that cup of tea she hadn't finished. As she started down the stairs, she realized she was hungry for more than a cookie. Maybe a little psychoanalyzing of a certain intelligence officer working for Victor Dupé's violent crimes taskforce. That job sounded extremely interesting. What made him tick?

Her pulse sped up at the idea of digging under Agent Holden's skin. Outside of Will, she hadn't evaluated anyone but child clients in a long, long time. The concept of adult conversation with a sexy stranger who posed no danger... Well, that might make her night and then some.

Agent Holden was trying to keep up a solid front. Underneath that snarky, tough exterior, lay an emotional guy dealing with some deep, dark, painful shit. She'd bet her multiple degrees on it.

Lucky for him, deep, dark, painful shit was her specialty.

CHAPTER THREE

Dr. Collins returned in a flourish of smiles and a fresh-from-the-shower citrus scent. The two dogs didn't smell nearly as good.

She'd left her hair down, soft curls falling over her shoulders as she hustled down the stairs. With the dirt and straw gone, Mitch now noticed streaks of blond in the curls. Her jeans were well-worn and sported a fashionable rip on one thigh, but he had the sense that it wasn't fashion so much as life on a ranch that had caused it.

Nothing special about her shirt—just a picture of a horse and a rider on a plain yellow tee. Except the cotton was tight across her chest, emphasizing full breasts he hadn't even noticed when they'd been under the robe. The yellow brought out her pretty eyes.

Pretty eyes? Jesus, he was fixated on those damn things.

"How's the coffee?" she asked, blowing past his watchful stance at the front door on her way to the kitchen.

His gaze fell to her ass like a magnet drawn to steel. He absentmindedly petted the Labs as they greeted him once more.

Tearing his gaze away, he hardened his will. "Weak," he said, the good manners his mother had taught him once again absent. For some reason, he liked jabbing her. Liked the fact he couldn't seem to rile her up.

"Hmm," was all she said.

Obviously, he needed to try harder.

The first floor was secure; he'd seen no signs of unwanted visitors lurking around outside. Phones and sat towers were still having issues, but an e-mail from Dupé had gotten through. He'd been delayed for another hour.

The sounds of banging cabinet doors and soft humming drew him to the kitchen.

A cup sat on the counter, the tea kettle on the stove heating. Collins was digging in the cookie jar. She pulled out two chocolate concoctions with white chips in them and grabbed a napkin from a stack on the small table nearby. Her lips, now the color of fresh strawberries, closed over the edge of a cookie as she took a bite. She pointed to the empty coffee cup in his hand. "Would you rather have tea? There's still coffee, too, of course, and I couldn't help but notice that although you thought it weak, you drank it. Perhaps you'd like more?"

"No thanks."

While she'd been upstairs, he'd kept thinking about her motorcycle comment. *Too bad,* she'd said. Was she feeling like him, wishing she could ride the hell out of here and never look back?

Didn't seem like it. She plopped into a chair and eyed him, chewing her cookie. "Any update on Chris?"

"No."

"Would you like something else while we wait? A soda? A sandwich?"

What was wrong with her? "There's a murderer on the loose and all bets say he's coming after you. Instead of tea and cookies, I suggest you get your stuff and we bug out."

She swallowed, flipped a lock of hair over her shoulder. "I'm not leaving."

Oh, crap. "I thought we were past the stranger-danger shit."

"Stranger danger?"

"You let me into your home. You made me coffee and offered me cookies. If you have a problem going somewhere with a 'strange man', you can put that fear to rest now. I'm not a stranger anymore. I'm the good guy trying to save your ass."

She smiled at him, not a happy smile, but a patient, tolerant one. Her slender fingers worked over a napkin. "This is my home. I have horses, dogs, a man who lives on the property. Clients who depend on me and need their therapy sessions. I can't simply pack up and leave, Agent Holden."

A man lived on the property? Interesting. Employee or something more? Was that why she didn't want to leave? "If you end up dead, what good are you to any of them?"

"You are blunt, aren't you?" She took another nibble of her cookie. "I won't let Chris Goodsman kill me. At least not without one hell of a fight."

Forget her ass that he couldn't keep his eyes off of, those lips were a thing of beauty. She had a couple of cookie crumbs on the bottom one. He suppressed the urge to reach out and wipe them off.

The kettle whistled. Collins left her chair, licking her lips and catching the crumbs on her tongue, nearly making Mitch moan. She poured hot water over a tea bag. "I understand this puts you in a tight spot with Victor. I'll talk to him and let him know it was my decision and you did a fine job of trying to talk me out of it."

He didn't care about Dupé and his assignment at the moment. What person in their right mind would put themselves in harm's way for no good reason? "It's only until Goodsman is caught."

"Which could be hours or it could be months."

Months. Thank God all he had to do was get her to the safe house and then he could be done with her.

She played with her teabag, hurrying the steeping process. "There's no guarantee he's coming for me. He may already be at the Mexican border and the authorities will never catch him. Meanwhile, I'm supposed to live in fear and give up my life? Sorry, that's not going to happen."

"Do you really believe that? That Goodsman will run and disappear and never come after you?"

The tea bag stayed in the cup as she returned to her seat, sipping at the warm liquid. "Chris lives for fame. Going into hiding and living a life of seclusion doesn't seem like his style, but sociopaths are often unpredictable."

Then why the hell would she sit there drinking tea when the man might be outside? "Pack your bags and let's get the hell out of here, Dr. Collins. The safe house is very nice, I assure you, and I've got to be honest, even with those guns you say you have, you're no match for a guy who killed his fiancée and managed to escape jail."

"Haven't you been honest all along?"

What? The woman was a loon. She was also his responsibility until Dupé showed up. "At least go with me to the house tonight. We can come back in the morning and take care of the animals, check on your…the man who lives here…and reschedule your clients."

"So you *haven't* been completely honest with me."

"What does my honesty have to do with any of this?"

"You're good at deflection, aren't you? Turning things around so you don't have to reveal anything about yourself. Except by doing that, Agent Holden, you're actually telling me a great deal."

"Stop psychoanalyzing me."

"Sorry, habit." She gave him that smile again, not looking sorry at all. "I'd really like to enjoy my tea and talk. I don't get many visitors who don't need my services. What branch do you work for under National Intelligence? Or is that top secret?"

She leaned forward, her eyebrows waggling.

Seriously? Mitch rubbed his eyes. He couldn't force her to leave. All he could do was keep her safe until Dupé arrived and then he could bail. He'd have to text Dupé and give him the news—Dr. Collins wasn't going anywhere.

Yeah…that news could wait. He needed a break from NI,

and he liked working with the taskforce. No way he wanted Dupé to know he couldn't handle this simple matter. He preferred getting through the holidays by focusing on the arsonist, but for now, he had to ride out the force of nature sitting before him.

Maybe he could still get Collins to that safe house. If he played nice, got her to trust him, he could talk some sense into her. Dupé never had to know he sucked at being a bodyguard.

"I'm sort of a...subcontractor," Mitch said. "I work for different agencies, depending on the situation and what they need."

"That sounds fascinating. Doing what?"

Positioning himself at the back door, he stared out the slender window at the night. The wind had kicked up—bad for the wildfires—but other than trees blowing around, nothing else moved. He glanced back at her. "Let's call it...threat management analysis."

She chewed her cookie and rolled a finger for him to go on.

Talking about job specifics was a no-go. Ditto for talking about himself. He stayed quiet, giving her only a mirror impression of her fake smile.

Giving up wasn't in her nature. Either that, or she refused to take the hint. "How did you end up on loan, as you called it, to Victor's taskforce?" she asked.

Victor. Again with the first name that suggested a certain level of friendship, of intimacy. Mitch never thought of Dupé—the freakin' director of the FBI's West Coast division—as *Victor.*

The taskforce wasn't a secret, although keeping the identities of the agents on the taskforce under wraps was crucial. If he watched his p's and q's, he could give her a little background on them and up his chances of getting into her good graces. And, maybe if he was lucky, he could gain her trust and be the one asking the questions. She seemed to be in a chatty mood. Anything to convince her to leave. Get her to that safe house and out of his hair.

"The Southern California Violent Crimes Taskforce deals with drug kingpins, gun runners, human traffickers, and the like," he told her. "Many of the criminals they're after have dealings with terrorists and people on Homeland's watch list. My expertise with national security and counterterrorism comes in handy on occasion, and sometimes they need a warm body to fill a hole when a bunch of them are undercover. Dupé requests my assistance, and if I'm in country and available, I make every attempt to meet that request. Gets me out here in the sun and surf."

"Do you analyze threats to the United States or to the taskforce itself?"

"Both." Time for *quid pro quo.* "How do you know Director Dupé?"

She gave him that smile again, letting him know his deflection wasn't going unnoticed. Fuck that. He didn't care.

"Victor and I met at my first criminal trial," she said, her hands around the tea cup. "I was an expert witness for the defense; he was an expert witness for the prosecution."

Mitch could imagine those fireworks. Time for some reverse psychology. "How'd that turn out?"

"Like I said, it was my first trial. I was wet behind the ears, as Victor loves to remind me, but I knew my subject matter well. The defendant suffered from disassociate amnesia and had no memory of committing the murder she was charged with. Victor, on the other hand, had profiled her and believed she was a serial killer who'd gotten away with multiple murders over a span of several years."

Keep her talking. "Who was right?"

"We both were. The court ruled the defendant mentally unstable at the time of the crime and she was remanded to a psych hospital for further evaluation. There, under hypnosis, it was revealed she had multiple identities and one of those

27

identities admitted to several other murders. That personality took over and committed the crimes, and she had no memory of them."

"Damn."

"Classic textbook for both of us, yet neither Victor nor I suspected she suffered from disassociate identity disorder. I had interviewed her but she didn't fit the classic DID model, so I ruled it out. She claimed there was no deep trauma in her past that would cause such a mental break. We had no records of other physical or mental issues."

"So what caused it?"

She shrugged. "We don't know. I believe there might have been a trauma in her early childhood that caused a break with reality. Probably happened to her around age two. Unfortunately, no amount of therapy or further hypnosis was able to identify the original cause, but I suspect she witnessed the death of her grandmother who died in the home around the time our perpetrator was two years old. The grandmother supposedly died in her sleep, but me being me, I could spin another story that would fit with the defendant's psychosis. She may have witnessed one of her parents killing the grandmother, or she herself may have been playing—experimenting with a pillow or something—and somehow managed to asphyxiate the grandmother, who was quite frail according to reports and regularly took a sleeping pill."

She obviously relished retelling this case, but an exit was beginning to look further and further away. "Wow, you have quite the imagination. Who did the gal kill?"

"She was a nurse standing trial for killing a patient in the long-term care facility of the hospital she worked for."

"The others were patients too?"

"Every one of them. Frail, older people, on many medications that extended their life, but certainly not the quality of it." She kept her hands wrapped around the teacup but didn't drink. "Victor and I crossed paths again down the road with Chris Goodsman. Marlie Klein, the woman he killed, was actually Susie Warren, a girl who went missing from Gum Pond, Arkansas, back in 1997. She was five years old. The FBI believed her mother's boyfriend kidnapped her when her mother ended up in jail for a petty crime. The mother never reported her missing. Somehow, she ended up in Los Angeles, living in a commune of other people much like her—outcasts from society with dubious backgrounds. Chris met her while she was waitressing at a club he frequented."

If she was going to recount every detail, he was going to have to make other arrangements in case trouble came to them first.

"I don't remember any of that coming out when she died."

"Victor kept it quiet. He was hoping to catch the man who had kidnapped Susie. It's his One—the case he never solved. He was a field agent in that area when it happened, and it still eats at him after all these years and all of his career success." She seemed to know Dupé better than he did. In that case, he would know how difficult she could be.

Back to reality and the here and now. "If we're going to continue to stay here, we should move to a safer room. I'll kill the lights."

"You're good at your job, aren't you? Hyperaware of everything, even while carrying on a conversation with me."

"You really should get a security system—cameras, motion sensors, the works."

She sat back and studied him, tea still cupped in her hands. "The dogs are my security system. They alert to strangers."

Dogs *were* a good alert system. "That's great if you're scaring off a burglar, but two dogs alone won't stop a killer."

She gave him an amused look, even though her eyes went hard. "That's what the gun is for."

Damn, she was stubborn, and he was bent, because that look on her face was turning him on. She wasn't scared in the least. Accepting, yes. Ready to defend herself, absolutely. But could she take on Goodsman and make it out alive?

Mitch's phone rang. Turning his back on the doctor and doing a stroll through the main floor of the house, he answered. "We're good," he told his boss by way of greeting. "Collins is safe."

"Are you on your way to the safe house?" Harris asked.

"Not exactly."

"What does that mean?"

There was no way around it—he had to tell Harris the truth, but he still hesitated. Failure sucked. "She refuses to leave the ranch."

For the next minute or so, Mitch listened to Harris rant. He tried getting in a few words, but Coop was on a roll. Dupé would have both of their hides for this, yada, yada, yada.

By the time he'd checked all the doors and windows a second time, and satisfied himself that there were no unwanted visitors creeping in the shadows outside, he'd walked two full circles around the first floor. On his second round, he realized the house was dark. The kitchen light was off.

His pulse sped up, his eyes—already adjusted to the dark—scanned the room for Collins.

She wasn't there.

Mitch pulled the gun from his holster and lowered his voice. "Coop, I got to call you back."

He hung up on his boss, praying he wouldn't have to call him and tell him Collins was gone. Or dead.

Not on my watch.

Raising his weapon, he listened for her or the dogs. Heard nothing.

Stepping into the living room, he swept his gun around the room. His heart almost stopped when she came into view, sitting in a rocking chair near the fireplace, the shotgun from above the front door lying across her lap.

The dogs were asleep on the floor near her feet. She rocked slowly in the chair, a soft popping sound coming from it as it adjusted to the movement.

Her gaze was fixed on the door as she sipped from her cup. "If Chris comes after me, he'll want to make a dramatic entrance. Dollars to donuts, he'll come through that door."

She was just crazy enough, Mitch feared she might have unlocked it after his last pass. The doorknob held, though, when he tested it. The deadbolt was in place.

He joined her, sitting in the matching rocker in the dark. One of the dogs lifted his head and thumped his tail on the ground. Mitch leaned over and patted the top of the dog's head.

Collins handed him a cup from the table next to her. A reading lamp towered over a pile of books, their titles difficult to make out in the darkness. Psychotherapy nonsense, most likely.

The cup was warm in Mitch's hands, the smell of very strong coffee rising up to meet his nose.

She clinked her cup against his. "Cheers."

He sighed. "What are we toasting to, dare I ask?"

"We're alive."

He sipped his coffee and mimicked her, settling his gun in his lap. The shadows were comforting. Her odd presence, along with that of the dogs, was comforting as well.

Honesty bubbled up from his chest. "I'm not sure that's worth celebrating."

She let go of a soft chuckle. "Neither am I, but it's the best I can do at the moment."

They both sat in the dark, rocking. "Why do you hate Christmas?" he finally asked.

"I don't."

"Could have fooled me."

She snorted. "It reminds me of a great loss, and I can't...go there. So I've declared this house a Christmas-free zone."

"I like it."

"So do I."

They clinked cups again.

After a few minutes, Collins put down her tea and stood, the shotgun hanging by her side from the crook of her arm. "I want to show you something."

This should be good. "What is it?"

"Come with me."

Before he could stop her, she unbolted the door and walked out into the night.

The stars were out, the moon nearly full. Fingerlike streaks of smoke cut through the distant sky to the northwest where the wildfires raged on. They were moving away from her ranch, and for that, she was grateful. Emma, shotgun swinging loosely at her side, strode for the barn.

Salt and Pepper took turns running ahead, then doubling back to her. Their eyes caught the flashlight beam here and there as she kept it on the path in case of snakes or other nocturnal critters she'd rather not run into.

"Where are you going?" Agent Holden quickly caught up to her. "You shouldn't be out here."

She handed him the flashlight and threw open the barn door. "I want to show you something."

His voice was flat, tight. "You're making yourself a target."

"If Chris is around—which I very much doubt he is—he'll confront me face to face, and wouldn't that be nice? Between the two of us, we could shoot his ass and put an end to this before it even gets started. You could be home before sunrise."

She smiled sweetly, and saw his jaw twitch. Not even the shadows could hide it. Annoyance? Oh, yeah. But maybe a touch of humor too.

"Are you always like this?" he asked, helping her move the big barn door out of the way, his eyes scanning the interior as well as shooting a look over his shoulder.

"Helpful?" she supplied.

"Bullheaded."

Still smiling, she led him into the barn, flipping on the overhead lights and passing the stalls of her other horses to get to Second Chance's. The foal was standing next to her mother, both of them lifting their heads and pinning the newcomers with their dark, soulful eyes. "Hope," Emma said.

Agent Holden's gaze inspected the barn, skimming over the stalls, tools, hay. "A smelly barn and some horses equals hope?"

It did to her. She pointed at the pair in front of them. "Hope is my new foal. Born a few hours ago and look how beautiful she is already. Strong and sleek. She almost didn't make it. Her mother might have died, too, during the birth, but they both lived and they're doing fine."

As if on cue, Hope swished her tail. She raised her head and whinnied at them.

"That's nice," Agent Holden said. He studied the horses for a moment, shifting his weight between his feet as if itching to be anywhere but in the barn with her.

"This is my Christmas present," she said, ignoring his restlessness. "Hope. She embodies a fresh start, a new year. An innocent joy I haven't felt in a long, long time."

Shyly, the foal ambled over. Emma stroked her nose. Both Labs inched closer and Salt put her nose up against the stall's open slats, sniffing. The curious foal dropped her nose to do the same.

Holden's eyes kept cutting to the barn door. Was he worried about Chris showing up or was he planning his escape? "She's...cute."

Cute? Hmm. His heart was colder than the Grinch's. "New life represents hope. Babies, puppies, kittens...they all make us feel happy and optimistic."

"If you say so."

But he couldn't seem to resist when the foal shifted her nose to him. One of his large hands reached out and rubbed her between the ears. He'd been that way with the dogs too. He couldn't seem to ignore animals.

In Emma's book, that made him even more likable.

Work your magic on him, Hope.

"Are you always like this?" she said, mocking his earlier question to her.

His lips twitched as he played along. "Charming and smart?"

"Detached and grumpy."

The lip twitch turned into a frown. He checked his phone, scanned the barn door again. "Only when I'm trying to keep someone safe and she's making that extremely difficult."

He liked a challenge; she could see it in the way his eyes danced. "Constant vigilance must take a toll."

"I'm not used to playing bodyguard."

Maybe not, but she would bet he guarded his own heart and his feelings closely. "Victor must trust you a great deal, then, and feel confident that you're up for the job."

A soft chuckle escaped his lips. "I was the closest warm body when the call came in. Nothing more than that."

Self-deprecating. She liked that. "Lucky me."

His roving gaze landed on her face, his eyes boring into her as if deciding whether she was being sarcastic or not. "We should get back to the house. I need to make contact with my boss and Director Dupé to let them know you're not going to the safe house tonight, which I have to state for the record, is a terrible idea."

His stare was too intense, sending a tiny shockwave up her spine. How long had it been since a man had looked at her like that?

Too long apparently because she couldn't hold his gaze. She broke eye contact and patted Hope's neck. "You've made that clear, and I appreciate your dedication to keeping me safe. However..." A deep breath helped her clear her head, steady the hand petting the horse. "Chris Goodsman has already taken something very dear from me. Something I will grieve over for the rest of my life. He's not chasing me away from this ranch. He's not taking anything else from me. Ever."

Swallowing the tightness in her throat, she glanced up at the good agent. "Do you understand?"

He petted Hope too, his fingers brushing hers when the foal raised her head and whinnied. His pause hung in the air like electrically charged ions after a flash of lightning. "I'll do my best to protect you, Dr. Collins, but there's something I think you should see so you understand that this is no joke on Goodsman's part."

Her hand holding the shotgun tightened on the stock. "What is it?"

Removing his phone from his pocket, he stared at it a moment before turning the screen toward her. "My boss found this in Goodsman's cell after he broke out."

Red slashes formed words on a beige wall.

Her fate is death. Her destiny is death.

The Resistance knows.

Collins dies bloody.

Chills raced over Emma's skin. The real Chris Goodsman—the man behind the charming persona everyone loved—was still hiding behind his role. What was he really planning? "Huh."

"That's it?" Agent Holden put an elbow on the railing and leaned toward her. "He leaves this message on the wall of his cell and that's all you got, Doc?"

More shockwaves rippled up her spine—because of Holden's closeness or because of the danger she was in? "Something has set him off again. He's misleading everyone like he did before, wanting them to believe he's had another break with reality similar to when he killed his fiancée."

She tore her gaze from the phone's screen. "Did they say what precipitated this? Did he have an argument with someone? Get into trouble? More importantly, did he know he was going to have an opportunity to escape and set this up ahead of time?"

Agent Holden shook his head. "Like I said, I don't know the

details, but I can find out if I can ever get through to Coop or Dupé."

Cell service was hit and miss on a good day at the ranch. With the fires, it was mostly miss right now. "I have a CB radio if that would help."

His face lit up. "That might. In the meantime, I really wish you'd reconsider the safe house at least for a night or two. You said you had a guy living here. He can take care of the horses and the dogs until it's safe for you to return, right? But who will take care of the place if you're dead?"

They were heading for the barn door when Will appeared, making an imposing figure in the doorway. He took in the agent, then dropped his attention to the shotgun in Emma's hand. "Everything okay, boss?"

How to answer? "Will, this is Agent Mitch Holden from the SCVC Taskforce. One of my former patients broke out of prison and Agent Holden, here, came to check on me because there is a possibility the man may come here. Agent Holden, this is my employee, Will Longram."

"It's Mitch." He held out a hand.

Will's eyes narrowed. He ignored Mitch's hand. Lady appeared, her old hips keeping her always a few steps behind. "Is Emma in danger?"

Holden nodded. "She won't leave."

"That true?" Will said to her. "How dangerous is this guy?"

Great, now they were ganging up on her. "The only thing that's going to chase me off this ranch is the wildfires. If you're worried, Will, you're free to leave. No hard feelings. Either way, you'll have a job when Chris Goodsman is caught and things return to normal."

"Goodsman, huh? I saw a blip on the news about that waste of a human being. Heard he escaped. You think he's coming after you?"

"Most likely he won't," Mitch said. "But we can't take that chance."

Will nodded. "I'll take care of the horses, keep an eye on the barns and outbuildings. You need anything, Em, ring me on the walkie talkie."

"I will. Thank you."

He gave Mitch another once-over, then walked away. Lady took her time getting to her feet, then trailed after him.

"Charming guy," Mitch said.

Emma smiled. He'd described himself the same way. "Apparently, I'm a magnet for them."

CHAPTER FOUR

Mitch used Emma's CB radio to get hold of the local police, who were able to get a message to Victor Dupé. He kept it short and sweet:

Collins refuses to leave.
I'm staying.

Whether or not Dupé sent reinforcements was up in the air. With the current situation, getting anyone to the ranch to relieve him might take a while. Knowing Cooper Harris and the SCVC Taskforce, someone would show up eventually, even if they had to walk through fire to do it.

At least he had Will and the dogs to help with security. He'd worked with less and made it out alive.

The good doctor had taken her shotgun and gone to bed. For some strange reason, Salt and Pepper had stayed with him.

Emma didn't seem the least bit worried. He liked that about her. Most people would have freaked out and been eager to go to the safe house. His job would have been easier from that standpoint. Her refusal made the situation more challenging, but also more interesting.

What *did* frighten her? For some reason, the question kept circulating in his head.

He retrieved his laptop from his truck with the footage Dupé had sent the previous day of their potential arsonist. *Could be a long night.* Might as well get started on his real assignment.

He took the laptop, a fresh cup of coffee—better now that Collins had doubled the grounds—and headed up the wooden stairs to the second floor. Better vantage points from up there. Emma's bedroom was the best, but she was sleeping, and he didn't think she'd appreciate his presence.

Across from her master bed and bath were two decent sized bedrooms and a guest bath. Both bedrooms had sweeping views of the ranch. He could see the entire drive stretched out below, as well as the barn, pasture, and horse runs. A stream ran on the east and south sides of the property at the foot of the hill. Woods along the east side as well, intermingling with the stream.

He put Pepper in front of Emma's bedroom door and told him to stay. He'd finally learned their names before Emma had retired. The Lab stretched out across the threshold of the closed door, laying his chin on his paws. Salt followed Mitch to the first bedroom, a large, airy space that had been turned into an office.

Bookshelves lined one wall. A sturdy Arts & Crafts desk sat facing a bank of windows that overlooked the driveway and valley beyond. Under the window was a big, comfy couch with pillows and a folded afghan draped over one arm. Next to the couch was a matching chair and ottoman. Probably where the doctor grilled her patients when they weren't riding horses.

Horse therapy. *Yippee ki yay.*

Mitch peered outside. All was dark out, a blanket of ash and fog rolling into the low spots. In the distance, the orange glow of fires threaded across the top of the hills.

Mitch set up his laptop and opened the video file. The security camera footage was clear enough, but the man's face was half hidden by a baseball cap and hoodie drawn up over it. The FBI's facial rec program had identified him as Sean Gordon.

Gordon was on foot, carrying nothing more than a small backpack, entering the park at dusk.

Mitch calculated the distance from the entrance to the point of origin of the fire. Three miles. Six miles, round-trip.

Even sticking to the main roads, a six-mile round-trip through a national park at night was no picnic. Using the trails, seasoned hikers and campers had been known to lose their way, run into wild animals, twist an ankle. Though around the holidays, there were fewer visitors in general.

The drought had caused massive wildfires throughout the northwest and extended the fire season beyond normal. Millions of acres from Washington State down through California up in smoke, lost lives, homes and businesses destroyed.

Mitch fast-forwarded the footage, estimating the time it would take Gordon to reappear leaving the park. He reran the footage and watched again.

Nada. The man in the hoodie never left, at least not on foot through the main entrance.

Had someone been waiting for Gordon inside the park to hustle him out after he started the fire? Had he taken a different way out? Was he still inside the 1800 acres of pine and cedar trees?

The motorcycle gang the man belonged to was part of a survivalist/homegrown terrorist group who called themselves The Reckoners. They claimed to live off the grid and yet their group ran several websites and blogs for doomsday preppers and survivalists, recruiting more people to their cause via social media. A few of their members had been busted for gun running, sales going down inside the park in some of the lesser traveled areas.

Mitch clicked the laptop to connect to Emma's wireless network but the slow satellite service struggled to find a local tower. He sat back and watched the bars on his laptop's digital antenna fade in and out.

If he'd had his kit, he would have set up a mobile hotspot and boosted it with his own portable satellite dish. Emma's house had a nice southern exposure that would have worked great. Unfortunately, the kit and satellite dish were back at his hotel, two miles from his childhood home.

Whatever gods existed took pity on him, and the fog in the atmosphere momentarily cleared enough for the satellite hookup to work. Sitting up, he connected to the Internet and typed in a search.

The wildfires were headline news across the country, right under the breaking news about Chris Goodsman. The actor's escape had trumped the danger to people. Go figure.

Scrolling past the Goodsman news, Mitch found links to dozens of articles on the wildfires as well. Expert analysis was mixed in with plenty of opinions on how the fires had started and the best way to put them out.

Mitch logged into the various blogs and forums used by The Reckoners. While there was plenty of banter about the fires and the government's inability to contain them, no one in the group claimed responsibility. Not that he'd expected them to, but it would have made his job easier.

The Deep Web held more information. He trolled a few forums under his fake accounts, found lots of discussion about fire raining down from Heaven, the Second Coming, and biblical quotes. Apparently, it was the end of times. Folks argued about the true identity of the antichrist: the president or the Pope? Vitriol spewed from commenters hiding in the anonymity of false usernames and imaginative avatars.

For his job with National Intelligence, Mitch regularly monitored forums and blogs, looking for the vigilantes, the crazies who were motivated enough to take action. He'd seen it all, but the depravity and hate that one human being could have for another still shocked him at times.

His gaze stopped on a username. One he'd seen pop up in multiple end-of-the-world forums. Mary Monahan. She believed she was the mother of a boy who would save the world.

Her belief wasn't based in any kind of reality. It was based on a sci-fi movie franchise where future cyborgs traveled through time to kill a man who would lead the human resistance in The Last War between humans and computers.

The movies had spawned the popular cable show Chris Goodsman had starred in for ten years, *Resistance: The Mary Monahan Chronicles.*

Mitch shook his head as he read the username TheRealMary's post:

For it is written, the true believers will not be touched by fire from the machines.
Fate will not guide them; truth will.
Their destiny is resistance.

The dish on Emma's roof lost its connection to the satellite. Mitch's screen locked up.

Chris Goodsman isn't the only psycho out there.

Sighing, he clicked out of his browser and went back to the zip file Dupé had sent. One folder contained a map of the national park, including topographical and satellite versions. Mitch studied the landmarks outside of the park area, the various entry and exit points.

Gordon could have left from multiple spots, or someone could have driven him out. With his survivalist training, he could be camping inside the park, but that was risky with so many firefighters and first responders combing through it.

Mitch began looking for motorcyclists leaving the park that day, especially those with two people on them.

The satellite made a connection, his laptop signaling him that service was once more available. He opened up his browser and started to go back to the forums to look for chatter amongst the homegrown terrorists' groups when he decided to type in *Resistance: The Mary Monahan Chronicles* instead.

The search engine brought back ninety thousand results. Mitch went to the Wiki page about the show.

A list of cast and characters appeared along with an in-depth description of the plot backstory and summary about the main characters, Mary and Tom. The show had won dozens of awards, spawned thousands of fan fiction stories, and catapulted the originally unknown cast into super stardom during its ten year run.

Several of the reference notations at the bottom of the page listed links to Goodsman's trial and conviction. Mitch clicked on the first one and started reading.

Two hours later, he caught himself drifting off, the swirl of information overload turning his brain to mush. Moving to the sofa near the window, he set his watch alarm for a nap and fell asleep with the laptop on his belly.

───────────

Mitch woke with a sudden *oh, shit* jerk, the smell of bacon and eggs assaulting his nose.

He sat up, dumping the laptop off his chest and finding his face inches from a plate with soft blue flowers and his favorite breakfast on it.

"Good morning, Sleeping Beauty," Emma said. Salt and Pepper sat on either side of her, tails wagging and tongues hanging out, gazes locked on the food. "I thought this might wake you. Never known a man who could resist bacon."

She was freshly showered, dressed in jeans and a flannel shirt. Her hair was pulled back in a ponytail, her smirking lips once more the color of strawberries.

Mitch ran a hand over his face. "What time is it?"

"Nine-thirty. Your watch alarm went off at five, but you didn't wake up, so I finally shut it off."

"Why didn't you wake me?"

"You apparently needed the sleep."

She set the plate in his lap, picked his laptop up off the floor and placed it on her desk. "There are clean clothes in the bathroom if you'd like to shower. No underwear, I'm afraid." The glee in her tone told him she was enjoying the fact he'd have to go commando. "Coffee's on downstairs."

"Did Dupé arrive?"

She headed for the door, the dogs torn between following her and staying with the bacon. "He did not."

Mitch reached for his phone and realized it was still on the desk. "Shit, he's going to kill me."

She turned back. "For what, falling asleep? Being human?"

His morning hard-on was painfully thick between his legs as he hustled to the desk. Trading the plate for his phone, he saw he'd missed two calls and three texts. "For not answering my goddamn phone."

"I spoke to Victor shortly after I shut off your watch alarm. He's joined the taskforce searching for Chris. I assured him I was safe here at the ranch with you and Will. He doesn't like it, but he knows better than to argue with me."

She winked and marched out. The dogs took one last look at Mitch and his bacon, and followed.

Victor Dupé knew better than to argue with her?

Mitch shook his head, grabbed a strip of crisp bacon and stood for a moment chewing it. His head was still clouded with a dream, one that included Emma and his motorcycle.

Total fantasy. She was a ball buster and he had no time for that kind of woman in his life, even if it was just sex.

But he sure as hell wasn't happy about spending more time with her.

Except in his dreams. If those pretty lips of hers ended up on certain parts of his body in the safety of his dreams, so be it. Since Mac's death, he'd had a hard time sleeping at all, and when he *did* fall asleep, he usually ended up suffering horrible nightmares. To dream about a sexy woman doing him on his bike was a welcome reprieve.

The bacon was cooked to perfection, and suddenly Mitch

was starving. Snatching up a second piece, he hit the head, washed up, and ignored the clean clothes. One way or another, he'd be out of here by sunset. He'd get back to his hotel room and take a nice, long, hot shower. Then he'd get to work on nailing Sean Gordon's ass to the wall. Hopefully, he could take a few of the man's brothers-in-arms down with him.

Seeing the clothes Collin's had laid out for him gave Mitch pause. Well-worn men's jeans and a flannel shirt not much different from the one she wore. He fingered the shirt, wondered about the man who might have worn it. A brother? A lover?

A husband?

Emma hadn't been wearing a ring. There were no pictures of her with anyone else. He didn't have a file on her. No background at all, except what she'd told him and the mentions on the internet about her in conjunction with Goodsman's trial.

Who was this woman? Independent, not afraid of a killer on the loose, and one who went toe-to-toe with an FBI God and didn't even flinch.

She profiled criminals, treated them, and recommended their incarceration or release. She raised horses, saved dogs, and provided therapy to juvenile delinquents.

Taking his plate, he went downstairs.

Emma looked up from her place at the kitchen table, a pair of reading glasses on the end of her nose. A file was spread out on the table in front of her.

Sun shone through the window and the smell of bacon and coffee filled the air. The toaster snapped and two pieces of lightly browned bread popped up.

"Toast?" Emma shuffled her papers together and laid her glasses on top of them. She crossed the room to the counter and started buttering. "There's plenty more bacon if you'd like."

"Where are the dogs?"

"Running around the ranch like they do every morning. Why?"

"You let me sleep in, and you let the dogs leave you. Still not taking your safety seriously, are you?"

She stopped buttering long enough to open the drawer next to her hip and flashed a Smith & Wesson peashooter at him. "There's a .380 Beretta taped to the underside of the kitchen table. I like the revolver best so I keep it handy."

She grinned like the Cheshire cat and went back to buttering the toast.

Mitch helped himself to the bacon piled on a plate near the stove and snagged some coffee. It pained him to admit his shortcomings, but he owed her some gratitude. "Thanks for helping me out with Director Dupé."

She gave him that noncommittal smile and kept buttering.

None of my business, and yet, he needed to know. "So you and Victor...?"

He let the question hang.

The knife went into the sink with a clatter. Emma glanced at him as she brushed crumbs from her hands. "Me and Victor what?"

The jeans and shirt upstairs certainly didn't look like Victor Dupé attire. She hadn't said anything about the man that made Mitch believe she'd slept with him. And certainly not with her hired hand, Will.

And yet...

The thought of her with Director Dupé wouldn't leave his mind. From her story the night before, she obviously thought highly of him and there had been a touch of awe in her voice.

He raised one eyebrow and shrugged. "You seem to know him well, that's all."

An odd look crossed her face. She tilted her head slightly. "We're friends."

"Dupé doesn't have friends."

"Is that so?" Two more pieces of bread went into the toaster and she pushed the lever. "Well, if you're concerned about the status of my relationship with him, I suggest you talk to Victor about it."

Right. Like *that* was going to happen.

She'd shut him down, yet there was no subterfuge, no embarrassment. If anything, she seemed amused by his little display.

He suspected he'd put his foot in his mouth. The clothes upstairs didn't belong to Victor, nor had Emma ever had an affair with the man.

Good to know.

Not that he cared.

"Is Goodsman as wacky as they say?" he asked after a sip of coffee.

She handed him a piece of toast. "Define *wacky.*"

"He encourages his fans to believe in the fantasy world of Tom Monahan, cyborgs, and the Resistance. He glamorizes that world and glorifies anyone who claims it's real. He even has a fund set up to bail fans out of jail who've committed a crime in the name of Tom Monahan. Who does that?"

The second piece of buttered toast made its way to the table with her. She took a bite as she put her reading glasses back on. "He's clever, but I assure you, he's sane by psychology standards."

"I don't know." Mitch sat and started on one of the eggs. "I think there might be some validity to that psychotic break he had when he killed his girlfriend. He perpetuates the idea that he's still Tom Monahan."

She shuffled papers, read, and chewed. "When it fits his purposes, it's easy for him to pretend he's the fictional character Tom Monahan. His fans and the press eat it up."

"You don't agree with the other experts who claimed he has grandiose delusions that he's the savior of the world?"

"Oh, I believe he has grandiose delusions, but they're bigger than the Tom Monahan world and they are firmly based in reality."

"What do you mean?"

She gathered up her file and her toast and headed for the stairs. "Chris is extremely convincing, and the most dangerous liars are those who believe they are telling the truth, but during my one-on-one interview with him, I saw a crack in his facade. I saw past the lie. So what I mean is Chris Goodsman is the best actor I've ever seen."

Disappearing from his sight, her footsteps echoed overhead as she hoofed it up the steps to the second floor.

Bending over, Mitch took a peek under the table. Sure enough, there was a .380 pocket pistol taped to the underside.

He couldn't keep the smile off his face as he finished his breakfast. A minute later, Emma reappeared, heading for the tiny mudroom off the kitchen. She pulled on a barn coat, flipping her ponytail out from under the collar.

Mitch jumped up and stuck his plate in the sink. "Where are you going?"

She tugged on a boot. "I have a client at ten."

"Seriously? Not only are you putting yourself in danger but you're willing to risk the safety of your client?"

"Good one." She winked at him and pulled on her other boot. "But it's not going to work. My client is coming from a juvenile detention center where her health and well-being are at risk on a daily basis. Trust me, even if a killer is on the loose here at the ranch, my client is safer with us than where she currently lives."

Mitch rolled his eyes at her back, then followed her out the door.

CHAPTER FIVE

Emma felt Mitch's eyes on her.

He watched her from the fence near the horse barn as she led Twinkie through his paces with Danika on his back.

The girl was especially broody today. Seeing the new foal had brightened her eyes for a few minutes, but the holiday season was tough on criminals too. Especially young juveniles. Separated from family and friends and unable to participate in the normal holiday festivities, their moods plummeted like Santa coming down the chimney.

Emma glanced over at the far field. Hope was doing well, prancing by her mother's side. Second Chance seemed to have taken to her new role as mother with ease and a certain pride. She lifted her head from grazing and stared back at Emma for a moment before flicking her tail and nuzzling Hope.

Will was cleaning out Twinkie's stall, Lady by his side. Salt and Pepper lounged in the sun near Mitch's feet.

Danika's guard roamed the area near the house, keeping an eye on the girl while getting some fresh air. Officer Carla Moses had confirmed Emma's observation about Danika's mood. "She's off her feed," the woman had told Emma, using a term they both understood as Danika had made her way to the barn to see the foal. "Was cryin' about her momma last night."

Not surprising. Most 14-year-olds would miss their mother at Christmas, juvenile detention or not. The fact that Danika had accidentally killed her mother only added to the girl's misery.

"Take him to a trot, Danika," Emma instructed her.

Danika sat up a bit taller and nudged the horse's side. Twinkie responded, moving into a faster gait, his gold and white mane lifting and falling. Danika guided the horse around the fenced-in area, as the wind blew her dreadlocks and the horse's movements provided a brief sense of freedom.

Around they went several times, each pass peeling back another layer of the girl's mood until she was smiling. Emma caught the girl's eye on the fourth pass and motioned her in.

"Get the molasses treats," Emma said after Danika dismounted. "Let's work on the tricks you learned last time."

Over the next ten minutes, Danika instructed Twinkie to lower his head on command, step in and out of a Hula Hoop lying on the ground, and lift his front feet when she pointed at each one. Finally, she took the horse through a simple obstacle course.

"Can I braid his hair?" Danika asked when they'd completed the circuit. Her gaze was downcast, her soft voice barely above a whisper.

That would cut into their time on the couch today, but time with the horse was just as important. "After you brush him down, you can do a single braid, okay?"

The girl nodded and led the horse to his stall, freshly cleaned and ready for him.

Emma followed slightly behind, giving Mitch a small smile as she passed. The wind caught his bangs, lifting them, his lovely gray eyes staring her down. No return smile, no shift in the broodiness that matched Danika's.

The fresh air and horses didn't seem to change his perspective at all, which surprised Emma. Animals and nature did the trick with almost everyone she'd ever encountered. She'd seen hardened criminals turn into saps over a puppy, stone-cold killers lose their hard edges when planting a garden.

Mitch fell into step behind her as she entered the cool shadows of the barn. Officer Moses appeared at the far end where the other barn doors were open. Her gaze touched on Danika and the horse, then on Mitch. Emma had caught the woman watching him several times.

Hard not to. All that masculinity in slouchy jeans and his black shirt. His jaw had a light sprinkle of whiskers this morning.

He looked like a motorcycle rider. Not the type that hung in gangs, but a lone wolf who needed the freedom, who was addicted to the rush.

Danika led Twinkie to his tie-up, and Emma stopped just inside the doors to give the girl some space as she went through the steps of brushing the horse down. Danika spoke softly to Twinkie and smiled when he nudged the treat bag hanging around her neck. More than once, she gave in and snuck the horse a molasses treat in between brushes.

Mitch sidled up next to Emma, saying nothing. He hadn't changed into the clothes she'd laid out for him, but had rolled the sleeves of his shirt to his elbows, revealing muscled forearms.

Taking him breakfast this morning had been more for her sake than his. When she'd stolen into the office to turn off his watch alarm at five a.m., she'd caught herself staring at him as he slept under the moonlight coming through the window. One arm had been thrown up over his head, his hair looking like he'd ravaged it with his fingers. His strong jaw sported a hint of whiskers lining his face, the lines around his eyes had been relaxed for the first time since he'd arrived. Sleeping in the monochrome light of the moon, he'd seemed younger, almost...playful.

And sexy as hell.

Long legs stretched out on her couch, that broad chest of his rising and falling with his slow, even breaths, her fingers had itched to touch him, to feel his strength. He seemed so peaceful, so unencumbered at that moment, she'd wanted to lie down right there with him. Curl into his strength and protection and sleep like she hadn't slept in a long, long time.

How long she'd stood there, she didn't know. She'd been mesmerized by his beauty, his solidness. Finally, he'd shifted in his sleep and she'd fled, embarrassed. If he'd woken and seen her hovering over him, she would have been mortified at the least, but worse he would have seen her vulnerability.

Come morning, she'd hesitated about going back in to wake him. She might get trapped in that gravitational pull of his and end up watching him again while he slept.

So she'd made a plan. He'd been sleeping so peacefully, she'd hated to wake him, but she brought food, hoping it would do the trick of keeping her focused until his nose detected a different kind of wake-up alarm.

His hair still stood up from all the hand raking he was doing. Was it out of frustration with her or because he wanted to get out of here?

His morning erection had been impressive, even when contained behind his zippered jeans. He'd looked the epitome of the morning after a night of debauchery, only she hadn't gotten the benefit of that debauchery.

Her cheeks heated. Good thing they were standing in shadows.

Too long without a man. She really needed to get out more. Go into the city, grab a random guy and work out her sexual frustrations.

But that *so* was not her. She needed a connection with a man to be attracted to him.

So why am I attracted to the man next to me? Outside of disliking the holidays, they didn't seem to have any connection.

Mitch stood watching Danika comb out and braid Twinkie's mane. "That poor horse," he mumbled under his breath.

Emma sent him a side-eye. "Poor horse?"

"You named him Twinkie and he's getting his hair braided. Do you emasculate all the males in your life?"

Ouch. "He came with that name. I didn't give it to him. He was a trick horse for a traveling show for nearly ten years, and then his owner got old and sick and couldn't care for him properly anymore. Twinkie was getting up in years too, but he was perfect for a therapy horse. Besides, he's butter yellow with a white center. He does resemble a Twinkie."

"You should rename him."

"Like what?"

"George, Carl, Dan, who cares? Just as long as it sounds manly."

"Like Mitch?"

"Mitch is a good, strong name."

Yes it is.

"Got a text from my boss," Mitch said. "They had a spotting of Goodsman forty miles south of here."

Her pulse did a skip. "That's good news, right? He's moving away from me."

"Could be a false sighting."

"Could be." But she was going to hope it wasn't.

Danika finished and they went inside. Officer Moses followed, staying downstairs as Emma led the way up to her office.

"I'll hang down here," Mitch said and Emma smiled at the way Carla's face lit up.

"Help yourself to coffee," she called to the guard. "And Agent Holden knows where the cookies are."

The two of them disappeared into the kitchen and Emma felt a twinge of jealousy when she heard Carla laugh a moment later before she shut the door to her office.

Which was entirely ridiculous.

Focus on what's in front of you.

"Who's that man downstairs?" Danika asked. She stood looking down at the rumbled cushions on the sofa.

"He's uh…" Emma snatched up the pillow Mitch had slept on and plumped it with her fists. His scent wafted up and she caught her breath. "A friend," she settled on.

The girl sat on the couch, curling her feet under her and staring over the back out the window. "He a cop?"

Emma returned to her desk and set up her pocket tape recorder. The light on her phone was blinking. Six messages.

The media was all over Chris's escape. She'd been expecting them to hunt her down, even though her number was unlisted. They were always after a statement. "He works for the government."

The girl slowly swung her gaze around, her dark eyes meeting Emma's. "You in trouble, Dr. Collins?"

Big trouble if I'm sniffing pillows and feeling jealous of Carla Moses.

The worry in Danika's eyes sobered her. Nonattachment was challenging with her patients; the kids often found it challenging as well. Without a mother figure in her life, Danika looked at Emma sometimes as if she cared for her. Maybe she did, but it was most likely transference. Danika didn't have a single role model or person in her life to support her. She looked to Emma for that sense of self.

"Agent Holden is here to help me with work, that's all."

Danika's expression barely changed, but it was enough to tell Emma she saw through the lie before the girl once more turned her focus to the view outside. "I seen the news."

Emma fiddled with the recorder, didn't turn it on. "About what?"

Danika's nonresponse was telling. She'd been watching the wildfire coverage.

Which was ill-advised. The child was under enormous emotional stress, something that could trigger her desire to set something on fire.

Emma could hardly recommend putting the girl in lockdown, but she would have to say something to Danika's social worker about limiting the girl's exposure to the wildfire news. "It would be best if you didn't watch the news right now."

Danika stared out the window. "I seen them talking about that actor dude that escaped. He doesn't like you."

That's an understatement. The phone blared and Emma hastily turned off the ringer. Damned reporters. "I'm sure the police will catch him soon. Let's talk about you."

For the next hour, Emma drew Danika out of her shell and touched on emotions triggered by the holidays. No surprise the girl was depressed. At one point, she point blank stated she had nothing to live for except seeing Twinkie.

"Will and I are having a cleanup day here at the ranch on Wednesday." Emma said on a whim." Would you like to come and spend the afternoon helping us?"

The girl's eyes brightened, but she hesitated. "That's Christmas. Why you working on Christmas?"

Why, indeed. "The horses don't care what day it is and the barn needs an in-depth cleaning."

"Are you going to have ham and potatoes for dinner? My momma always made ham and potatoes at Christmas."

Hmm. Should she humor Danika or break that trigger to the past and help her move on? Create a new tradition? "I'll see what's in the deep freeze and we'll go from there. You might end up with eggs and biscuits if I don't have anything else."

The girl shrugged. "I s'pose."

Emma took it as a good sign when Danika's steps seemed lighter as she bounced out of the office and down the stairs. She had something to look forward to now, but Emma wasn't taking a chance. She would alert Carla and Danika's case worker that the girl was borderline suicidal. That type of emotional overload was sure to trigger her desire to set a fire.

Downstairs, they found Carla alone in the kitchen. "Where's Mitch?" Emma said, then corrected herself. "Agent Holden?"

Carla cocked a thumb at the front of the house. "Had to take a call and said the reception in here was bad."

Emma followed Carla and Danika out the side kitchen door to the transport van in the driveway, keeping an eye out for her bodyguard. Unfortunately, she couldn't see him if he was out front. Once Carla had the girl secured inside the van,

Emma recommended increased surveillance through the holidays. "I'll send an official recommendation to your supervisor and Danika's case worker with today's eval. Her current mindset is unstable because of the holidays and the wildfire news coverage she's been allowed to watch. I suggest she return Wednesday to help with cleaning up the stables to keep her occupied."

"Working on Christmas?" Carla shook her head. "You need a life, Dr. Collins. So do I, though. I'll be the one to bring her, since I caught holiday duty again this year."

Emma waved them off and turned around to find Mitch watching her from a few yards away. Salt was on her back, trying to get him to cop a belly rub.

His face was grim as she approached. He held up his phone and showed her a picture. "Recognize this gal?"

Straight brown hair, pale skin, plain dark brown eyes. Behind those eyes, though... "That's Linda Brown."

"Linda Brown, a.k.a. Mary Monahan, correct? At least she believes she's Mary Monahan."

A slither of worry traced down Emma's spine. "What about her?"

"Dupé confirmed she was in the truck that ran Goodsman's transport van off the road yesterday. The van had a video camera on it and caught Brown on film. There was a man with her, but he wore a stocking cap and has yet to be identified. Goodsman escaped with them."

"Linda is Chris's number one fan. Or, I should say, she's his character *Tom's* number one fan."

"She believes she's his mother."

"You've done your homework."

"A little light reading. She's as crazy as he is, correct?"

"Crazy is technically not a mental health term."

Mitch just stared at her.

Emma let go a mental sigh. He was so sexy, standing there totally exasperated with her. "I've not had the pleasure of analyzing Linda in person, so I can't attest to her true mental state, but she appears to suffer from delusions of grandeur. Meaning, she believes she is the famous character, Mary Monahan. Chris, on the other hand, wants everyone to believe he had a psychotic break and suffered from a similar delusion of being Tom, but believe me, he's simply a sociopath manipulating the system."

"So you've said. This woman is dangerous, Dr. Collins. She's willing to kill for him."

"I doubt she did any killing herself. Not her style."

"She has a beef with you, does she not?"

Boy, did she. "She believes Chris is her son and he's here to save the world. I'm a roadblock to that."

"So that's a yes?"

Emma looked down at Salt and Pepper, both lying at Mitch's feet again, panting and watching her. "Yes."

"I have to strongly recommend once more that we leave here and get you to a safe house."

Never. Running from Chris was one thing. Running from Linda was out of the question.

She will not drive me from my home.

Of course, not heeding Mitch's warning was stupid. Which was exactly the look he was giving her—the *how can you be a complete imbecile* look.

Emma steeled herself. "Two years ago, one of Chris's fans upended my life. He took everything from me—the people I cared about, my home, the future I was planning. Please try to understand that this ranch, and everything I've built here, is the one thing that saved my sanity. Leaving here, giving Chris and Linda that kind of power, is the one thing I cannot do."

Leaving Mitch, she went inside. The kitchen felt warm and cozy, and she leaned her backside against the counter for a moment, drawing in deep breaths. He followed, the dogs trailing behind him.

Yanking out the drawer beside the sink, she grabbed a bag of

M&Ms from her secret stash. "I'm not scared of Linda Brown," she told him around a mouthful of chocolate. She always went for the M&Ms when lying. "Let her come."

"Is there anything you are scared of?" Mitch asked, his eyes serious and thoughtful.

"Sure," she said, popping another M&M. "Plenty of things. The one thing I'm not scared of is crazy people."

Collins was either brave or incredibly stupid.

At this point, Mitch was pretty sure she was both.

The doctor hustled up the stairs, M&Ms in hand, acting like her pants were on fire. He'd seen the lie in her eyes, the tremble in her hands as she shoved the colorful chocolates into her mouth like a starving woman.

Now, he watched her from the bottom of the stairs, trying not to enjoy the tight fitting jeans and the way they hugged her curvy ass.

Damn, she was a handful.

He sort of liked it.

When was the last time a woman had told him no? The last time one had presented this much of a challenge?

He couldn't remember.

"Where are you going?" he yelled up the stairs after her.

"I have to record my notes from Danika's session," came her reply.

That was it. The door to her office closed with a solid *thunk*.

The ranch was too spread out for him to watch every inch and she had no security system. If she wouldn't leave, the best he could do was stick to that sexy little ass of hers like glue.

Travesty, that.

Maybe if he became her shadow, didn't give her a minute's

peace, he could convince her to go to the safe house. Drive her crazy and make her give in.

He could drive anyone crazy. His mother always said it was a gift. She hadn't meant it in a good way.

Grinning for the first time in a long time, he climbed the stairs after Emma, the dogs on his heels. By the time he was done with the psychologist, she'd beg him to take her to the safe house.

The moment he swung through her office door, not bothering to knock, the grin fell off his face.

She stood immobile, eyes locked on her landline phone on the desk. The M&Ms had been dropped, the candies scattered at Emma's feet.

A woman's voice filled the air. *"While the world sleeps, Dr. Collins, Destiny plans. You will not take Tom from me again."*

Mitch strode to the desk and mouthed, "Who is that?"

She punched a button on the phone to mute their end. Her voice was low as she answered. "Who do you think?"

"Linda Brown?" At her nod, he grabbed her hand. "Threatening you?"

Her focus stayed on the phone. "In her own way."

"What does that mean?"

"In your terms, it means she's crazy."

A smile. Was she making a joke?

The woman was still talking in the background. "How did she get this number?" he asked.

"Good question." Her gaze came up to his. "It's unlisted."

He cocked his chin at the phone. "Let me talk to her."

"Reporters have the number, too. I have six messages from various media outlets wanting my comment."

"So someone got the number and shared it."

She nodded and unmuted the phone.

Mitch interrupted Linda's diatribe. "Linda Brown, this is Special Agent Mitch Holden. Why don't you stop with the Monahan Chronicles verbiage and tell me where you're hiding Chris Goodsman?"

The woman hesitated for a second, then her voice filled the room again, rising with her words.

"'And the cyborgs will come to destroy Him, but The Chosen One will be protected by the Resistance, carrying fire in their hands. Fire will consume them, and He will rise from the ashes of their destruction.' While the world sleeps, Dr. Collins, destiny plans. You will not take Tom from me again. I know who you are underneath your human skin. I know you're the leader of the cyborgs. You will not succeed. I will stop you."

The call ended, a dial tone taking over and Linda's voice echoing in the office.

"I'd say that constitutes a threat," Mitch said, picking up the handset and slamming it down for good measure.

Emma pulled her hand from his, bending down to scoop up the scattered M&Ms. Both dogs whined and nudged Emma's legs, her hands. Dumping her collection of the candies in the trash, she brushed her hands together, then petted their heads and leaned on the edge of the desk. "It's not credible. She's bluffing. She won't come after me unless I get in her way. She's all talk."

"She ran that transport off the road and killed the driver."

"I doubt she drove or pulled the trigger. She wanted you to see her face so all the 'resistance' fighters would know she was involved in the rescue when the video was released to the media, but she's not one to do the dirty work, even if she claims to be a resistance fighter. That much I have ascertained from studying her social media habits."

"That so?" Mitch pulled up the text from Dupé he'd received earlier and held it out for her to read.

Second armed guard, severely injured. Reports Brown shot driver point blank.

Her body language didn't change, yet he sensed she was controlling it on purpose. "I'd like to see the footage."

She tried to take his phone and tap the video clip attached to the text but Mitch held tight. She didn't need to see the camera catching the driver's calls for help. He'd been pinned by the steering wheel, unable to do more than pull his gun from its holster as Brown busted in the door, pronounced some of her TV show mumbo-jumbo, and shot him point blank.

Emma's fingers were warm against his and her eyes rose up to meet his gaze. Something sizzled between them. For a second, they stood like that, each vying for the phone without actually moving a muscle. Underneath the conquest of the phone was something else. Raw. Sensual.

Power of will was a funny thing. Mitch had learned that in the field, seeing injured soldiers ignore busted knees, broken wrists, and gunshot wounds in order to save one of their own. Hell, he'd carried a few men himself across enemy lines to safety, willpower the only thing keeping his injured body moving.

But not Mac. There'd been nothing left of Mac to carry home.

Emma released the phone and broke eye contact. Cleared her throat. "Linda is no doubt enjoying Chris's company and not worrying about me, other than to throw out threats. It empowers her. Makes her feel in control."

"He's with her right now, isn't he? So if we hunt down Linda Brown, we'll find Goodsman."

"It's possible."

Mitch pulled his cell out and dialed Cooper. The call went nowhere. "Dammit, the cell tower's out again."

"Try this." Emma scooted the desk phone toward him. "The landlines were out yesterday, but they're obviously working today."

Mitch picked up the handset and started to dial, dropped it back into the cradle. "No dial tone."

"It will come back."

"Do you have any idea where Linda might hang out? Where she might hide Goodsman?"

"No clue, but maybe something will be said in the fan forums. She'll want to gloat about rescuing Chris."

"I didn't see anything last night when I was researching, but

I'll check out more in-depth stuff while you write up your notes."

Mitch grabbed his laptop and plunked on the couch. Emma stared at him. "What?" he said.

"I dictate my notes. You'll need to go downstairs."

"Sorry, Doc, not gonna happen. Where you are, I am."

"Patient confidentiality requires—"

"Protecting *you* requires I stay within five feet of your physical presence."

"Since when?"

He gave her a snarky smile. "Since I deemed it necessary five minutes ago. You have two potential stalkers at this point who've both made threats against your life. I'm not going anywhere, and no offense, but I couldn't care less about your patient, so suck it up."

"You don't need to be in the same room with me. At least step out into the hall and give me some privacy."

Pepper came and laid down at his feet. Salt stayed by Emma. Both of them watched her as Mitch opened his laptop and searched for the satellite connection. "Nope."

The dogs looked at him.

So did Emma, giving him a penetrating stare as she drew out her chair and sat. "Why are you being difficult about this?"

Back the dogs' heads went to look at her.

Difficult? She hadn't seen difficult yet. "You're the one refusing to let me take you somewhere safe. This is the best compromise I can make."

"Did you throw temper tantrums when you were little and didn't get your way?"

And *ho-boy*, how did she know that? "Who's deflecting now? Do you always redirect the situation to psycho-analyzing when you're challenged?"

There it was, that patient smile. "You *did* throw tantrums, but someone somewhere along the way taught you the strategies of passive-aggressive behavior."

Thank you, Mommy Dearest. "Actually, it's not passive-aggressive behavior I'm practicing right now. It's called a tactical maneuver and I learned it from my brother. If you want me to give you some space, pack up your things and let me take you to the safe house. I'll give you all the space you need once we're there."

No patient smile this time. Her glare was pure frustration.

After a tense moment, it passed. She clicked a key on her computer keyboard and Mitch heard a faint ding.

Emma Collins started dictating.

Holden 1, Collins 0.

CHAPTER SIX

An hour later, Emma removed her pistol from the gun cabinet where she'd locked it prior to Danika's arrival. She stuck the handgun in her leather holster, grabbed a box of bullets, and returned the shotgun to its home over the front door.

"Where are you going?" Mitch said as he followed her outside.

The midday sun was warm overhead, though smoke from the fires clouded the sky. She headed for the barn, the dogs running ahead. "Shooting practice."

His long legs ate up the ground, keeping up with her with no problem. "Excuse me?"

"I thought it might be a good idea to brush up on some target practice."

"You've got to be kidding."

"You're welcome to join me."

The bullheaded son-of-a-bitch was cute but annoying. He'd sat and scanned fan forums, complaining nonstop about her lousy satellite Internet service while she tried to concentrate and dictate her notes. Finally, in order to drown him out, she'd slapped in her earbuds and cranked some meditation instrumentals to lower her blood pressure while she typed up an analysis of Danika's mood and emailed it to the girl's caseworker.

It took three tries, but finally the e-mail went through.

The landline and cellular service continued to play havoc with communications and Mitch had been unable to speak to

Victor or his team of fellow agents. He'd sent several e-mails and texts but hadn't received any replies.

"You have a secure shooting range out here?" He shaded his eyes as he looked around the property.

There was nothing in the woods but wild animals, so *secure* was a matter of perspective.

The barn was cool and shadowed. Twinkie raised his head at the sound of them entering. Second Chance and her foal were still outside.

"In the woods." Emma stroked Twinkie's neck as she went by, murmuring soothing words to him as she hauled his saddle from the wall and secured it on his back.

"The woods." Mitch crossed his arms and looked at her like she'd grown an extra head. "That seems like a safe place to go when two people are gunning for you. What are you, a glutton for punishment? A too-stupid-to-live heroine in a horror flick? There's a killer on the loose who's coming after you, and oh, yeah, there's a forest fire blazing out of control a few miles from here, so let's go into the woods."

The sarcasm in his voice could have peeled the paint from the barn walls if they'd had any. Emma tightened the cinch on Twinkie's saddle and made sure his bit was secure. "My woods are on the southeast side, a half mile or so from the ranch and even farther away from the forest fires than we are right here. We're both well-armed. I don't see how that compares to a movie heroine with questionable decision making skills or someone with a victim or martyr complex."

He stood there, staring at her as if she suddenly turned into an alien or was speaking a different language. "I stand by my earlier assessment that you're nuts."

She half smiled to herself, grabbing a second saddle for Igor, the old gelding standing in a patch of sunlight. "I understand your reluctance to be here, Agent Holden, and I hope we can resolve this situation soon, but until then, would you rather I cower in the house or take you out for a round of gun practice?

Special agents like yourself have to stay sharp, right? Regular practice at the range and all."

Glancing over her shoulder as she saddled up Igor, she saw the slightest tick in his jaw. "We should be figuring out where Brown and Goodsman are hiding out, what kind of vehicle they might be driving, and who might be helping them."

"You said there was nothing more in the fan forums, and we have limited internet access, so that seems like a further waste of time to me." Emma patted the gelding's neck and handed Mitch the reins. "Agent Holden, meet Igor. After we get back from target practice, I'll give you my notes on Chris from my sessions with him. I also have quite a collection of research on Linda and her obsession with the show. Maybe it will give you insight. Deal?"

A heartbeat of silence. "Would you really shoot Goodsman if he showed up here?"

She hauled herself up onto Twinkie's back. "I can and I will if necessary."

"What about the shotgun? I thought you were going to use that to do it. What's with this sudden need to take your pistol out and shoot it?"

The truth felt like a rough pebble in her throat. "I haven't shot my Smith and Wesson in two years. It saved my life then and it may have to again."

She forced herself to meet his gaze. The tick in his jaw sped up. His face hardened even more but his voice came out softer, more sincere. "Goodsman's fan? The one you mentioned earlier?"

"Someone attacked me and I stopped them. I don't take shooting anything—human, animal, even a can—lightly, but in the event that my life, or the life of someone I love, is threatened, you're damn skippy I'm pulling the trigger."

A sly grin crossed his lips. "I like you, Dr. Collins. You're as crazy as your patients, but then maybe you have to be to survive all that shit you have to listen to from them."

He didn't know the half of it. "You're starting to get the picture, Agent. Have you ever ridden a horse before?"

"Couple times." He kicked a boot into Igor's stirrup and hoisted himself up. "You a good shot?"

A laugh bubbled up from her throat. "Hell, no. That's why I use a shotgun."

He raised an eyebrow at her. "Then maybe we oughta bring that shotgun, you think?"

She steered Twinkie out of the barn. "You're my shotgun on this trip."

———————

The forest was quiet. Too quiet.

Mitch's nerves were already on edge, and the absolute, unnatural silence amplified every twig snap under his horse's feet, every snort the animal gave as they wound their way along the creek, then across it to the other side of the woods.

Mitch kept an eye out for animals, saw none. Not a bird tweeting, not a rabbit munching grass or a mouse scavenging for food. Scared off by the wildfires, most likely.

They were going in deep, Emma leading the way through spruce and fir trees on Twinkie.

Twinkie, Igor, Second Chance. Salt, Pepper, Lady.

Three adult horses, three dogs. Symmetry.

The doctor seemed to like that. Everything in her house had a symmetry to it—the pictures, her clothes, the way she laid food out on a plate. Even the cadence of her voice, the way she walked. All of it was in balance with life, her environment. She was currently working hard to maintain that, and after what he'd gleaned from the information she'd given earlier, plus the police report he'd managed to pull up from two years ago, he now fully understood why.

It was no wonder she was fighting so hard not to leave the

ranch and show fear or uncertainty. A part of him understood that. He respected her staunchness. He'd been there a few times himself.

But God Almighty, he wanted to pick her up, throw her over his shoulder, and get the hell out of here.

Balance and stability were not qualities he'd ever admired. His mother had tried to create that type of life for him and Mac. On the surface, she'd succeeded, but at great personal cost. All the struggling to pay bills and make ends meet had meant they hadn't seen her much. He respected the fact she'd worked her tail off to keep them in decent shoes and food on the table, but when she'd had downtime, it had never involved them. She never came to a baseball game or a school event, never took them anywhere. When she was off work, she stayed in bed or went out with a man.

Boyfriend of the week, he and Mac had dubbed the ones who'd hung on longer than one night. A few of them actually made it longer than a week.

Up ahead, Emma let Twinkie walk at his own pace, her soft voice talking sweetly as she guided the poor horse on a dirt path as narrow as a stripper's G-string. No fear in that woman. Even though Cooper had alerted Mitch to the fact they'd had a call from a witness saying they'd spotted Goodsman and Brown forty miles south of the transport van incident, Mitch wasn't letting his guard down. Eye witnesses were often wrong. Until Goodsman was in cuffs and back in prison, Mitch was keeping a close eye on his charge.

Emma wasn't backing down, foolhardy as it was. No cowering on her end. Instead, she was going to brush up on her use of lethal force.

His kind of woman.

"Where does this trail lead?" he called.

She didn't slow, didn't look back. "It meanders around for a few miles, then merges with an old logging trail into the park. The logging trail was used before the park became state owned."

Hmm. "How far is it until you enter the park?"

She shrugged. "Seven or eight miles. Maybe more. Why?"

Mitch's gaze landed on her braid, dropped down to her ass cupped in the saddle. The sway of the horse's body rocked hers, showcasing her comfortable posture and sexy curves. "I'm supposed to be figuring out who set the fire in the park and which way they went."

His mind drifted back to the dream he'd had the previous night. Emma on his motorcycle, naked, her long legs gripping the seat, then gripping him as he pounded into her. His imagination took over, bending her over the bike seat so he could get his fill of that sweet ass of hers.

A bird called from far off, bringing him back to reality and making his tension ease a bit. A bird was good. Meant the fires were far enough away that animals felt safe again.

A hundred yards ahead, he saw a clearing with a felled tree and a collection of tin cans on the ground. He dodged a low-hanging pine branch as Igor plodded along on the not-so-smooth trail.

Emma guided Twinkie off the path to a small outcropping of bushes. She hopped down and tied the horse to a tree. "We'll leave the horses here. They're used to gunshots, but no sense agitating them unnecessarily."

He'd known her less than two days, but already he recognized her modus operandi. Calm, patient, serene—keeping those around her, whether animal or human, the same way.

Was it pretense or did it come naturally, this even-tempered, unruffled persona? What would it take to make her lose it, he wondered.

He also wondered if he had it in him to find out.

Mitch tied up Igor, shutting down his errant, pornographic thoughts and keeping an eye on the woods around them. Twigs and pinecones snapped under his feet. The trees were good cover and the underbrush would give away anyone who attempted to sneak up on them.

Another plus.

Emma left him behind, heading for the felled tree and tin cans. As he watched from the protection of the trees, she set up the cans on the log, then backed up twenty paces and checked her gun.

Satisfied, she eyed her target. Her chest expanded, then stilled as she raised the S&W and aimed at the first can.

No rushing. A balanced stance. Self-confidence radiating off her. She looked as competent as any agent at the firing range.

Pfft, the gun discharged, a bullet whizzing at her target.

Dead pine needles and dust mushroomed into the air where the bullet hit the ground.

Another breath and she moved her hand ever so slightly, realigning.

Pfft.

Another miss, this one coming closer and digging into the dead bark of the tree.

A sigh of defeat escaped her lips and she looked over her shoulder at him. An embarrassed, tight smile trembled on her lips. "See what I mean?"

"Do you need your glasses?" he joked.

It wasn't really a joke. He hated that frustrated smile, the defeat in her voice. Everything she was doing seemed spot on. Her vision, however, might not be the culprit. He'd seen it plenty of times before.

"Only when reading," she replied. "Distance vision is 20/20. Any other ideas?"

Walking over to her, he checked her weapon's site, found nothing wrong. "Take your firing stance again."

She did and he tucked himself behind her, peering over her shoulder. She smelled like citrus and horses and good, clean air, and hell on wheels, he breathed that sweet scent deep into his lungs, letting his eyes fall closed for a moment.

Snap out of it.

But he couldn't. It'd been so damn long since he'd been

intrigued by a woman. Since he'd found one who was good at getting him to forget the never-ending pain and grief lodged under his breastbone.

"Mitch?"

Her soft voice brought his eyes open. He cleared his throat. She glanced at him from her peripheral vision, keeping her gun aimed at the cans. "Is everything alright?"

Wanting to touch her, he put his hands on her shoulders—just a light touch—to make her relax a bit. "See that bird on the red can's label?"

Her breath hitched, her body tightening ever so slightly under his touch. She swung her gaze back to the can, her voice coming out higher, lighter. "Yep, got it."

"Let the can, the tree, everything else fall away." He removed his hands but kept close to her, enjoying the feel of her heat, the way his presence had the pulse under her ear jumping. "Concentrate on the eye of the bird, Emma. Just that and that alone."

She gave him an almost imperceptible nod. "Have you taught many people to shoot?"

Too many. Hell, he'd taught Mac all those years ago, and look what good that had done.

Blinking, he barred the ugly memories from derailing this moment in the woods with a beautiful woman. Moments like this were too few and far between. "Focus."

Another tiny nod. Her fingers flexed as she adjusted her grip. Deep breath—

Mitch stepped back.

—*Pfft!*

The clang of the bullet hitting the tin can rang out, echoing in the clearing.

Emma lowered the gun and whirled, a giant smile on her face. "I did it!"

She hadn't hit the eye, but she'd nailed the can, and that was what mattered. He smiled back, liking the bubble of delight enveloping her face as she laughed. "You doubt my coaching skills?"

"You're a fine teacher, Agent Holden."

Oh, the things he wanted to teach her. "A teacher is only as good as his student."

She stepped toward him, still smiling. "Did you learn that in agent school?"

The teasing was heavy in her tone. No one had teased him in a long time, and she was good at it. Initially, he'd found it annoying, but now...

Still, he took a step back, needing space to keep him from grabbing her and kissing her. "Actually, I learned it from a superior."

"Victor?"

"Cooper Harris."

She took another step toward him and he suddenly felt like a mouse being preyed on by a cat. "Sounds like quite a guy."

He stood his ground this time. "He is."

Her gaze traveled over his face. She licked her bottom lip and the sweet, hot flare of desire shot to his groin. "Any other tips you want to share with me?"

He could think of a few. Or a hundred. All of them involving her with fewer clothes on. "Practice, practice, practice."

She *hmmed* on a smiling sigh. "I think it's your turn, isn't it?"

Silence hung in the air between them. God, he wanted to kiss her. Wanted to back her up against one of these ancient pines while he kissed that coy smile off her face. His body ached to find relief in her steady comfort. Her patience.

Even her teasing.

As she stood before him, waiting, totally open with no hidden agenda that he could detect, and every one of her nonverbal cues giving him a green light, he still hesitated. This was a job, not a quickie in the woods with a woman he could walk away from when they were both satisfied. He was here to protect her and instead, here he was, completely distracted by her.

Her life depended on him; that's why he was here.

The sharp knife of guilt, always mixed with his inexplicable grief, stole his breath for a moment. Mac had needed him, too. Had been depending on him to keep him safe, alive.

His brother was dead because of him.

Clenching his jaw, Mitch looked away from Emma. His attention snagged on the cans, then flitted to the trees, back at the horses.

"Um," she said, suddenly uncertain, "go ahead. I'll get out of your way."

The smile fell off her face and she moved several feet back, checking her gun and ignoring him.

Shit. Now he'd done it.

But what could he say? What could he do?

Certainly not kiss her.

Taking his Glock from its holster, he strode across the pine needles, took his stance, and aimed.

His neck and shoulders muscles knotted. *Too tight to be shooting.* He needed to relax.

Couldn't.

Breathe, goddammit. Breathe.

He blanked his mind, imagining the bastard who'd dropped the bomb that killed his brother standing before him instead of the cans.

Bam, bam, bam, the shots echoed in the forest and the tin cans rose into the air, suspended for a brief instant before they toppled, one right after the other.

Release came then. His neck. His shoulders. His whole body.

Emma strode up next to him. "Impressive. I wish I could shoot like that."

"Practice," he said, his voice coming out stronger than he'd expected. "Lots of practice."

"Do you mind if I shoot some more?"

He glanced at her face, found that calm, serene smile on it. His lungs filled and he found he could smile back. "I'll set up the cans."

He'd only gotten two of them back on the log when he heard the distant sound of a shotgun. Emma's head swung around to look over her shoulder in the direction of the ranch. "Was that…?"

Mitch hauled ass across the distance, grabbing her by the elbow and together they ran for the horses.

CHAPTER SEVEN

Igor might be old, but the animal still had spunk. As Emma kicked Twinkie's flanks and followed Mitch, she was impressed by the agent's ability to maneuver the aging horse through the woods at a healthy gait and at Igor's ability to meet Mitch's demands.

The dogs ran ahead of all of them. Once Mitch and Emma broke free from the trees, Mitch gave Igor his head, turning the animal loose to run, and Emma prodded Twinkie to follow suit. The horses' legs worked quickly to carry them both back to the ranch.

Will waited for them, Emma's shotgun in hand.

"What happened?" Mitch demanded as they wheeled up to the corrals.

"Stranger," Will said, eyes scanning the area east of the barn. "Saw him slinking behind the stables. Called him out and he took off for the rocky area out there."

Mitch jumped down from his horse. "You hit him?"

"Nah. Scared him off, but the shot was more to get your attention."

Emma guided Twinkie around so she could get a better look at the path leading to the pond and the direction the stranger had taken. "What did he look like?"

"Get down," Mitch demanded, grabbing Twinkie's reins and holding the horse steady. "We need to get you in the house."

"Shouldn't we go after him?" she asked, scanning the tree line and hills.

Will held the shotgun like a baby in his arms, but he was ready for another round. "I didn't get a good look at him, but if it was someone we knew, they wouldn't have been pussyfooting around the place. Figured it was better to shoot first and ask questions later."

Mitch nodded, pulling out his weapon. "Good call."

"We should go after him," Emma insisted. "Find out who it is. It might not be Chris. It might be someone displaced by the fires who was looking for help."

Mitch shook his head. "Get down, Dr. Collins, and get your butt in the house."

Curiosity demanded she find out who it was. She hated living in fear and had made a vow never to do so again.

But truth was, she didn't want to go running off into the woods in search of a stranger. She wanted to make a cup of tea and think about what nearly had happened with Mitch under that oak tree.

Sighing, she gave in. The saddle creaked as she ignored Mitch's hands and used the horn to swing off the horse's back.

The ground should have felt solid under her feet. Instead, her knees gave a little. Her vision seemed to close in on her.

Fear. God, she hated that damned emotion, making her weak and shaky.

Not all of her bravado was false—she'd trained her mind and her emotions for the past two years and she never intended to go back to being a victim.

But there was something unnerving about the seriousness in the look Mitch kept giving her. Something about hearing that gunshot that had made the unnerved sensation go straight to her stomach.

Vulnerability.

Her heart beat a high, rapid tempo against her ribs. There had been a strange man—possibly a man who wanted to kill her—roaming her property. The old flash of terror, embedded deep in her bones, came flooding back with sudden ferocity.

Realizing Mitch might be right—that Chris and Linda were actually coming after her—pissed her off as well.

Anger was a better emotion. She could work with that, not let it freeze her up.

Stay angry. "Will, can you take care of the horses?"

"Happy to," he said. "Long as you do as the agent here asks and get yourself tucked safely into the house."

Pulling her Smith & Wesson from the holster, she took off the safety and gave the property one more scan. Nothing but the leaves on the trees blowing in the wind. Birds sang and the dogs meandered around in the grass, unalarmed.

Mitch moved in front of her, and started to take her elbow. She jerked away. "I'm going, but I want to know who the hell that was."

"Soon as I put up the horses," Will said, "I'll see if I can pick up his tracks."

Mitch was torn, she could see it in his eyes. He wanted to do some tracking himself, but his mission was to stick close to her and make sure she was safe.

That was his issue to work out. She moved away, heading for the house, the dogs falling in beside her.

She heard Mitch mumble something to Will but couldn't make out what he said. He caught up to her halfway across the yard. She tensed, waiting for the lecture about how they needed to leave.

It didn't come.

On the porch, Mitch caught her hand before she could grab the doorknob. His big, strong hand held hers immobile.

The rest of her body went immobile too. "What are you doing?" she asked, trying to pull away.

"Shh," he said, drawing her close. "I go in first, make sure it's safe. You follow."

His eyes told her the reason why. The stranger behind the

barn might have been a decoy. Chris or Linda might actually be inside.

She couldn't stop the involuntary tremble that snaked down her spine.

His hand tightened on hers. "I'll protect you, Emma."

His voice was low and controlled. Totally confident.

Emma.

He'd used her first name instead of Dr. Collins or Doc.

Progress? Or a tool to make her feel safe?

His confidence was not simply a show of bravado. He truly believed in himself. It hadn't even been twenty-four hours and she believed in him too.

"I'm okay," she lied. She didn't want to, but she found herself returning the hand squeeze. She liked the strength, the control that simple movement gave her. "Let's get this over with."

Which was another lie. A part of her didn't want it to be over with because then he would let her go. Right now, his hand was the only thing keeping her grounded. Keeping her knees from giving out.

I am nuts.

She told the dogs to stay, gave him a nod.

He raised his gun and nodded back.

Her clinical mind came to the rescue. As he opened the door, she watched him, analyzed his movements. He flinched at the noisy squeak of the door and she made a mental note to oil the hinges.

Mitch Holden was something to behold as he entered her house. His body was that of a panther stalking its prey, ready to strike. Ready to defend her. His lanky body glided with silent ease.

As he pulled her behind him, he went right, sweeping his gun in front of both of them, his gaze taking in every detail. At one point, he stopped and cocked his head to listen to something. She cocked her head too, but heard nothing except the hum of the fridge.

They moved on.

The tightness in her chest loosened. He'd kept her with him. That said something, didn't it? He could have shoved her in a closet or the kitchen pantry and told her to stay put, but instead, he kept hold of her hand and allowed her to trail after him.

Mimicking his position, she kept her gun pointed at the ceiling and her senses attuned to the environment. *Don't screw this up.*

After clearing the first floor, they climbed the stairs. Emma locked her gaze on Mitch's back, trying to be as quiet as possible and amazed at his ability to avoid the weak points in the wooden stairs whereas she seemed to find every spot that groaned and creaked.

The price you paid for living in an old farmhouse.

The last room they cleared was her bedroom. Her bed was still unmade, a breeze coming in the open window and billowing the curtains.

"Did you leave that window open?" he growled.

Her pulse skittered under her skin. "I opened it this morning to let in some fresh air. The house smelled like bacon. I forgot to close it."

Mitch released her hand, checked the closet and under the bed. "Luckily, we're all clear. Did you notice anything out of place or missing while we were going through the place?"

She shook her head, already embarrassed at the fact she'd left that damn window open and that she'd clung to him like a scared little girl all through the house. "Everything looks exactly as I left it."

He closed the window, locked it, and pulled the shade. "I'm going to check the attic."

"I'll go with you."

Mitch pulled the attic stairs down from the ceiling at the end of the hall and Emma flipped the light switch. The bare bulb up above threw soft light down on them. As they climbed the narrow steps, dust swirled in the air, tickling Emma's nose.

She hadn't been up here in a few weeks. Mitch hit the landing and did a visual sweep of the scattered boxes, the old desk, and her telescope, pointed at the northern sky.

Hiding places were minimal, save perhaps if you were the size of a mouse. Mitch's gaze took in the telescope for a brief moment before he looked back at her. "Do you use it?"

Her throat felt like she'd swallowed cotton balls, which was silly. It wasn't like she was spying on her neighbors—she had none. She cleared her throat, focused on a box near her feet. Some old college texts books. Why was she hanging on to those? "On occasion."

"You have a good sky view from here, I bet."

"On clear nights, I can see a long way."

They left the attic, clomping down the stairs. Mitch shoved the collapsible steps back up and turned off the lights. "Can you get that file for me? The one you have on Goodsman?"

"Sure." Back to business, but she smelled like sweat. Like fear. "I need to change my clothes first."

He looked at her funny, then nodded. "Stay away from the windows."

He walked out and Emma plopped down on the bed and blew out a long breath.

On one hand, she felt slightly ridiculous. The stranger could have been anyone. Like she'd said in the yard, it could even be someone displaced by the fires. They might have had car trouble or been hiking in the park and got lost when the fires started. They could be exhausted, hungry, injured.

But a part of her knew Mitch was being smart to keep her secluded. It could be Chris. While the actor's personality and normal MO didn't point to him being a stalker, she knew better than to believe it was completely out of the range of possibility. Anything was possible. She'd learned that two years ago.

Putting the safety back on her gun, she set it on the nightstand and went to the closet. Pulling on fresh jeans, a tank, and a flannel shirt, she felt better. Will had sent the stranger running, his show of boldness scaring the person off. Mitch was in the house with her, and he wouldn't let anyone get in and hurt her.

Fluffing her hair, she looked at her reflection in the full-length mirror on the back of her closet door. Her cheeks were flushed, her eyes bright with new-found confidence. She smiled at herself and started a mental to-do list.

Find the file on Chris.

Make tea.

Cancel appointments.

She hated that last one. Like Danika, the kids she was working with this week all needed extra attention, but she couldn't endanger their lives by bringing them to the ranch. Maybe she could arrange to visit them instead. It wouldn't be the same without the horses to aid her, but it was better than nothing.

Back at the nightstand, she opened the drawer to stick the gun inside and froze, her world tilting once more on its axis.

"Here," Emma said, shoving a well-worn green file at Mitch. "This is everything I have on paper. I also have computer records I can copy to a USB if you want them."

Seated at the kitchen table, he moved his cookie aside to make room for the massive file. He'd raided the Snoopy jar and was on his third oatmeal chocolate chip.

Salt and Pepper thumped their tails at Emma's entrance, but she ignored them. Tenseness radiated from her body. Her face was as white as the refrigerator.

"You okay?" he asked.

She turned on her heel and headed out. "Yep, peachy."

"Where are you going?"

He heard her footsteps pounding up the stairs. Her voice came back muffled. "To pack."

Wait. *What?*

Pack, as in leave the ranch?

He knew she'd been rattled by the idea that someone had been on her property, but in the heat of the moment, she'd seemed normal. In denial mostly. Inside the house, she hadn't flinched when he'd taken her room by room to make sure there were no intruders.

So why the sudden change of heart?

Leaving the cookie and the file on the table, he followed her up the stairs.

He found her in her bedroom stuffing a couple of T-shirts into a pale blue overnight bag.

Okay, kiddos, what's wrong with this picture?

Fuck if he knew.

On one hand, he was relieved she was finally coming to her senses. On the other…the woman hastily throwing clothes into a bag wasn't the same Emma Collins who'd been driving him nuts for the past day. The one with a telescope in her attic and a fondness for lost causes.

"What's going on?" he asked.

"I was wrong," she said with a shrug. She'd changed clothes and returned the gun holster to under her arm. "You were right. I should leave the ranch for now and go to a safe house."

And yep. Mind blown.

This woman. He couldn't get a handle on her. One moment, she was sitting in a rocking chair downstairs with a shotgun on her lap refusing to leave, and the next her butt was on fire to get away from the ranch as fast as she could.

Not only did no woman, *ever*, tell a man he was right, this woman definitely never admitted she was wrong.

Her change of heart, along with her absolute mechanical movements and lack of eye contact, was starting to freak him out.

"Emma, what's going on? Why the sudden change of heart?"

She off-handedly pointed over at her nightstand. "Someone *was* in the house. They left me a message."

On the nightstand, he saw a lamp, a stack of books, and a box of tissues. Nothing looked different from his last foray in the room only minutes ago.

He moved closer. The plastic green toy next to the base of the lamp was so small, he almost missed it.

Removing a tissue from the box, he snatched it up and took a closer look. An army man, like the kind he and Mac had played with as kids.

On closer inspection, he realized what he was looking at. "Is this what I think it is?"

"One of the many Tom Monahan resistance fighters marketed to kids around the world. I hear they're collector items among adults as well."

Her voice was neutral; her jerky movements not so much.

The green army man was a replica of Tom Monahan in a famous scene at the end of Season Five. Mitch had seen it while researching—one of the most valuable of all of the collectors items. The Tom figurine held an Uzi in one hand and had a patch over his right eye. In his other hand, he held up the severed head of a cyborg.

Great for kids.

"Goddammit," Mitch said under his breath. No wonder Emma was now ready to leave. "Did you touch this?"

Her sharp gaze snapped to his. "Yes, sorry."

"I'll bag it anyway and we'll get it dusted for prints."

"Does it matter whose prints are on it? I mean, it seems pretty obvious who put it there, doesn't it?"

"It's all evidence for when we catch this sick bastard and his accomplices."

She nodded. "I have a few things I need from my office, and I'll need to alert Will I'm leaving. Hopefully, he'll stay and take care of the horses. Do you think he's in danger?"

"He seems quite capable of handling things."

"Can I bring the dogs? Not Lady, she won't leave Will. Just Salt and Pepper."

As always, the Labs had followed him and now lounged together in a patch of sun on the bedroom floor.

"The safe house is for people, not pets, but…"

"But you like them and you know I'm right. They're a good security system on top of whatever the safe house might have."

If it would get her out of this house and to a place where protecting her was easier, he'd stand on his head. "I'll grab their food and throw it in my truck."

"Thank you."

"The sooner we leave the better."

"Give me five."

He nodded, took the toy, and headed downstairs. The plastic Tom Monahan went into an evidence bag he pulled from of his truck. He tossed a giant bag of dog food from the mudroom into the back.

Will came across the yard. "Buggin' out?"

"Seems our stranger was in the house. He left Emma a little gift."

"Ah, shit. What was it?"

Mitch held up the bagged toy. "Not a lot of doubt in my mind who's behind this."

"That actor guy, huh?" Will frowned and rubbed his chin. "Doesn't seem like the type to hike around in the woods, does he?"

"I'd go looking for him and whatever vehicle he got here in, but her safety comes first."

"Not much traffic getting in and out of the valley from what I've heard on the CB. Think he came in on foot?"

"Dangerous with the fires and smoke."

Will nodded, looked off in the distance. "Bastard. He had to have transport, but you can't just drive around out there. I didn't find anything for tracks, human or motorized, but I'll take another look, see if I find anything that hints at horses or motorcycles."

Motorcycles. He needed to get back to hunting down his arsonist. "Might not have been Goodsman, but one of his fans who believes he's a resistance fighter. They're into survival shit, right? You may be spot on that he hiked in and out. Either way, Emma's finally decided to go to the safe house. She's worried about you and the horses."

Will grunted and patted the dog who was attached to his leg. "I can handle myself against some milquetoast, pansy actor or anyone who thinks they're part of his *resistance* fighters. Tell her not to worry. The horses and I will be fine."

The two men shook hands and Mitch went inside.

Emma was waiting, overnight bag in hand. "Will's going to stay?"

"He is," Mitch said, gathering up the file on Goodsman. The last of the cookie went into his mouth. "You ready?"

She took a long look around at the kitchen, then walked into the living room and took down her shotgun. Meeting Mitch's eyes, she nodded. "Ready."

Maybe the old Emma was back. He felt the corner of his mouth twitch as he opened the front door and scanned the area. Satisfied all was clear, he motioned her outside. "Let's go."

CHAPTER EIGHT

"Sorry, agent." The state trooper looked haggard, deep creases around his eyes and bracketing his mouth as he studied Mitch's credentials. "Roads west and south are closed because of the fires."

Emma sighed silently, feeling slightly claustrophobic at the mass of cars and people. All four lanes in both directions were backed up. No one was moving.

"What about north?" Mitch said.

"Ten-car pile-up five miles from here has shut down evacuation efforts for now."

Her bodyguard gripped the steering wheel so hard his knuckles turned white. "How soon before it's cleaned up?"

"Could be hours. Lot of people injured, possible fatality from what I heard on the radio. Emergency medical personnel can't get to them because of this traffic jam and they're already tied up with other casualties."

Emma wondered if she would have to pry Mitch's fingers from the leather-covered wheel. He held his agitation in tight, most likely from his training but possibly a learned response from his upbringing.

His gray eyes cut to the jam-packed road of cars and trucks stretching from one horizon to the other, back to the trooper. "Thank you, officer."

He wheeled the truck around and they headed back toward the way they'd come, going off-road to get around the tangle of cars trying to merge onto the highway.

"What now?" Emma asked. "Back to the ranch?"

"We passed a motel a mile back, didn't we?"

"The Lazy 8? I wouldn't board my horse there."

"Goodsman and Brown wouldn't suspect you're there either, I'm guessing."

Her cell rang and she jumped, not expecting a call, especially since the towers were so hit and miss. "It's from the ranch," she said checking the ID.

"You've got service?"

"3G, but yes."

He wheeled farther off the road and parked, pulling out his cell as she answered.

Will sounded out of breath when she answered. "I've got a problem," he said. "I wouldn't have called, but..."

"You saw the stranger again?"

"No, not him. It's Second Chance."

Emma's stomach plunged. In her peripheral vision, she saw Mitch do a fist pump as his call must have connected. "What's wrong with her?"

"She's listless. Keeps sitting on her haunches and won't let Hope nurse. I called the vet, but she can't get out here. Said the roads are shut down."

"They are."

"Hell in a hand basket, I'm so sorry."

She so didn't need this right now. "Will, this is not your fault."

"I'm cursed, Emma."

"You're not cursed, for Heaven's sake."

Mitch bailed out of the truck, but the driver side window was still down from his conversation with the deputy. "Coop?" she heard him say. "Yeah, I've been trying to get through to you and Dupé. We can't get out. I finally convinced Miss Bullheaded to split, and now we're stuck. The highway's jammed front to back."

Miss Bullheaded? *He should talk.*

"What do you want me to do?" Will said. Panic laced his voice. "I keep urging her to her feet, but she never stays long, and she's completely off her feed. I have no idea what's wrong."

Post-foaling problems ran the gambit. Hopefully, it was nothing serious. If it was, they were in trouble with no vet to help them out. "We'll be back in a little bit. We can't get out of the area anyway. Try to keep her up and moving if you can."

"I'll do my best."

They disconnected. Emma continued to eavesdrop on Mitch's conversation. He'd brought his boss up to date on the stranger who'd paid them a visit. "...couldn't pick up any tracks. No idea how the guy got there or got away. Maybe he didn't. Gordon's a survivalist. He and this guy both may still be hanging around in the forest. The fires traveled west and north. It's burned a lot of acres so far, but there are still thousands untouched."

Tension coiled low in her stomach. The best way in and out of the valley at a time like this was on a horse. Did Chris know how to ride?

"I'm shooting for a hotel that's not far from the ranch," Mitch said. "That's my only choice."

Think about Second Chance, not yourself.

Emma leaned toward the open window. It was easier to focus on Second Chance than herself. "We're going back to the ranch. My new mother is having problems and our vet can't get out to see her. I need to check her out."

Mitch covered the end of the phone with his hand. "We're not going back to the ranch." He removed his hand and spoke to the man on the phone again. "Yeah, I took a look at the maps Dupé sent and the video footage from the park. Our pyro probably had someone inside who helped him."

"Agent Holden, this is serious," Emma spoke over him. "We need to get back to the ranch. Second Chance could die."

This time he ignored her as he spoke into the phone. "I need to see the ignition site, but evidence will be hard to come by since the fire probably burned up any that the arsonist left behind."

People in the cars across from them stared at her and watched Mitch as he paced beside the truck door. The tension in her stomach pulled tighter, a wire about to break. What if Chris and Linda were in one of the cars out here, watching them?

"Please get back in the truck," Emma said to Mitch.

He must have heard the trepidation in her voice. He leaned down, cocked a brow at her.

"Please," she said again. "We need to go."

"You're kidding." But he wasn't talking to her. He was responding to something his boss had said. "Dammit. Should have figured that. Is there any way you can get a helo out to the ranch? Lots of National Guard in the area. Take her out that way?"

He listened, sliding into the truck seat and shifting into drive. Emma's rapid pulse slowed a fraction. Her stomach was still tied in knots.

The truck shot forward. Mitch blew out a disappointed sigh. "Yeah, I know, I waited too goddamn late. We'll hunker down at the ranch until Dupé can scare up transportation. Hell, I'd take an army transport at this point… Yeah, I'll handle it. Trust me…" He glanced over at her. "The good doctor here is one tough lady. She can handle a gun, a horse, and herself. Chris Goodsman tries anything, he'll have to get through me. If he manages that, Dr. Collins will still kick his ass."

The compliment made her flush. She looked away, studied the weeds and wildflowers lining the frontage road. The valley lay just ahead, gray clouds of smoke lingering on the horizon.

Mitch disconnected after a few more comments. "Hotel's booked, according to Coop, so we're out of options."

"No matter. I need to get back to my horses."

"What's wrong with Second Chance?"

"I don't know. Will said, all of a sudden, she's gone off her feed and keeps sitting on the ground. Could be something serious."

"You sure you're alright staying at the ranch?"

The toy version of Tom Monahan sat in its plastic evidence bag between them in the cup holder. A part of her wanted to toss it out the window. The other wanted to make Chris Goodsman eat it.

"I'm fine."

Mitch said nothing more until they were back in front of her house. It took longer to get back, since they had to go against the flow of traffic, but they made it, Will waving to them from the pasture where he was attempting to lead Second Chance around. She balked at the harness, trying to back away from him.

The dogs jumped out of the back and went to greet Lady. Emma left her overnight bag for later and started to follow.

"Okay." Mitch scanned the area, seeming satisfied there were no strangers. Still, he pulled his gun from its holster and flipped off the safety. "Let's go see about this horse."

They started across the yard toward Will. "I hope it's nothing serious or we're in for a long, sad night," Emma said. "If Second Chance didn't expel all of the placenta or has a uterine tear, there's nothing I can do for her. We'll probably lose her."

"Yeah, about that," Mitch said, as he continued to sweep the surrounding area with his focused attention. "I can probably help."

———

"It's colic," Mitch told his eager audience. He'd checked Second Chance's vital signs and listened to her gut sounds. The only thing left was a rectal exam.

He could hardly wait.

Rubbing a forearm across his forehead, he wished he hadn't opened his mouth. "Probably due to stress from foaling."

"Colic." Emma gave a nod. "Is that all?"

"Colic can be serious." He wiped his hands on his pants, gave the horse's belly a pat. "Depends on what type it is. If it's impaction or displacement colic, she needs surgery. If it's a gas buildup, I can relieve that with a tube."

"We've got one of them naso tube thingies," Will said. "Will that help?"

Mitch wanted to say no. Why was he doing this? "Nasogastric?"

"Yeah, that's it. Doc Jane left it here with some meds early on in Second Chance's pregnancy in case the horse had bowel issues."

"She show you how to use it by any chance?"

"She did."

Looked like he would at least have help saving the damn horse. "Go get it. The meds too."

Will trotted off to the other end of the barn. Emma crossed her arms and gave Mitch a curious stare.

"What?" he said.

"You know a lot about horses, Agent Holden."

This wasn't his job. He shouldn't be worried about this horse instead of Dr. Collins, but something in him wanted to save the damn animal just for her. "Cleaned my share of stalls growing up."

She entered the stall and rubbed Second Chance's nose. "You grew up on a ranch?"

"Sort of."

When he didn't come forth with anything else, she chuckled. "Seems like you picked up more than the basics of cleaning stalls if you can diagnose what's wrong with a horse."

"I'm no vet, just seen a lot of this sort of thing. Sweating, bloating, the sitting down. Classic signs of colic."

"When I brought you out here the other night, you acted like you didn't care for horses. You said you'd never ridden a horse."

"I said I rode motorcycles." He leaned against the rail. "And you're right, I don't care for horses."

Her brow furrowed as she stroked Second Chance's ears and jaw. "How is that possible? How can you not appreciate these beautiful creatures?"

Will returned, saving him from talking about it, handing him the medication. "Will this help?"

Banamine. Good enough. "Yep. Let's get that tube in her, see if we can get the gas and fluid accumulation out. Then we'll administer a dose of this stuff."

Guiding a stomach tube into a horse's nose and down her esophagus into her stomach was not exactly a walk in the park. She fought them for a good, long time, and Mitch didn't blame her.

Will managed to get the back flow of gas going and she settled down. Probably because she was finally getting relief.

Thank the stars. He wouldn't have to do a rectal.

He wrapped things up, giving the horse a dose of the meds through the tube. Then they removed it.

Second Chance seemed like her old self, moving around without issues and nuzzling Mitch's shoulder as he wound up the long, flexible hose. Hope was nursing a minute later.

"That's amazing," Emma said, smiling at him and Will. She stood on the lower rung of the railing, her arms propped on the top, looking over at the horses. "You two make a good team."

Will blushed and hustled off, muttering, "Better go do my perimeter check. I'll be back in twenty to see about her."

Mitch needed a shower. As he backed out of the stall, he also wished for a decent change of clothes.

"You ready to head in?" Emma said.

"More than ready."

Night had fallen once more. Mitch readied his weapon and kept Emma behind him as they made their way to the house. Salt and Pepper waited on the porch.

He let her follow him through the house, her tiny gun in her hand as they made sure the place was clear. In her bedroom, the last room they went into, she stared at the nightstand and rubbed her gun arm with her empty hand.

"You okay?" Mitch asked.

She nodded without looking at him. "Why don't you grab a shower. I'll make us some food."

His stomach seconded that idea. A beer would be good too. "Stay clear of the windows, don't open the door for anyone but Will."

Turning on her heel, she headed for the stairs. "The clothes I laid out for you are still in the bathroom. You're smelling pretty ripe. Might want to wash the clothes you have on. Toss them out the door and I'll throw them in the wash."

It had been a damn long time since a woman had taken care of him. "I appreciate it."

A simple dip of her chin and she disappeared down the stairs, slow and deliberate as if she were descending into the depths of hell. Salt and Pepper sat on the landing, watching her. Both dogs turned in unison to look at him.

"Go," he muttered and jerked his head toward her.

In a scramble of toenails, wagging tails, and panting, the two Labs took off.

In the bathroom, he stripped down, turned on the shower, and eyed the clothes neatly folded on the sink. Who did they belong to? Unanswered questions made him nuts.

Why do you care?

He tossed his dirty clothes outside like Emma had instructed, then leaned his forehead against the closed door. He hadn't cared about much of anything or anyone in long, long time. He'd buried himself in work to keep from thinking about the things—the people—he didn't have. Could never have again.

Loneliness swamped him. Irony too. All the places he'd been in recent years that would have been great spots to settle down and grow roots, yet he'd run from every one of them.

Dupé and Harris had offered him a permanent spot on the taskforce, which was the perfect job for him, but he'd turned them down. Need, impulse, drive...something kept him on the move. Now here he was, stalled on his latest case and needing to get Emma off the ranch and to safety so he could get back to finding the arsonist, and all he wanted at that moment was to stay.

The water was hot, the soap smelled like Emma. Citrusy. But now that he was rubbing it on him, he realized it was lemongrass—which was far better than something girly.

He made quick work of cleaning himself up, not wanting to leave Emma for long. Even though Will hadn't seen anymore of their stranger, the guy could still be out there.

The clothes were too tight for his liking, but they would do until his own were clean and dry again. A hunger pang struck and he finger combed his wet hair.

He hadn't had time to go through the Goodsman file or work up his own profile of the guy. Was Emma right? Was Goodsman just a damned good actor, or was there merit to the idea that he was psychologically unbalanced enough to buy into his fictitious identity as Tom Monahan? His motivation to break out of jail was viable, except wasting his freedom to come after her seemed out of character. Like Will had mentioned, a spoiled, rich actor on the lam didn't suddenly turn into a survivalist who traipsed through forest fires to get revenge on the psychologist who'd petitioned against his release.

On the other hand, if Goodsman truly believed he was Tom Monahan, leader of the Resistance, he just might.

Mitch jogged downstairs, the smell of a home-cooked meal filling his nose. Meat, potatoes, yeasty rolls. Damn, he hadn't had anything that good since his last Sunday meal with his mother.

Which had been at least three years ago.

The dogs were stationed by the back door, Emma humming over a cutting board where she chopped vegetables and threw them in a skillet with beef tips. A glass of wine sat on the counter by her side, a soup pot filled with cut-up potatoes simmering on the stove. The light inside the oven revealed the rolls he had smelled.

"On the TV show," Mitch said, snagging a carrot from the cutting board, "did Goodsman have a trainer? One of the articles I read said he did some of his own stunts."

Emma didn't miss a beat, sipping at her wine as dinner cooked and the washing machine churned in the corner of the mudroom. "It's rumored he did some of his own stunts until he was injured in Season Six. The producers deemed him too important to the show to allow him to take any further risks, but his fans loved it. I think it made him feel more like a man when he could say he did his own stunts."

"If he had the proper equipment, do you think he'd hide out in the forest?"

She thought about it as she rinsed the cutting board in the sink. "The show often went on location to film, so he's no stranger to woods or the desert, although he hardly had to rough it. Stars like that have a trailer with full amenities, even when on location. I believe they used horses, ATVs, and motorcycles in several episodes throughout the different seasons. My guess is, he knows how to ride them all."

Mitch leaned against the counter and smiled.

"What?" Emma asked, turning off the boiling potatoes and dumping the water. A stick of butter went into the hot pan, followed by milk. "You have an evil look on your face."

Evil. Yeah, he'd learned how to trick the enemy in more than one way during his time in the service. "Just working on an idea on how to capture this weasel."

She handed him the potato masher. "I'm all ears."

The boiled potatoes turned to mush under his ministrations. "Let me stew on it a bit."

"Is it dangerous?"

"Possibly, for you."

Emma raised her wine glass to him. "Well then, I would love that."

CHAPTER NINE

"Tell me why you hate the holidays," Emma said around a bite of mashed potatoes. They were extra creamy tonight, thanks to Mitch and his muscles. She could never get them that creamy unless she pulled out her blender.

He finished a mouthful and pointed his fork at her. "You first."

They ate by candlelight; Mitch deciding they didn't need to make themselves anymore visible than necessary to whoever might be watching the house. Lights were out and the candle flickered, throwing shadows on the wall.

She liked it. It softened Mitch's hard angles, made it easier to talk about sensitive subjects.

He looked good in the flannel shirt she'd laid out for him. The lapis blues of the fabric made his gray eyes the color of the night sky and, in the candlelight, they looked almost black. He'd probably not like that Victor Dupé had once worn that shirt, but she wasn't sure if he'd be jealous or simply weirded out.

"I already told you," she said.

"No, you didn't. You said you lost everything and everyone you cared about. I assume someone you loved died close to Christmas?"

Her heart pinched and the food on her plate no longer seemed all that appetizing. If he'd researched Chris Goodsman, surely he'd come across the media reports about the break-in that cost her so dearly.

Emma had declared their dinner a Chris-free zone. If she started talking about him and his fans, she wouldn't be able to eat.

Now it looked like she might not stomach her food anyway.

Mitch seemed to understand her silence. "Hey, it's okay. I don't like to talk about my past shit either. New subject?"

She moved some veggies around with her fork, her brain searching for a safer subject. "Where did you learn about horses?"

He mimicked her earlier statement. "I already told you."

Two could play that game. "When I asked if you grew up on a ranch, you said, *sort of.* That's not an answer."

"I spent summers working at a livery. My brother and I both did. The owner was…a friend of my mother's."

Her internal therapist radar pinged at the way he hesitated before using the word *friend.* "But you claim you don't like horses. I imagine that was a sucky job for you."

He wiped his mouth on a napkin, sat back, and tossed the napkin next to his plate. "I lied. I like horses just fine. It was the situation—the people—that I didn't much care for."

It was obvious he liked animals of all kinds. "People often are the cause of situations we don't care for." She took another bite of potatoes. "Did the owners treat you poorly? Or your brother?"

By the look on his face, it might have been both. "It wasn't about us."

Ahh. "Your mother, then?"

His gaze, previously glued to the center of the table, came up to hers. She could see him wrestling with how much to tell her. "The owners were rich. Big shots. Mom worked as a hostess for them in her off hours when they threw parties. That's how she got Mac and I our summer job in the stables."

Nothing too telling in that statement, except the fact he didn't like that his mother had catered to the "rich" people, working as a hostess. The hostess job didn't jive with her and the owner being friends.

So something had happened between his mother and the owner during that time which now he negatively associated with horses and probably all rich people. "You're close to your mother?"

A derisive snort. "That was Mac's job."

A job? Was—past tense. "Mac is your mother's favorite, I take it?"

She'd meant it to sound lighthearted. A bit of teasing. Mitch picked up his fork and stabbed a piece of meat. "Yeah, you could say that."

"Older or younger? Do you have any other siblings?"

"Older. No other siblings."

Prickly, but using present tense for the brother again. "If I'm clear on all of this, your job, your dislike of the holidays, your mother, and your brother are all off limits for us to discuss." She waved her fork in the air. "How about this weather? There's a safe topic. Crazy for December, isn't it?"

For a moment, he didn't react. Then he laughed softly under his breath. "I'm sort of a mess, Dr. Collins, if you haven't already figured that out."

Back to Dr. Collins. The candlelight played across his cheekbones and cast circles under his eyes, now downcast to his plate.

"We make a good couple, then," she said off-handedly, finding herself hungry again. "I wouldn't want it to get out since it could ruin my career, but I'm a bit of a mess myself. You already know that, however."

Another chuckle. His eyes locked on hers over the glass beer bottle as he tipped it to his lips, then he set the bottle down softly. "Psychologists aren't allowed to have issues?"

"No." She smiled sweetly, the smile she had perfected over the years to keep probing minds at bay. "If we can't handle our own issues, how can we possibly help others with theirs?"

Light flickered in the depths of his eyes. He toyed with his beer, turning the bottle in circles on the table. "Don't you go to each other for psychoanalyzing?"

"I haven't found the right colleague yet for that."

"I'd assume with your contacts, you'd have access to more than one who would qualify."

"I have colleagues who are friends, but you can't go to a friend and expect them to treat you."

He looked thoughtful. "That's a pickle, isn't it?"

She shrugged and chewed a bite of beef tip. "I'll handle it on my own. I always do."

Whoops. She'd said too much. Behind his eyes, she saw the wheels turning. Analyzing. Another sip of beer. "You shouldn't bear your grief alone. It will eat you up. Take it from me, I know."

"Have you sought therapy for your issues?"

"Hell, no." The face he made was laughable as he slapped the bottle down on the table. As if she'd suggested he try waterboarding for fun. "But you aren't me. Therapy could help you, I bet. Me? I'm a lost cause."

She'd once been teased about all the people, pets, and ideas she constantly tried to rescue. *Emma Collins, the patron psychologist of lost causes.* "It's a myth that everyone can benefit from therapy, you know. Only those who *want* to engage in therapy will actually find it helpful."

"Ah, there's the rub." He grinned, leaning forward and pointing an accusatory finger at her. "You don't want to talk about what happened with anyone, not even a fellow, trained professional."

"Exactly."

He sat back, looking pleased with himself, and tore into a bun. "I get it."

She felt a bit pleased as well. Damaged people usually understood each other. "I thought you might."

"It would be like me going to one of my coworkers and talking about a failed mission."

"Not just any failed mission. One that cost someone close to you their life."

His fingers stilled, a piece of bun in each hand. "Yeah. Like I said, Doc, I get it."

So he'd lost someone close to him and blamed himself. "If you decide you'd like to talk about it, I'll be happy to listen. As a friend, of course."

His Adam's apple bobbed. "Not gonna happen, but thanks. I appreciate the offer." And then, "Why as a friend? You don't take adult clients anymore?"

Honesty warred with politeness. What did she have to lose by telling him the truth? He would be gone from her life in a matter of days. "I'm afraid I'm too...attached to you to be a proper therapist at this point."

"Attached?"

"You're not a stranger anymore, remember?"

The grin. The flippancy in her tone. It should have made him grin back.

He didn't.

He stared. He smoldered.

Damn. She made work of grabbing her napkin from her lap and wiping off her mouth, her fingers. *Stay professional.* "The current situation has caused us to..." She groped for a neutral term, couldn't find one that conveyed her meaning without it coming out wrong.

"You've grown on me," she blurted.

His smile was slow, lazy. "You like me."

"I find you quite annoying and contemptuous, but underneath your irascible attitude...yes, I like you. I think we could be friends, and if I'm your analyst, I can't be your friend."

The smile froze. He jabbed at his food. "I don't need a therapist, so it's cool."

They ate for a few minutes in silence, and Emma let go a mental sigh. He was irritated at her again, but she had to be honest with herself, his irritation was easier to deal with than his sexy, probing gaze.

She'd learned long ago that the feeling of safety was a

condition of the mind, not the body. Her mind was telling her she was safe. Physically, at least.

Emotionally...that was another story.

The damaged, vulnerable man across from her was working his way past her carefully constructed walls. Sure, she felt sympathy toward him, but this was more. This was...

Sex, her mind volunteered. *Lust.*

Ah, yes. Two wonderful human traits.

His physical attractiveness, his standoffishness, his skill with everything from a gun to a horse, was downright sexy as hell.

Her toes tingled, her cheeks felt warm. She stared at her plate, forking food into her mouth. She didn't taste it. All she could think about was the light in his eyes, the teasing note in his voice. His very nearness at the small table filled the air with his personal, very potent brand of electricity. It stole around her in the dim shadows and tickled her skin. Desire sizzled and wove around her spine, rising up her back, brushing her neck.

The scrape of chair legs on the floor startled her.

"Good dinner," Mitch said, crossing to the stove where he helped himself to seconds. "Want some more?"

He held up the slotted spoon over the skillet, looking back at her.

She'd imagined spending these nights leading up to Christmas alone. Eating alone, sleeping alone, grieving alone. Now here she was with a near stranger in her house, making himself at home, sitting at her table, saving her horse.

Protecting her.

She hadn't realized how lonely she'd been. It was a gift, this simple act of sharing a meal with a man who understood her neuroses and who didn't think less of her for admitting her failures.

It just so happened that this gift was smoking hot.

Surprisingly, she'd eaten all of her mashed potatoes. She nodded her head and smiled. Not the practiced smile—she couldn't work that one up. "I'd love some more of your potatoes."

The spoon lowered; his gaze on her sharpened. "There's my girl."

It was said softly, so softly she almost didn't hear it. "Excuse me?"

He looked away and grabbed the bowl with the potatoes in it, bringing them to the table. "You're a good cook, Emma."

First name, again. He flip-flopped back and forth; perhaps the intimacy of the meal and candlelight had relaxed his boundaries.

Fiddling with her napkin, she focused on the mound of potatoes he plopped on her plate. "I like to cook, but I can't take credit for these. You're as handy in the kitchen as you are in the stable."

He chuckled, returning to the stove and refilling his plate.

She hadn't had a man wait on her in a long time. The kitchen, even in the shadowy light, seemed lighter, cheerful almost, regardless of the lack of light. Her heart pinched at the thought he wouldn't be here much longer.

Mitch returned to the table, dug in. Emma picked up her fork and toyed with the potatoes. *There's my girl*, he'd said. What did that mean?

She was hardly a girl, and the statement seemed quite out of context. She couldn't help stealing a glance at his face and wondering: what made this man tick?

As if he felt her stare, he glanced up.

Caught. "You are quite the renaissance man, cooking, saving animals, protecting the womenfolk," she said, once more trying for humor. "Keep this up, and I'll have to hire you."

A smile. One that made her pulse hop. "You don't want to do that."

She was pretty sure she did. "The case you're working on now—I heard you say something about the wildfires and a pyromaniac. You think the fires were intentionally started?"

He moved food around on his plate. "I can't really talk about it."

"That's why you were curious about that trail into the backside of the park, isn't it?"

"Could be."

"I don't need to know the details, but I have worked with multiple, criminal fire setters. I could share some insight into the workings of their minds, if you think that would help you with your case, Agent Holden."

His eyes caught hers over the candlelight. While his gaze was serious, penetrating, his voice held a note of teasing. "Mitch. I'm not a stranger anymore, remember?"

"Mitch." She forced herself to hold that piercing, perceptive gaze of his. *Focus on the work.* "Fire setters often get started as juveniles. Their minds are quite fascinating."

"The suspect is part of a homegrown terrorist group who has a perpetual beef with the government. His mindset isn't that difficult to figure out."

"Perhaps not in relation to why he started the fires, but a little insight into his psyche might determine if he is a pathological fire setter or simply following the command of someone he believes has authority over him. It could assist you in capturing him."

The corner of one eye narrowed slightly as he studied her. She had the feeling he was about to shoot her down again when he bobbed his chin and went back to his food. "Sure. Why not? Can't hurt."

Progress. He was letting her in, even if it was in relation to a case. "Then we best finish up here. We have a lot of analyzing to do after dinner."

Raising his beer bottle, he held it out in toast. "To taking down the bad guys."

Like the previous night's toast, clinking her glass against his made Emma happy.

Silly, really. He was with her another day or two at most. She'd never see him again after that. No sense in getting attached.

But loneliness sucked, and for now, he was here, and his hostility and antagonism had dwindled to almost nothing. Was it wrong to wish for more than a friendly exchange over dinner? "To taking down the bad guys," she echoed.

The sexual tension between them had been palpable all day. Mitch got a hard-on every time he thought of that smile she'd given him. The one at dinner. The real Emma Collins—not the head shrink, not the horse whisperer. The woman behind all the masks.

Tucked away in her upstairs study, the clock counted down the hour to midnight while Emma read by candlelight. She sat at her desk, her reading glasses perched on her nose and her hair in a messy bun, schooling him on the inner workings of a pathological fire starter.

The sexy librarian of his fantasies before him, Mitch found it difficult to concentrate on what she was saying.

"As with certain other behaviors, pyromania is an impulse control disorder," she explained. "Pathological fire starters start fires to relieve tension or for gratification. It's emotional for them. They get a kind of euphoria from fire and it can reduce the buildup of stress in their system. In your case, your suspect may not be a pyromaniac. He may simply be a criminal arsonist, setting the fire inside the national park as a means to an end for someone other than himself. The leader of his group, in other words."

"Mmm-hmm."

Emma lowered the glasses to the end of her nose and shot a look over at him where he sat on the couch. "Are you tired, Mitch? Should we call it a night and pick up here tomorrow?"

He wanted to call it a night, all right. He wanted to pull the clip from her hair and lay her out on her desk. Unbutton that soft flannel shirt and see what hid underneath. "I'm good. Just thinking."

Not about what she was saying, but it wasn't a total lie.

She waited, as if expecting him to go on. When he didn't, she sat back in her chair. "Is it still your feeling he's a criminal arsonist?"

Yepper, but he wanted to keep her talking. "He has three priors, all for setting fires."

"Any juvenile history of fire setting?"

Mitch scrolled through the file he had on his laptop. "The first incident that resulted in an arrest was at the age of nineteen. He was part of a small-time motorcycle gang in Oceanside who broke into some old lady's house, stole her stuff, and killed her. He set fire to the house to destroy any evidence."

"So he probably had juvenile incidents and those records are sealed. Was he sent to prison for the murder?"

"Nope. He did time in a psych unit. He wasn't there when the murder occurred, according to courtroom documents. He was called in afterwards by the leader to burn the house, so he got off on a technicality and was sent for a psychological eval. He spent six months at the county detention center in the psych ward."

"And his other arson charges? What happened there?"

More scanning. "Empty buildings. No one was injured in either place."

Emma removed her glasses and put the end of one earpiece in her mouth as she rocked in her chair. "Those don't sound like he was destroying evidence. What type of buildings were they?"

"One was a church, the other was an abandoned fire station that was being converted to a community center."

More rocking, her teeth nibbling on the end of the ear piece. "A church. That's interesting. What religion?"

"No idea." Mitch forced his eyes away from her lips. "Living River Freedom Church was the name. Small congregation, no affiliation on the notes I have. It appears he had a partner working with him both times. He's also suspected in six other cases where fire destroyed property."

"The church is often perceived as a source of authority, and for many, represents damnation as much as salvation. Then there's the symbolism. Burning in the fires of hell, fire shall destroy the earth, the burning bush and Abraham, etc. As for the fire station..." She set down the glasses. "Was the suspect's father, or any other male family member, a fire fighter? Or a minister perhaps?"

"I don't have the guy's life story, here, only his criminal history." But something she'd said triggered a connection in his brain. "Fire shall destroy the earth...the end of times? Is that the Biblical symbolism you're referencing?"

"Yes, why?"

"Tom Monahan and the apocalypse, ring any bells? Remember that garbage Linda Brown was spouting on the phone... 'The Chosen One will be protected by the Resistance who will carry fire in their hands. Fire will consume them, and He will rise from the ashes of their destruction.'"

"Many fables and most religions have resurrection stories that begin and end with fire. The creators of the show used a host of metaphors to come up with The Chronicles: the phoenix rising from the ashes, Christ's resurrection, the Book of Revelations..."

"Chris Goodsman was in jail when the wildfires started, but Linda Brown wasn't."

"You think Linda Brown started the wildfires? That's a huge leap."

"I'm brainstorming. The fires certainly benefitted Brown and Goodsman. Maybe Brown didn't start them but she had help. Someone who understands how fires, wind direction, that sort of thing, all work."

"Your suspect."

Mitch nodded.

"But why? How would setting a forest fire in the park have

anything to do with her delusions of being Mary Monahan?"

"She's acting out what it says in The Chronicles, and it worked, didn't it? She got Chris free."

Emma's face took on a look of sheer shock. "Oh, my God, you're right. But she couldn't have known that the fires would spread in a direction that would cause the evacuation of the prison."

Maybe not, but something told Mitch he was onto something. "Have you ever used that trail we were on today to get inside the park?"

"I've ridden that far a time or two when I needed to clear my head, but it's a rocky one. Not for the faint of heart, and you have to access it on horse or foot. A couple of places it's washed out by the stream that curves around my land, and there's more than one outcropping that makes the trail dangerous to anyone who's not familiar with the layout."

"But a survivalist could navigate it, right?"

"A survivalist like your suspect?"

He nodded and she stared at him for a moment, her brain getting on the same page with his. Mitch scratched at his chin. "I need to have a look at that trail."

Emma nodded. "I'll take you."

Boy, he wanted that. More than anything. Watching her lead the way, her sweet backside tantalizing him with every step of her horse. Plus, he might figure out how Sean Gordon had slipped out of the park and escaped.

But he couldn't do it. His case would have to wait. "Too dangerous, forget it. I'd go alone and leave Will here to guard you, but if anything happened…"

"You couldn't live with yourself?"

Her grin was mocking. The tone of her voice as well.

The trail was already cold. Another day wouldn't matter. "No, I couldn't."

She sobered, folded her glasses and stuck them in her top drawer. "We'll head out at first light. Will and the dogs will come with us. I'll be perfectly safe with the two of you, and it's not like anyone could follow us without us knowing it."

She stood and shoved her chair in. "I'm going to turn in. I've made up the bed in the spare room. You're welcome to it."

He didn't want her to go, but he didn't want to argue with her either. No way he was letting her take him to the park tomorrow, but right now, he just wanted her to sit back down and keep talking. "Who does this shirt belong to, Emma?"

She turned back at the door, a weird look on her face. "Does it matter?"

Yeah, it did. For no good reason, he was jealous. "I'm a curious guy."

"Last Christmas, a friend stayed with me to help me through the holidays. He left a few clothes here in case he found time to return. This place is kind of a refuge, I guess you could say, for people as well as animals."

His gut bombed. A man had stayed with her. Probably held her and let her grieve in his arms.

Mitch wanted to hit something. Then he wanted to shred the shirt. "I see."

"He's a good man, one who's been there for me when things were rough. It was only a few days, but it meant a lot to me."

He closed his laptop and shoved it away. Stood. "Are my clothes dry yet?"

"Yes, I'll get them for you."

"Don't bother," he said, walking past her. "I'll get them myself."

CHAPTER TEN

Emma overslept, then hurried through her morning routine. *So unlike me.*

She was doing a lot of things that were unlike her.

How weird that with everything going on, and the fact Chris, Linda, or someone else had been in her bedroom yesterday, she had slept like the dead.

She might have *been* dead if not for Mitch.

His presence is why you slept so well, dodo.

Salt and Pepper weren't in her bed when she woke, nor did she see them now as she left the bathroom, pulling her wet hair into a ponytail. Down the hall, she discreetly looked around the corner to peer into the guest room, prepared to use the dogs as her alibi for snooping, but neither they nor Mitch were in sight.

The bed was made, the shade open to the bright morning sun pouring in.

Had he even slept in there last night?

The sound of a pan knocking against something in the kitchen echoed up the stairs. Emma cocked her head at the top of the stairs and listened.

Whistling, soft and upbeat, met her ears, along with the sounds and smells of frying meat.

Mitch was making breakfast.

How nice.

Nice? It was flippin' awesome.

What am I doing? Falling for a guy because he makes me breakfast?

There was more to it than that, of course, but Emma knew the signs of transference. Mitch had come into her life during a fragile time of year and had proven to be adept at dealing with everything she, and the world at large, had thrown at him. Add that to the fact he was tall and sexy, damaged and mysterious—what woman in her right mind wouldn't have a crush on him?

Dangerous waters, doctor.

Calling up her professional persona, she descended the stairs.

The dogs had tag-teamed Mitch, Salt taking up the position by the door, Pepper by the table. Both gave her a cursory glance and a weak tail wag and went back to keeping their laser-locks on the man with the food.

He wore the clothes he'd arrived in, and gave her a tight smile from his station at the stove. "Hungry?"

She'd told herself last night that she had to be mistaken about the jealousy she'd witnessed on his face when she'd told him about Victor helping her through the holidays last year. But the same expression still clouded his eyes and sat heavy in the faint creases around his mouth. "Smells delicious. I'm sorry I overslept. I'd love some breakfast, but I should check on the horses."

"No big deal about oversleeping." He flipped a sausage, grease splattering. His attention darted around between the frying pan and another skillet with eggs. "Will and I fed the horses and let them out to pasture. Relax and have some breakfast. We've got all day."

Mitch respected Victor, saw him in an elevated light that Emma knew many others did too. It didn't seem right to divulge that Victor was a kind man under his badass, FBI director persona. His agents knew he was fair and dedicated, but she wasn't sure they realized what a softy he truly was. Revealing the fact he'd stayed with her, even though nothing inappropriate had happened, seemed too intimate—for both her and him.

She helped herself to the pot of coffee, watching Mitch from the corner of her eye. "Did you get any sleep?"

"Plenty."

Somehow she doubted that. "Are we going to the park today?"

"The fire burned north from the ignition site, but it's still too dangerous to go into the park without proper equipment and clearance from the fire chief." He scooped up an egg from one pan and slid it onto a plate, then two sausage patties, and handed it to her. "All I want to do is check the trail and see if it was a possible escape route for the arsonist."

An adventure. She was almost giddy. This one would be far more suited to her than yesterday's excursion in Mitch's truck, trying to escape the madness of a stalker and the chaos brought on by the wildfires. Today, it would be sunshine, horses, and Mitch.

Her psyche loved that idea.

Her body didn't mind it either.

She sat at the table, eyeing the delicious smelling food in front of her. "Will and I can saddle up the horses after breakfast."

"I've already prepped Harry. You're staying here with Will."

Emma's forkful of egg stopped halfway to her mouth. "Harry?"

Mitch plopped his plate on the table and dropped into the seat opposite her. "I refuse to ride a horse named Twinkie. When I ride him, he's Harry."

She almost smiled. "I'm not staying here. I'm going with you."

"No, ma'am, you are not."

Stuffing the egg into her mouth, she chewed slowly and eyeballed him. "I know the trail, you don't."

He dug in, avoiding her glare. "I served two tours in the

Middle East, and no, I don't want to talk about where or any details concerning my job there. I only mention it in order to assure you I know how to navigate rougher terrain than you have here in California. I'll find the trail and follow it to the park, do my investigation, and be back before sunset."

She stewed for a few long moments, watching him eat. He was a magnificent creature, reminding her of the horse he insisted on calling Harry. Twinkie, too, had an independent streak that reared its head on occasion. When he'd first come to her, he'd been neglected and didn't trust strangers. Only his handler had been able to get the horse to cooperate. It took Emma months to gain the horse's trust. With patience and kindness, she'd taken the damaged trick horse and returned him to the gentle soul he'd once been.

She wondered if the same patience and kindness might work on Mitch. "You believe that I will be safer here with Will in this house, where we know Chris or one of his fans entered yesterday, than on the trail hidden in the woods with you?"

His gaze flickered up to hers, dropped again. "I do."

It was a lie.

But why? Why was he suddenly so emotionally distant and trying hard to create physical distance between them again?

Jealousy.

He'd let down his guard and actually started liking her. Realizing she had spent last Christmas with a man had made him retreat behind those walls again.

Petty and childish. Did he think her a nun? A saint?

"Nothing happened between the man who stayed here last year to comfort me while I grieved, and it's juvenile of you to treat me this way because you fear something did."

He froze, then set his fork down. "It's none of my business what you do here, or who you spend time with, Doctor. My only mission is to keep you safe until they catch the man after you."

"Last night, we were friends. After I told you about the

owner of the clothes you were wearing, you became distant and cold. Why is that, Mitch?"

He jumped up from the table and refilled his coffee cup. "I apologize for any misunderstanding, but I have other things on my mind besides being your bodyguard. I'm trying to solve a crime I can't get all the evidence on, or even get in to view the scene where I believe the arsonist started the fire. I can't solve crimes from remote distances."

He returned to the table, sat, and gave her a hard look. "My attitude has nothing to do with the clothes or your friend. I'm simply battling a no-win situation, stuck here with you, and trying to make the best of it."

He could add lying to his skill set. Most people would believe him by the look on his face. The earnestness in his voice. The way he didn't fidget or glance away as she held his gaze.

The most dangerous liars...

"I'm sorry you're *stuck* here, Agent Holden. Safe travels to the park and back."

Picking up her coffee, she stood and pushed in her chair before she headed for the stairs and the sanctity of her office. "I hope you find what you're looking for."

He was a goddamn ass.

Shoving the rest of the breakfast into the dog dishes, Mitch berated himself for hurting Emma and lying to her. As the dogs sucked up the eggs and sausage meant for her, he tossed her dish into the sink and started scrubbing up the mess he'd made.

Except nothing could scrub clean his conscience. Not over what he'd just done nor what he *hadn't* done five years ago.

His mother still had all of Mac's shirts, all of his uniforms. For some reason, Emma's hanging onto a shirt her "friend" had left behind hit a raw spot with him. A raw spot he couldn't put into words but suddenly understood all too clearly.

He was jealous of his dead brother.

Fuck, what is wrong with me?

Parents often hung onto their dead child's clothes, refused to change anything in their bedroom. He knew that.

And yet, for some reason, his mother seemed to prefer living in the past, pretending Mac might come home, rather than enjoying the son she still had.

Stupid shirt.

Crazy didn't begin to cover what he was for letting a harmless piece of fabric turn him into a jackass.

He ran the hot water until it scalded his hands and created more bubbles than necessary. He scoured the dishes and the skillet beyond what was necessary to clean them, then rinsed them. Checking drawers, he found a dishtowel with faded horses printed on it and went to work drying and putting the dishes away.

The table still needed cleaning, but he left it and took the stairs to Emma's office.

The door was ajar and he could see her working at her desk. Her reading glasses perched on her nose as she made notes by hand in a file.

His chest hurt over alienating her. He *had* been jealous, like some horny teenage boy, last night. But then he'd realized it was more than jealousy. Much more.

And not just because of the reminder of Mac's shirts hanging in his mother's house.

There was no accounting for what he was feeling right now. *I don't even know her.*

But his gut didn't lie. He was drawn to Emma in a way he'd never been drawn to another woman.

Rapping on the wooden door with two knuckles, he wasn't surprised when she didn't look up. Disappointed? Hell yeah.

"Leaving now?" she inquired, continuing to write in the file.

"Not yet."

When he didn't continue, she glanced at him over the rim of her glasses. "Did you need something?"

"Yeah." He started to walk into the room, stalled out in the doorway. His feet just wouldn't move. "I need to apologize."

Carefully, she laid down the pen and sat back in the chair, giving him her full attention.

He stammered, so unlike him. "I, uh... I was rude downstairs. I'm sorry."

"Thank you."

Silence hung between them. That was it. Nothing else.

Except that stare of hers. Penetrating but nonjudgmental, making him want to step inside and explain more fully.

Sweat beaded along his hairline. The dogs had ambled up and now stood near him, Pepper reaching out to angle his head under Mitch's hand.

Taking a steadying breath, he dropped his gaze to the dog's soft brown eyes. "It's not jealousy," he said. "I mean, at first, yeah, it was a little, but you know that's crazy, because why would I be jealous of some guy staying here? You had a life before me, and I've only known you a day or so, and well, it makes no sense to me, as I'm sure it doesn't to you. But I felt protective of you, and I like you, so it didn't sit well with me thinking about some other guy being here. You know, having a relationship with you and then hurting you."

She removed the glasses from her nose and tossed them on the desk. "Why did you assume he hurt me?"

"He's not here any longer and you still have his clothes. If you'd thrown him out, I'm guessing the clothes would have gone with him or been burned." He continued to pet Pepper, the dog leaning into his leg as if offering support. "Then, this morning, you said nothing happened with that guy, but it sounded cliché, and I guess I was already entrenched in my normal mode of operation, so I had a hard time believing you."

"Your *normal* mode of operation?"

He made eye contact, wondering if she was analyzing him or asking out of politeness. "I don't let myself get involved with anyone, anymore. I keep people at a safe distance, even friends."

"So they won't hurt you?"

"So I don't hurt them."

"And how do you imagine you would hurt me by being my friend?"

"My track record at keeping people safe is abysmal, and if I get emotionally attached in any way, well, the odds of me successfully protecting you go down even farther. I need to be clear-headed and detached so I don't let emotions interfere with your safety."

She was quiet for a long moment, her attention falling on Pepper and the way he was petting the dog. "You've been a bodyguard before?"

"Not in the strict sense of the word, but…"

His throat shut down, pressure forcing it closed.

"But you felt intrinsically responsible for someone and that person got hurt?"

Was he really doing this? He scanned her face, saw the neutrality in it. Her eyes slowly came back to his, and he nodded. "My brother. He…died."

"You believe it was somehow your fault."

Another nod. "It was."

She tilted her head. "How so?"

His guts crawled. The story ate at him, night and day, always there, hovering.

"Mac is—was—*is* my twin. Older by a minute."

His sweat turned cold as the image of Mac's face swam in front of his eyes. The look of relief on that face he had known so well. "Mac was a Green Beret. His squad got ambushed in a showdown between some local gangs in a Yemen border town. I was nearby in Saudi Arabia on an intelligence mission with another Special Forces group and we got the SOS Mac sent out."

"You went in to rescue him," Emma said, softly. Her voice barely penetrated his memories. "But something went wrong."

Mitch could still feel the brotherly slap Mac had given him right before Mitch had told him to haul his injured ass over to the rundown building nearby while Mitch covered him with gunfire. "I had analyzed the situation and ran best-case scenarios on the way there—that was my job. It was a ground fight, and there were only a dozen or so shooters. Once my team arrived, we split up. Me and three other guys went to get Mac's men into a nearby building, stabilize the injured men, and the second group would concentrate on taking out the gang members."

"Mac didn't make it to the building?"

"He made it." Mitch's ears rang with the distinctive sound of a fighter jet bearing down on them. His knees shook from the way the earth trembled when the bomb hit the building...

A fireball erupted. "No!" Mitch yelled.

"Mitch?"

Suddenly, his ass was on the floor and stars danced on the edge of his vision.

"Mitch, look at me." Emma was suddenly in front of him, her hands on his shoulders as she shook him. "You're here, in my office. You're not in Yemen. Look at me. You're safe."

A warm, rough tongue licked his face, causing him to refocus and shake off the sticky cobwebs of memory. He blinked, concentrating on the smooth skin and tiny freckles dotting Emma's face.

His tongue felt thick, his face hot. He hadn't had an episode in months, and here he was, getting sucked into the past and nearly blacking out. "Oh, fuck."

Emma shooed Pepper back and checked the pulse in his wrist.

He snorted derisively and yanked it away. "Sorry, I have these flashbacks and then I... I'm okay, really."

Her countenance said she thought differently, but she didn't argue. She sat facing him and petted Pepper, who crawled halfway into her lap. "What happened? To your brother?"

Mitch ran a hand over his face, through his hair. For a minute, he couldn't speak. Emma didn't say anything, patiently waiting for him to get his shit together.

"I was laying down cover with the other two guys in my group. All of Mac's men made it to the building and then... The building was bombed."

"Bombed?" Her shock was evident. "By one of the gangs?"

He shook his head. Salt had found her way into the group hug and settled with her head in his lap. He stroked her head and tried to breathe. "The Yemeni government claimed they had intel that the gangs were involved with the Taliban and were rioting. They believed the building was a hideout, so they bombed it without verifying there were no military ops going on in the area."

She continued petting the Lab, her face clouded with a mix of emotions. He waited for her to tell him it wasn't his fault. Instead, she asked, "Do you have these flashbacks often? The blackouts?"

Thank God, no. "Not as often anymore."

"How long has it been since your brother died?"

A creeping relief stole over him when she didn't offer platitudes or arguments about where the responsibility for his twin's death lay. "Five years. Today."

Christmas Eve. The most awful time of the year.

Emma nodded. "Pretty impressive."

"Excuse me?"

"The twin connection runs as deep as any I've encountered. Five years of anger, grief, and blame and no therapy? You know how to bury things deep in order to keep functioning, Agent Holden."

She didn't know the half of it. "I don't remember what happened afterward. They say I blacked out from the concussion caused by the explosion, and I ended up with some shrapnel in my chest, but I don't think it was any of that. I felt like…" The clamp in his chest turned, cranking his heart down another inch. "I felt like I exploded along with that fucking building."

"Your twin died in front of your eyes. You blacked out from the shock it had on your system—physical, emotional, mental. You couldn't process it. You're suppressing the emotions, which is what rises up and knocks you on your ass when you recall what happened. You're caught between a rock and a hard place, Mitch. If you let yourself remember the incident, it overwhelms your system like it did on that day, and everything shuts down. Unfortunately, suppressing those emotions keeps you from processing that day and moving on with your life."

He tried for a lighthearted tone. "Let me guess, I need therapy."

She smiled, but it was full of pain. "Don't we all?"

He scrubbed a hand over his face. "Everyone told me it wasn't my fault, that I shouldn't blame myself, but I'm the one who devised the plan. I'm the one who calculated the risk and sent Mac and his men into that deathtrap."

Silence descended. Was she waiting for him to continue? Was she analyzing what he'd already said?

The clock on the wall ticked quietly and Mitch felt the clamp on his heart releasing pressure. His hand was buried in Salt's fur and her eyes were closed as she drifted to sleep, head still on his lap.

"How many times afterwards," Emma said softly, "did you consider ending your own life?"

Good God, how did she know that?

"Four." The word spilled out, easy and sweet on his tongue. Salt whined in her sleep. He stroked her side, watching her chest rise and fall with her breathing. "Every Christmas. All I can do is think about Mac. The flashbacks, the memories, they make me wish I'd died with him. I usually bury myself in alcohol. Last night, that shirt… Well, it made me remember how my mother has all of Mac's shirts, and today, I realized I'm fucking jealous of my dead brother because she still worships him and ignores me."

Emma's lips pursed for a moment and Mitch's gaze couldn't help but zero in on them. So smooth, so full.

He felt warm all over. His fingers itched to reach out and touch her grounding presence.

"And this Christmas?" she asked. "Do you wish you were dead?"

Those hazel green eyes of hers were sad, but there was something else flaring in them. Hope? Yearning? He couldn't tell, but it tugged at his gut, made his chest expand, his blood pulse thick in his veins.

For the first time in a long while, he didn't want a drink or the sour oblivion that came from too many of them. He didn't want to collapse in a drunken heap, hoping he never woke up.

"Not this year," he admitted. His voice was ragged with grief, but he met her steady gaze head on. "This year, I want to live."

CHAPTER ELEVEN

Oh, this man. He was killing her.

Emma sat, heart thudding, as Mitch's eyes darkened with desire.

With life.

He wanted to live. Because of her?

A part of her knew his grief was simply running its course. Most people went through the five stages of grief in a year. For someone like Mitch, a man who'd lost his twin brother and blamed himself for it, five years wasn't outside of the normal parameters.

He needed help in a big way—in regards to his guilt, to his relationship with his mother, and probably to other things she still hadn't learned about. More help than she could ever give him, especially now since she was falling for him.

Slightly flustered, she felt paralyzed by his eyes. By the fact she was sitting on the floor, pinned down close to him by the dogs, and wanting to do nothing more than crawl into his lap and wipe that desperate misery off his face.

"I don't know what it is about you," he said. "You make me want to talk about things I haven't spoken of to anyone else, ever."

The sign of a good therapist. "Moving through grief is a very individualized process. Time works wonders, and the brain has lots of coping mechanisms. Not all of them are healthy, but…"

What was she doing? The mechanics of the brain and psychological babble weren't exactly seductive topics.

And yet, the sexy man in front of her had lust in his eyes and was grinning at her.

"I'm sorry," she said on an exhale. "Sometimes it's difficult for me to turn off the psychologist in me."

"Don't apologize. You're good at it."

She fiddled with Pepper's ear, feeling the urge to grin back at him. "Very few people find the brain and its inner workings as exciting as I do."

"You understand me because you've been through something similar, haven't you?"

He knew she had from their previous conversations, yet he was opening the door, inviting her to trust him like he was trusting her.

The sun shone through the picture window, cutting a long rectangle across the floor. Dust motes danced in the sunbeams.

Sitting on the floor made it easier, somehow. As if by lowering herself to the ground with the dogs and the dust, her secrets were both grounded and light as a feather. The heart space where her pain nestled had knocked her down to these very floor boards before. How many nights had she lain in here and cried herself to sleep, the dogs licking at her tears and cuddling their big, warm bodies up to hers?

"It was a child," she murmured through the old familiar ache. "I lost a baby."

"Emma." Her name came out quiet, a holy thing. "I'm so sorry."

The sympathy in his voice made tears well in her eyes. "I was engaged once. He insisted I quit my job, that it was bad for the baby growing inside me."

Mitch's hand crept forward and gently took hers. "What happened?"

A single tear slid down her cheek. "I didn't listen." She dashed the wetness away. "I miscarried after one of Chris

Goodsman's fans broke into our home and tried to kill me."

Mitch's grip tightened, a protective anger radiating from him. He remained quiet, giving her space to talk more if she wanted to. Quiet, if forceful support, if she didn't.

I could love him for that.

The thought hit her with the impact of a brick. She started to draw away, wondering what was wrong with her.

Mitch stayed her hand, keeping her close. His grip didn't tighten farther, he simply held her there, unmoving. "No wonder you understand how I feel. You're carrying the same kind of emotional shit."

Emotional shit, yes, indeed. She would always be bogged down with the guilt sticking to her legs like quicksand.

"I guess so." Staring into his solemn eyes, Emma snaked her free hand out to touch his heart through his shirt. "I have an imaginary ice pick buried right here. You?"

A somber nod. "I know exactly how that feels."

She didn't drop her hand. "It doesn't...hurt as much with you here."

He caught her gently by the back of her head, drew her face close to his. His breath fell warm on her cheeks, his pupils dilating. "Have you ever wanted something that you knew was wrong, but in some ways, it seemed like the only thing that might save you?"

The eyes might have been a window to the soul, but psychologists knew the pupils—and the way they dilated—were an honest cue to sexual interest.

Her pupils had to be dilated too. She knew exactly what he meant. Her lips trembled. Her hand rubbed over his shirt, feeling the solid wall of his chest under her fingers. She gave him a half-hearted smile. "You think we can save each other?"

His gaze dropped to her lips and she automatically parted them in anticipation. "Seems to me, doctor, that we either work on saving each other or we damn ourselves to another holiday of guilt and self-destruction."

Could this damaged, heartbroken man help her heal her wounds? Logic said no. Her heart said something else. "Therapy only works for those who want it to," she warned.

"And do you want it, Emma? Do you want me?"

How could she say no? He'd rekindled a fire inside her that had been cold and dark for two mind-numbing years. "Yes," she breathed.

He took her lips with a slow, deliberate press of his mouth, his body inching slowly toward her, disturbing Salt. The Lab shifted, as did Pepper, and Emma scooted toward Mitch, meeting him in the middle.

He caught her up in his arms, his mouth demanding on hers. She gave him what he wanted, parting her lips and allowing him access.

The hand behind her head supported her as he deepened the kiss, their tongues dancing. She swept her arms around his neck, dragged her fingers through his short hair.

Her brain yelled for her to stop, to regain her professional composure and put distance between herself and this man who'd swept into her life and turned everything upside down, but the woman in her shoved logic and reasoning out of the way and into a deep, dark hole.

Right now, all she wanted to do was feel loved. Desired.

Safe.

All three existed in Mitch's arms.

It was a relief to succumb to her baser instincts and crawl into his lap. His hands worked under her shirt, cupping her breasts through her bra. A gasp escaped her lips at the feel of his fingers kneading the sensitive flesh through the fabric, and then slowly teasing the lace back so he could touch her.

"Fuck, Emma," he whispered, tweaking a nipple between his thumb and index finger. "I've never met anyone like you."

Closing her eyes and arching to give him better access to her breasts, she smiled. "I suppose you're lucky then. I can be a handful."

He shoved her shirt out of the way and cupped both breasts fully again, squeezing and massaging them. "Yes, you are, and I love every bit of it."

She laughed and then gasped as his lips touched the top of one breast. He lifted the nipple and laved it with his tongue, pulling a moan from her.

She hung on, arching higher, loving the increasing manipulation from his mouth. A large bulge pressed against her pelvis where she straddled him. Needing more of him, she swiveled her hips and ground into him.

He moaned against her skin and satisfaction shot through her. That little bit of power, knowing that she could bring him some pleasure in return, spurred her on.

She reached for his belt, unbuckled it, and was about to start on his zipper when Salt and Pepper both came to attention. A second later, they were up and tearing out of the office and down the stairs.

Mitch broke off from his ministrations to her breasts and looked over his shoulder at where the dogs had disappeared. "Company," was all he said, his breath sounding like he'd been running a marathon.

Emma knew the feeling. Her breath was coming fast and hard, too, as she lowered her shirt and licked her lips.

Sure enough, a knock sounded on the kitchen door downstairs, setting both dogs off.

As the dogs barked and Emma tried to reengage her brain, Mitch deftly picked her up and untangled himself from her legs. Gaining his feet, he lifted her and set her on the corner of her desk, then adjusted the bulge in his jeans.

"Stay here," he said, planting a kiss on her forehead. "I'll see who it is."

Emma gripped the edge of the desk for balance as his sudden absence left her lightheaded. Her body leaned toward him even as he disappeared out the doorway.

Her lips stung from his kisses, her nipples were still hard

from his handiwork. Easing her bra back into place, she couldn't keep the silly grin off her face.

I think I'm finally ready for therapy.

Mitch stole across the kitchen floor, gun cocked and ready. Salt and Pepper came scrambling up behind him, but he stopped them with a hand gesture.

Well trained, they both sunk to their haunches and waited for his next command.

He didn't think Goodsman or Brown would walk up to the door and knock, but they were both loony as jaybirds, so he wasn't taking chances.

A peek out the window showed him a broad man standing on the porch wearing a hat and overalls.

"It's me, Will," Emma's ranch hand called. "Don't shoot."

Smart man. Mitch lowered his weapon and opened the back door. "What's up, Will?"

Will's eyes were wary as always, skimming over Mitch, then tracking over his shoulder. The Pit-mix sat next to his leg and started wagging her tail when the Labs rushed forward to greet her. "Emma okay?"

"Of course," Emma came bustling into the kitchen at that moment, face flushed. Her shirt was slightly askew and strands of hair had come loose from her ponytail. "Is everything all right with the horses?"

Will removed his hat and nodded. "Horses are fine. You didn't come out to check on the foal."

"Sorry, I overslept." She gave a slight chuckle that sounded forced. Her fingers worked the edge of her shirt hem and she kept biting the inside of her cheek. "Mitch said he helped you take care of the morning routine and that you had everything under control."

It was weird to see the doctor without her composure. She was cute, shifting her weight and brushing back a strand of hair as her eyes darted to Mitch and then away.

Will's gaze cut to Mitch as well, stayed there a condescending moment, then went back to Emma. "I wanted to ask about switching out Second Chance and Hope to the far stalls so I could start cleaning out the main barn."

Total bullshit. Mitch could tell by the way the guy was standing with his feet spread and his hands flexing and releasing on his hat brim that he was pissed. The guy was protective of Emma, which was good, but maybe there was more to it than that.

The stall cleaning was an excuse for him to get the lay of the land. To check up on Emma and see for himself if something was going on with her and Mitch.

Boy, was it. Mitch wanted to throttle the man for interrupting what could have been one hell of a start to his morning.

"Danika is coming tomorrow to help us clean out the main horse barn," Emma said. "It's part of her therapy. She's going to need plenty of hard work to keep her mind off the holiday, and it'll be good for me, too."

Will spun the hat in his hands. Flex. Release. Flex. "All right. I'll inventory the feed and do some mowing in the far pasture today. With the fires and all, I want to make sure we're going to have enough feed to last for the next week."

"Yes. Good idea." Emma gave him a nervous smile. "Mitch and I are going to ride the trail to the park and back. You'll keep an eye on things here, right?"

Will's eyes narrowed slightly at Mitch. "I thought you were going alone."

Mitch shot Emma a look. "I am."

She reached out and playfully punched his bicep. "No, you're not. I'm going too."

The woman was crazy. Sexy but crazy. What was he going to do with her?

Fuck her blind and then get the hell out of her life.

But it was already too late for that. He couldn't walk away from her so easily. She'd gotten under his skin, made him lower his defenses.

"I guess Emma is going too," he said to Will, barely believing he was saying the words. "Just so you know, it's a dangerous risk and I've advised strongly against it."

Will gave him a pitying look, as if he knew Emma's stubbornness all too well. "I'll ready Igor for you, Em," he said, even though he didn't take his eyes off Mitch.

"Thank you, Will." Emma headed for the pantry. "I'll get some food for the trail."

Mitch stepped out onto the porch next to Will and closed the door behind him. "She's a handful."

Will stared off in the distance along the long, winding drive to where it met up with the county road. "She is that. A spitfire, my mom would have called her."

"I'd cancel the ride into the park, but I need that intel for another case I'm working."

"Can you keep her safe?"

"Like I said, it's risky. If whoever was in the house yesterday is out there, they could get the drop on us."

"If Goodsman only wanted to kill Emma, why leave her a present? Seems like he's taunting her."

"It's probably not even him. Last I heard from my boss, he said they had a witness spot him forty miles south of here."

"So who was in the house yesterday?"

"No idea. Seems like they're playing a game."

"Maybe they want to scare her, drive the doctor a little crazy? Quid pro quo for something she did to them in the past?"

Well, well, Will was a smart guy. "Makes sense."

He stuck the hat back on his head. "My guess? Goodsman is getting some revenge and laughing about it from a place far away. I combed the woods last night and again this morning. There's nobody out there. Whoever left that calling card yesterday did it to throw Em into a tailspin, and then they bugged out."

"You think it's safe then to take her with me?"

"Odds are, yes." Will patted the top of Lady's head who still sat next to his leg. The Labs found spots in the sun to warm themselves, their eyes darting to Mitch every so often. "I'll keep out of sight, but I'll cover your six."

With Will behind them, Mitch could relax a bit. "On which horse?"

"Don't need a horse."

With that, Will and Lady left him standing there, both of them kicking up dust as they crossed the yard heading for the horse barn.

Inside, Mitch caught Emma in the pantry. "Which branch of the military was Will?"

She whirled in the tight quarters, protein bars in hand. "Why?"

He took the bars and set them on the shelf. "Was he Special Forces?"

She bit her bottom lip, looking up at him. "Yes, but it's his story to tell, so that's all I'm saying."

Mitch put his hands on her hips and drew her close. "That's all I need to know."

She grinned as he lowered his lips to hers. "What are you doing, Agent Holden?"

"Showing my gratitude." He nibbled at her bottom lip and felt his chest expand when she giggled and kissed him back.

"For what exactly?"

He didn't want to get serious again, but he needed to tell her the truth. "For the way you listened and didn't preach at me about letting all my shit go. I can't let it go. I won't."

She brought a hand up, her fingers light on his forehead as she brushed a lock of his hair aside. "I know, and that's okay."

In that moment of complete acceptance, peace filled his chest for the first time in a long time. "Why don't you want to change me, Emma?"

She gave him a sad, droll smile. "Your dysfunction enables mine. Why else?"

At least they could recognize the madness in themselves. Accept it. "I can't promise you anything."

"You don't have to. I'm a big girl. I know what I'm getting myself into."

Did she? Since he'd been here, he'd admired her guts and bravery, but she was a tad reckless. Him, even more so. That could spell disaster. "Is there any way I can talk you out of going with me on the trail today?"

"Nope, and don't even think of canceling because of me. We're going. I will not be held hostage in my house, and I can't sit here and do nothing. I'll go mad."

"I think you're crazy already, Emma."

Her smile turned happy. "Crazy attracts crazy, so what does that make you?"

"Is that a professional adage? Crazy attracts crazy?"

She laughed. "Absolutely. You ready? We better get going or we won't make it back before nightfall."

He kissed her then, long and slow, a part of him wanting nothing more than to stay here, in this house with her, making her even more happy.

After thoroughly telling her that with his kiss, he regretfully pulled back. She was right; if they were going to check out the trail, they needed to get going.

"Grab your shotgun," he told her, letting her out of the pantry and swatting her backside as she passed him. "And your pea shooter too."

"Yes, sir." She gave him a saucy salute and went to retrieve her weapons.

Mitch took a minute to revel in the feeling of peace permeating his chest, winding right around the old shrapnel buried there. It wasn't overwhelming but there was a spark of something—a feeling he hadn't experienced in a long time.

Five years to be exact. For the first time in five years, he couldn't care less about the holidays. All because of that little spark inside him.

Because of Emma.

Desire. Expectancy. Both warred with the grip of the past. The possibility that he could blot out the pain for a few minutes, a few hours—maybe even a few days—without the aid of alcohol or any other drug was welcome. He could get through Christmas sober this year.

But cleaning out the horse stalls wasn't in his plans.

Keeping a certain doctor in her bed all day long, naked and at his mercy? That was more like it. She deserved to be pampered, to feel appreciated and valued. To experience a Christmas like she'd never experienced before.

Feeling like a dirty-minded Santa, intent on giving Emma the best, most erotic Christmas of her life, Mitch grabbed the protein bars from the shelf and closed the pantry door behind him.

Time to get busy. He had a criminal to catch and a seduction to plan, and less than twenty-four hours to do both.

CHAPTER TWELVE

Face the past.

Deal with it.

Move on.

The goal of any good therapist was to help clients own their problems, deal with them, and then let them go.

In her years working with criminals, Emma had found few who were truly open to changing their lives. Sometimes they verbalized a desire to change, but more often than not, the hopelessness of life in prison and their past family conditioning won out.

Normal people living normal lives had trouble confronting and overcoming issues from their pasts. Those in the criminal justice system, where there was little support or hope for personal change, were usually doomed to fail from the start. Facing their past, mistakes and all, and then dealing with that past was only half the battle.

Letting it go...that was the true test.

The same held true for her, she knew, as she rocked gently in the saddle, Twinkie following Igor and Mitch ahead of them. Salt and Pepper ran back and forth, their noses to the ground, wagging their tails and occasionally barking at each other. She'd revisited her issues inside and out many times in an attempt to heal. Most days she felt strong and ready to move forward with her life. Others, she wanted to stay in bed and cry.

Grief was like that. It could hit you out of nowhere. Leave you bereft, even after all this time.

The sun was bright as it burned through a soft layer of smoke hanging high in the atmosphere. The day was warm for Christmas Eve, but then every day during this dry spell was in the low 80s if not warmer.

Adjusting her hat, she wiped sweat from her brow and calculated how far they'd come. They'd passed her makeshift gun range, Mitch promising her another lesson on their way back. She looked forward to his hands on her, helping her steady the gun. His voice close to her ear, murmuring instructions.

The memory of him guiding her the previous day made her shiver even though she was sweating. The kiss on her office floor had rocked her to her core. She hadn't been with a man since Roland. Being touched in that way, being kissed—it was a good thing they'd been sitting down. Mitch's kiss would have knocked her on her ass anyway.

As if he sensed her attention on his back, he shot a look over his shoulder. "Everything alright?"

Surprisingly, it was. As long as she didn't think too hard about him and his issues and the way his psychosis mirrored her own.

While she hadn't done a thorough, professional analysis of his personality or delved into all the things he hadn't told her about the day his twin had died, she didn't need to. She knew the MO of people like Mitch. Knew it like the back of her hand.

It was hers as well.

The people who wore their dysfunction like a badge of honor. People who identified so strongly with being a warrior, a martyr, a victim, that they couldn't let that identity go. To step out of that role and move on with a successful, productive, healthy life would be like cutting out the biggest part of their personality and kicking it to the curb. Who would they be then?

In her own life, she'd run away from the world she'd created with Roland. While she hated admitting that she'd been a victim, she *had* been one, and although she'd survived and dealt with ways to protect herself and give herself a sense of security again, she'd been victimized all over again by Roland's rejection. By the loss of their child.

Knowing something cognitively did not always translate to understanding it emotionally. That's what she'd learned through her ordeal. She understood it wasn't her fault she'd lost the baby. She understood Roland's difficulty in staying with her. Her mind accepted these things, but her heart didn't.

Mitch was in a similar situation. He'd faced his demons time and time again, but had yet to effectively put them to rest. Until he did that, he couldn't let the past go and move on. By day, he functioned well enough to be successful at his job, and that was probably the one thing keeping him afloat. Most of his emotions were closed off. Smothered. His defense mechanisms—anger and hostility—had become his armor, keeping him from getting involved in loving human relationships.

Figures he'd be attracted to me. While she sported a normal facade in order to make her clients and others comfortable enough around her to let down their guards, she was as angry and hurt over Roland's betrayal as she was at herself for putting her child at risk.

But if she could find a way to help Mitch through his damaged, dark state of being, she might be able to find her own way through the forest of demons she kept at bay every day.

They entered a clearing where the stream that bordered her property paralleled the trail. Because of the drought, the usually wide swath of water had been reduced to a slender, meandering trickle. Exposed river rock shone in the harsh sunlight. Cracks appeared in the ground in several places where the banks had dried out.

Mitch slowed his horse. "Let's give the horses a drink."

There were pink wildflowers here, their tiny heads blowing in the gentle breeze, oblivious to the fires that had ravaged the land only a few miles away. Emma dismounted and led Twinkie to the skinny stream, bending down and touching the flowers as the horse took his time sniffing the exposed river rocks.

"Nature's a bitch, but she knows how to give birth to beauty," Mitch said, looking down at the patch of flowers Emma knelt in.

Emma ran her fingers lightly over the pink heads. "The fires are a horrible thing. I can only imagine the losses to wildlife as well as those to people in the surrounding areas. It won't take long for Mother Nature to send up new grasses, flowers, and trees inside the park. Come spring, it will be a wonderful sign of hope and rebirth. I hope the locals can rebuild too."

"Destruction does wipe the slate clean." Mitch looked off toward the valleys south of them, but Emma had the feeling he was seeing something else. Something from his past. War, perhaps, or his brother's death. "But sometimes, not even Mother Nature can recover from it."

Did he really believe that? She stood, removed her hat, and used a hanky to wipe her face. Both horses stood together drinking. "Something new always rises from the ashes," she countered. "Something we can learn from, draw hope from."

He slanted a glance at her. "Perhaps."

For some reason, his concession, though mild, gave her a sense of satisfaction. "Human nature is much the same. Many people find ways to overcome tragedy and go on to use their experiences to help others."

"Like you," he said.

When she gave him a questioning look, he pointed at Twinkie and Igor. "The horses, the dogs, Will. You overcame your loss and now you work with juvenile delinquents and rescue trick horses. You've channeled your dysfunction pretty well, Doc, even if you've never sought therapy."

She laughed at that. "My penchant for rescuing things goes pretty far back. Like when I was seven and our neighbors moved off and left their cat and her newborn kittens. My dad forbade me from feeding that mother cat, but I snuck lunch meat and milk out to her every evening after supper. I found homes for all of her kittens too. Eventually, my parents gave up on punishing me for taking care of her. We got her spayed and she became my pet. Scout, I called her, after my favorite book heroine. She lived with us until she died at the ripe old age of thirteen."

"How many veterans like Will have you helped?"

Was he asking out of curiosity or something more personal? "Will is a unique case. Most of the vets I've worked with are in jail from extenuating circumstances stemming from their inability to reintegrate into a normal life once they return from their deployments."

"Can you fix them? The ones with PTSD?"

She squinted at him. "Fix them?"

"You know." He wiggled his fingers in the air. "Do that voodoo you do in therapy."

Touchy subject. One she'd been wanting to dig into deeper, but her work with criminal juveniles took up most of her time. "In most of the people I've worked with who suffer from PTSD—whether it's from military or other traumatic events—I've found they have a rift between their mental and psychological stability before the trauma and their mental and psychological stability afterwards. No surprise there, that's basically what it is. In my research, however, I haven't found a way to heal those dysfunctions. The best I've discovered most of my patients can do is manage it."

"So there's no cure?"

It saddened her to admit it, especially when she was pretty darn sure he was asking for himself, but she shook her head. "What happens to us becomes ingrained in our cells. If we suffer a trauma, our body never forgets it, even if our brain finds a way to disconnect from it. That's why, say, a woman who was sexually molested by her father or other male family member as a child may disassociate from the experience and forget it, her brain using a trick to repress the memory so she can continue to grow and function inside her family. Dependency can do that for us. As a child, she had no other option. She depended on her parents to take care of her, so her very survival relied on being part of the family. As a grown woman, she may be at a party or in a restaurant and smell a cologne or aftershave that suddenly triggers a flood of overwhelming fear, pain, and anger, but she doesn't know why. Snatches of the memory of what happened to her may even arise, yet she can't make sense of them."

"Because her attacker wore the same cologne."

"Exactly. Our sense of smell is the strongest at triggering memory recall. So even though our hypothetical patient's brain repressed the memory of the sexual molestation, it's buried in her psyche and the scent of the cologne brings it back up."

"And then what?"

"The psychotherapy community believes it's important for people to explore these repressed memories and bring them to the surface where they can be dealt with and then let go of."

Twinkie raised his head and ambled over. Igor followed. The two horses stood side by side, tails switching at flies while the Labs took their turn at getting a drink and running through the water.

"Almost sounds like you don't agree with that approach," Mitch said.

Emma stroked Igor's flank. "I've seen conventional behavior therapy help many people. I'm not arguing against it. I only know there are others, people I've dealt with in my own practice, where rehashing such devastating memories has a negative effect. It can create a tidal wave of stress and anxiety. Confronting an attacker can create more issues. In the situation where there is no single attacker—such as in a war—the client is left feeling frustrated. Take Will for example. He has no one single person to confront in order to heal his wounds. People like him often take out their frustration on themselves or their partners and children. In Will's case, he's somehow convinced himself that his unit's collective destruction was his fault. Back here at home, he's converted that horrible experience into something he can understand—he believes he's bad luck."

She kicked a pebble. "On the other hand, examining these past experiences does help a person understand self-sabotaging behavior. That can be very freeing." Didn't everyone want to understand themselves better? "I usually start there, helping my clients digest what happened to them in a way that helps them also understand how that experience created a negative habit or a self-sabotaging behavior. By forming new habits, they can find peace. Once they're strong and secure in themselves, then they can confront those who may have harmed them. Or perhaps find purpose from their trauma, such as military veterans who go on to help other vets deal with PTSD."

Mitch closed the few feet of space between them and stroked her cheek with a finger. "You've found purpose from your trauma, haven't you?"

Her purpose was staring her right in the face. Not a cure, but a respite. "I've found a balm for my pain."

He leaned down and kissed her gently. "Me, too."

The feel of his lips still came as a pleasant shock. "Sometimes," she said, looking into his beautiful, haunted eyes and feeling content, "that's enough."

One of the dogs barked sharply off to Mitch's left. Not the playful bark he'd heard before from both of them during the ride. This one was an alert.

Whipping around, he saw Salt lumbering toward Pepper who was several yards away. The black Lab had his nose to the ground, digging and pawing at something.

"Great," Emma said, returning her hat to her head. "He's

probably found another rabbit hole. I better chase him off before he brings me some poor little baby bunny."

Mitch hadn't seen or noted anything unusual on their trek so far. No one following them, no signs of anyone having been on the trail recently. Somewhere behind them, he could feel Will's presence. "The dog brings you rabbits?"

"He doesn't kill them." She started walking toward the dogs, Salt having now joined Pepper in his dig. "It's like he thinks he's saving them. He picks them up in his mouth and carries them carefully, bringing them to me. I've found more than one litter on my porch and had to raise them by hand."

Mitch fell into step beside her. "Dogs are intuitive. Maybe he knew the mom was dead, so he brought you the babies."

"Huh," Emma said. "Maybe you're right."

They came upon the dogs and Mitch grabbed Emma's arm to stop her. "That's no bunny hole."

Salt and Pepper had partially unearthed a fire pit, Pepper's nose now stuck in a red and black plastic bag labeled as beef jerky.

Emma looked around. "Someone camped here."

Mitch made out some tread marks near the pit, faint, but there. Probably from some type of hiking boot. "Yeah, and recently."

"How do you know?"

He motioned behind them. "Look at how close this is to the stream bed. If someone had camped here a few months ago, they'd have been in the water. And this jerky bag." He pulled the plastic bag off Pepper's nose and examined the date stamped on the edge. "It's not sun bleached and the expiration date is next year."

"Beef jerky expires?"

He'd eaten his fair share of it while in the field. That and MREs—meals-ready-to-eat—were two things he never wanted to see or taste again. "Store bought beefy jerky can last two years under normal conditions, but, yes, it will eventually go bad."

"Two years? Eww. That's gross."

Mitch moved the dogs back so he could inspect the rest of the tiny camp without them destroying any other evidence.

"So you think this might be your arsonist?" Emma asked. "Because why would anyone camp here and not inside the park, unless it was in the last few days while a fire raged in there, correct?"

Mitch looked at the dusty ground, noting where the sparse, dry grass had been folded down. "Someone sat here," he pointed to the spot, then cast his eyes around the fire pit area. "And someone slept over there. See the imprint in that yellowed grass?"

Emma followed the line of his finger and nodded. She pointed to the east. "There's another large imprint there."

They walked over to that one, both staring down at it.

"Two people or one who slept in two different places?" she asked.

Good question. It was hard to tell exact body size by the matted down grass. "The imprints are too similar to tell."

"Mitch?"

She'd done a one-eighty, now focused on a ring of river rock that someone had laid out in a three-by-three foot circular diameter at the base of a scraggly pine.

The hair on the back of his neck lifted as he took a step closer to her. "What is it?"

"An altar," she whispered.

Yep, the hair on his arms joined the hair standing at attention on his neck. "An altar?"

As Emma moved forward to take a closer look, Mitch stayed by her side. What he saw inside the ring of rocks made him want to grab her and put her back on her horse.

A half-burnt candle, a feather, some tiny, white bones. A pocket watch.

In the dirt, someone had drawn four symbols. In the center of the symbols stood a green Tom Monahan statue that matched the one Emma had found in her nightstand.

"Goddammit," Mitch swore under his breath. "The guy who broke into your house. This is where he camped, either before or after the break-in."

"Season Two, Episode Four," Emma said, her eyes glued to the collection of stuff. She pointed at the feather. "*The Hawk Sees.* Tom is visited by a hawk and has a vision of the cyborgs kidnapping his mother. He carries one of the hawk's feathers with him for the rest of the season, but it's stolen and burned by Calypso, one of the other kids in the original group, in an act of bullying. In a later season, when they're both grown, he kills Calypso when he discovers Calypso has been working with a cyborg to destroy their camp."

Her finger moved to the bones. "Season Five, Episode One. On Tom's fifteenth birthday, his group is starving. He goes into the woods and kills a squirrel. It's the first time he's had to kill anything. He wrestles with his conscience, but realizes in order to survive, he'll have to do a lot more killing."

"The pocket watch." Again her finger shifted. "That came late, Season Ten, I think. One of the few men who'd been with Tom and Mary through everything always carried a pocket watch and became Tom's surrogate father. In his last episode, he's mortally wounded by a cyborg and gives Tom his watch right before he dies."

Mitch withdrew his phone and snapped a picture. "And the drawings?"

They looked familiar, but he couldn't place why.

"Tom was captured by the cyborg colony at the end of Season Seven," Emma said. "The premiere of Season Eight opened with him being branded by one of the cyborg leaders and thrown into a slave camp. The brand was like a bar code reader, identifying him as a prisoner. Once he escaped the camp and made it back to his resistance fighters, he had his girlfriend turn the brand into a new tattoo. All the fighters then wanted one. It created a wave of fans in the real world getting them as well."

Mitch shook his head and fired off a couple more shots. "Keep the dogs away from here. I'll get a couple of evidence bags."

At his horse, he dug into the saddlebags and brought out his last two bags. He'd hoped to find evidence of his arsonist, but now had found more evidence of the Tom Monahan stalker.

Keeping an eye on the area around them, he sensed more than felt Will's presence, closer now than before. No doubt the ex-Special Forces soldier had seen them staring at the ground and knew something was up.

Mitch felt better knowing Will was keeping an eye on them, but with the find of the campsite, he felt fresh unease wash over him. He'd had alternative reasons for not leaving Emma behind, most specifically because he liked having her around, but it had been a dick move.

Emma moved back to the horses, calling the dogs after her while Mitch collected the evidence. When he was done stuffing the bags into his saddlebag, she hoisted herself up onto Twinkie and started toward the park once more.

"We should go back," he called to her.

She reigned Twinkie around to look at him. "Why?"

"Your Monahan nut may still be out here."

"It was Linda," she said. "I'd bet my ranch on it."

"Why?"

"She was featured in one of the fan magazines when the show ended. There was a picture of her in her house with an altar to Tom in her bedroom."

"Let me guess,"—he tapped his saddlebag—"it held all of these items."

Emma nodded. "And more."

Mitch looked north toward the woods where the park's boundaries lay. Linda Brown had been here. Helping Gordon or the other way around?

"'The Chosen One will be protected by the Resistance, carrying fire in their hands.'" Emma recited, as if confirming Mitch's

thoughts. *"Fire will consume them, and He will rise from the ashes of their destruction.'"*

"Brown and my arsonist worked together and started the fire, but was it to get to you or to free Goodsman?"

"Does it matter?"

"My money is on freeing Goodsman, but she wanted it to look like the resistance was after you. Why else would she get this close to your place and not set one of your barns on fire or your house? She picked the park, hoping the fires would go south and burn up your home, as well as cause the prison to have to move Goodsman. The fires veered around the ranch, but she got her favorite actor freed."

"That would be my guess as well," Emma said. "All we need is proof she was in that park at the time the fire started."

They might need more than that, but that would be a start. Mitch hopped up on Igor and touched the horse with his heels. Emma wheeled Twinkie back around and they headed for the park.

CHAPTER THIRTEEN

Emma sank her hands into the hot dishwater and found herself staring at the sheen of rainbows on the multitude of bubbles.

Rainbows. She hadn't seen one of those in a long time. Even in a sink full of dirty dishes from her evening meal with Mitch, the soft colors warmed her heart, made her feel happy.

They'd finished their journey to the park, the entrance on the south side nothing more than a footpath through the woods. A rusty gate that had once been green blocked the path, but there hadn't even been a sign announcing it was national park territory.

The chain and padlock on the gate hadn't kept someone from using the entrance—a bolt cutter had severed the heavy chain. Tire tracks from a motorcycle were hidden by brush that Mitch had pulled back. Probably where the arsonist had hidden the bike.

While Emma had stayed on her horse, Mitch had stood for a long time at that gate, sizing up the ground, the gate itself, and what lay on the other side, inside the park. He'd taken pictures of the broken chain and the scuff marks in the dry ground that showed the gate had been swung open and closed again. He took a million photos of the motorcycle tracks hidden under the bush.

Thankfully, that section of the park had not gone up in the fire, but it was still too dangerous for them to enter, Mitch had said. Emma figured he didn't want her and the horses messing up any potential evidence. He'd swung himself over the fence nearby in order to check the other side of the trail. He'd come back convinced that his arsonist had used this exit after setting the initial fire. He also told her he was betting his badge on the fact that Linda Brown had played a part.

On the way back to the ranch, they'd stopped at Emma's homemade gun range, but she'd been so nervous about Mitch's nearness, she'd given up practicing after 10 minutes.

The harder she'd tried to relax, the more anxious she had become. He'd been lighthearted, happy with his evidence, and had joked with her, laughed at her meager attempts, and seemed completely at ease.

Meanwhile, every look he gave her sent her heart fluttering. Every suggestive touch had caused her pulse to hopscotch over itself. Even with his instructions, she hadn't been able to hit a damn thing. She couldn't concentrate, couldn't focus on her mark. All she could see and zoom in on was Mitch.

As the apple pie in the oven warmed for their dessert, she admitted to herself that Mitch was a nice distraction. One that even now messed with her heart and emotions as he paced the living room floor and spoke in soft tones to his immediate supervisor, Cooper Harris.

"It had to be Gordon," Mitch said, "but he had help. There was one set of motorcycle tire imprints in the dirt at that old entrance, but there were two sets of footprints. One smaller than the other. Dr. Collins and I also found what she termed an altar to the Tom Monahan character from *The Mary Monahan Chronicles*. I'll forward the photos I shot of both sites, and as soon as I can, I'll get you the forensic evidence I nabbed. I'm betting Linda Brown was in on the arson as well as the accident to get Goodsman free."

There was a pause as Mitch listened. The smell of warm apples and spices filled the kitchen. Emma filled the coffee maker with decaf grounds and flipped the switch. As it brewed, she began washing the dishes.

All through dinner, Mitch had been quiet, his mind seeming to be distracted by the evidence they'd found. More than once, she'd felt his eyes on her, though, as if he kept circling back around to the tension between them.

They'd been at odds since he'd arrived, but everything had changed that morning in her office on the floor. It had been two years since she'd felt that kind of zing, that particular concoction of desire and need.

Mitch found her interesting; her analysis of him piquing his curiosity. He found her attractive as well. She saw it in the way he looked at her. Looked *into* her, as if he could see what her heart was made of.

She felt it in the way he touched her when he didn't really need to touch her. Gentle holds when helping her on and off her horse that only hinted at the power and strength inside him that could make her come apart a dozen times tonight if she wanted.

That interest had turned into something deeper. She stimulated his mind and set his libido on fire. He did the same to her.

In the old TV shows she sometimes watched, there was often a scientist who played with two inert ingredients, mixing them together and creating a concoction that could blow things sky high. That was how she felt when she got close to Mitch, when he stared at her with those sad eyes that saw past her professional smile and detached facade. If she let his volatile liquid mix with hers...*boom*. They might start their own version of a wildfire.

One that would burn her heart to a crisp and leave her in a pile of ashes.

Was it worth the risk? Her body hummed with a lust that wouldn't be quenched until she acted on it, her heart already layering on protective shields. *Another type of rift*, the therapist inside her acknowledged. Allowing her damaged heart to stay hidden behind those barriers of protection while the rest of her went on the journey of seduction.

If the female inside her was any good at reading the signs, her seduction wouldn't be all that strenuous. Mitch had sent out plenty of signals all day that he wanted more than a kiss from her. All she had to do was invite him to her room tonight.

Finishing the dishes, Emma dried her shaky hands. The dogs were fed, the horses taken care of. Night had come and the farmhouse was semi-dark, only lit by candles once again. The coffee finished brewing and the timer on the stove went off, alerting her that the pie was done. As soon as Mitch sent his photos off to his boss...

All mine.

Emma's heart quivered. She felt lightheaded.

What is wrong with me?

It wasn't like she was a teenaged girl seducing a boy for the first time. Nor was the subject of her quest immune to her. Mitch oozed pheromones and his body had no doubt been picking up on the flood of hers. Human nature was such that men and women understood the subtle cues of sex without great need for explanation. A look, a gesture, was all it took—especially since the stage was already set—to get her invitation across.

"I didn't mean to leave the cleanup all to you."

Emma jumped and whirled. "Oh, it was no problem. Really. I just... I'm glad you're here to share a meal with."

She gave him her practiced smile, hoping to create some distance between them for a moment. Her body might be ready to throw out its invitation, but her heart and mind were still catching up.

His eyes sized her up and he sauntered into the room. "That pie smells delicious. I haven't eaten this well in months. Maybe longer."

He stopped a foot from her, his intense gaze in the flickering shadows of the candlelight setting butterflies loose in her stomach. She took a step back and bumped into the counter. "It's nice to cook for someone besides myself."

Placing his hands on the counter on either side of her, he leaned in, not touching her, but totally invading her space. "I have good news."

She swallowed the tightness in her throat and wondered if he could hear her heart, it was thumping so loudly. "What?"

"In a little town southeast of Escondido, the police have surrounded a house where Chris Goodsman is hiding. Cooper said an FBI SWAT unit is in transit and he and a couple guys on the taskforce are headed there as well. A neighbor called it in, saying they saw Goodsman and Brown entering and leaving the house several times last night."

Her heart, already going crazy, stuttered in surprised relief. "So that sighting yesterday forty miles south of here was probably them."

The side of his mouth quirked. "Probably."

"And most likely my visitor yesterday was one of Chris's other followers, not Linda?"

"Brown no doubt helped my arsonist set the fires, but sent someone else to the house to frighten you while she's helping Goodsman get away. She was messing with your head, Doc."

Freedom. Up to this moment, Emma hadn't realized just how imprisoned her subconscious had felt by the threats Chris and Linda had made. Her body slumped slightly, her breath came out in a whoosh. "When is the SWAT team busting in?"

"Within the hour. Cooper will call as soon as Goodsman and his number one fan are in custody. Coop and Dupé will lean on them, and hopefully, this will wrap up my case with the arsonist as well."

"How so?"

"Brown will give up the goods on the arsonist. I'm almost positive Brown started the fire, and our fire starter snuck her out of the park."

He looked so happy, his eyes mirroring her relief. Emma's

arms moved of their own accord, snaking up to wrap themselves around his neck. "Funny how our lives intersected because of the two of them."

"Maybe it's destiny," he teased.

Her destiny is death. The words Chris Goodsman had written in his jail cell at Aleta Hills.

She started to say something about all the trouble Chris and Linda had gone to in order to freak her out, but she didn't want to spoil the moment. Who knew what Chris had been thinking when he'd left that message? From his past antics, Emma guessed it was nothing more than an insurance policy for him in case he got caught. He could once again make a jury, judge, and his fans believe he'd had a break with reality. That he had believed he was Tom Monahan when he'd left that prison, so when Brown, aka Mary, had shown up and rescued him, he'd gone with her willingly. She was his mother in that alternate reality, after all.

"Mitch," Emma said. "I know this is rather forward of me, but…"

The words were right there on her tongue, but if Goodsman and Brown ended up in custody yet tonight, and they gave up whatever evidence Mitch needed to solve his case, then he'd be leaving her.

On one hand, it should be all the incentive she needed to drag him upstairs and rip his clothes off. On the other…

His hands went to her hips and he pressed her back into the counter. His gaze searched her face. "What is it, Emma?"

Was he teasing her? Surely he saw the look on her face, the desire. "I, um… I want to ask you a question, but I've never approached a man like this."

A sexy grin played across his lips. "With a lead-in like that, I can hardly wait to hear the question."

He was so cocky, so confident. Good thing he had her backed up to the counter. Her knees were shaking as much as her voice. The therapist in her rose to the occasion, giving her some needed poise. "It's much easier to talk to you when you're being derisive and snarky."

He rested his forehead against hers, their noses brushing. "You know how to handle that, don't you? That's your comfort zone."

Her comfort zone was definitely being violated at the moment along with her personal space. Her breath was coming too fast, as if she'd run a mile. "I'm on the receiving end of snarky and derisive a lot in my line of work. Anger and hate as well."

One of his hands came up and rubbed the back of her neck. Goose flesh rose at his touch and shimmered down her spine. "This isn't work, Emma. Relax. You can ask me anything."

Deep breath. Relax. "Okay." She swallowed, her eyelids half closing at the exquisite feel of his fingers massaging the tight muscles in her neck. "It's Christmas Eve, and although I'd like to pretend that means nothing to me, there's a part of me that's eager to create a new memory. One that's happy and, well, satisfying, so I'd like to invite you to..."

At her pause, he tugged at the end of her ponytail. "Yes?"

She bit her bottom lip, forced herself to look him in the eye. "Since you no longer have to worry about guarding me from Chris, your job here is over, right?"

His fingers went higher, kneading the base of her skull and loosening her ponytail. "Potentially. Once I get word from Cooper that Goodsman and Brown are in custody. Why?"

Again, there was a teasing note in his voice. He knew exactly what she wanted to ask him, knew how he was affecting her.

God, it was hard to focus with his fingers massaging the back of her head as his body—a very hard, muscular body—pressed into hers. She was pretty sure one part of that hard body meant he was thinking the same thing she was, and at this rate, she wasn't going to make it upstairs to her bedroom before she ripped his clothes off. "You're not on the clock, technically."

He chuckled. "As in, I can hit on you and not get into trouble with my bosses?"

"Is that what you're doing? Hitting on me?"

He gently tugged on her hair, forcing her to turn her head sideways and bare her neck to him. His lips moved over her skin, raising a new wave of goose bumps. "Isn't it obvious?"

The fluttering in her belly settled as the female in her exploded. She raked her fingers through his hair, drawing him in even closer. "Thank God. I thought I was going to embarrass myself by begging."

"Oh, that sounds fun." His teeth nibbled at her earlobe. "Maybe I should make you beg."

"You're horrible," she said, but it made her laugh.

He kneed her thighs apart and she wrapped her legs around his waist, his erection acutely and strategically placed at the junction of her thighs. He lifted her and set her on the counter. "You love it."

"I do." She found his lips and kissed him, slowly, purposefully, hoping he understood just how much she wanted him. "You're exactly what I need tonight."

Emma's kiss was deep and wild—a surprise. The kiss on the floor of her office had given him a glimpse of this, but it had been restrained. Bashful, almost.

Not any longer. He kissed her back, rough and equally as wild and she moaned.

He loved it. Loved the way she made him feel.

Strong, powerful, free.

Free of the past. Free of the judgments and the grief and the anger.

I could get lost in her.

Her fingers worked at his shirt while his fingers unbuttoned her jeans. His shirt fell to the floor as Emma scored his chest with her nails. The satin fabric of her panties was wet.

Exactly what he wanted.

He wanted her wet and ready for him, because there was no going back now. No more dancing around this attraction. This bond they had with each other.

Hard and fast...he'd fallen for her much too hard, so goddamn fast, but there was no going back. He wanted—no, *needed*—to taste her, feel her, drive himself into her.

Drive away the pain.

He'd been lost for so long. Lost and afraid, imagining the rest of his life without Mac. A steady, aggravating burn under his skin.

In Emma's arms, he felt at home. Safe, grounded.

Happy.

The future no longer stared him in the face like an ugly, angry beast. Now all he saw was potential. Possibilities. An ease to his agony. He wanted to be a better man. A better man because of her.

Emma tugged on his hair, nipped at his collarbone. A little hellcat, urging him on. He slipped a finger past the satin underwear, sliding into her slick folds.

Her body arched and she whimpered, her hand smacking into the pots she had washed and stacked on the counter to dry. They clanged to the floor, raising a commotion with the Labs, but Mitch laughed and shooed the dogs away.

Emma's pretty eyes flashed in the shadows with lust and need as they looked at him through thick lashes. "I want to be..."—her breath came in gasps that matched the stroke of his fingers as he built a new rhythm—"more than friends."

She tried for a grin, but bit her bottom lip instead as he inserted a second finger. "Oh, Doc, I promise we're going to be much more than friends when I get done with you."

Those lashes of hers dipped down, her hands on his shoulders holding on tight. "God, I hope so."

She licked her lips and he caught the bottom one between his teeth, kissing her as she moved against him, her core tightening around his fingers.

Jesus, he needed to slow down, take her the proper way and make it good for her. Show her what this meant to him, his appreciation for the comfort she'd given him. He should haul her upstairs to her big, old bed, strip her slowly, and take his time memorizing her curves, the feel of her skin, the taste of her on his lips.

His cock had other ideas, especially when she unzipped his fly and slipped her hand inside.

Her fingers were cool and gentle, teasing him into the air. Once he was free of his pants, she gripped him firmly and gave a tug.

And god*damn* it. He was about to come just from that.

Distract her before you embarrass yourself.

He ripped off her shirt with his free hand, saw the sexy lace beneath. Peach, a shade or two darker than her skin. Nipples strained against the fabric, taunting, begging for him to take them into his mouth, like the previous day, before they'd been interrupted.

Grabbing her wrist and removing her hand from his too-hard dick, he bent down and suckled a nipple through the fabric.

She arched again, legs spreading wider. The hand that was still free grasped at his back, her nails digging into his shoulder. Shoving her wrist up to the cupboard overhead, he took his time laving her nipple through the lace, nipping at it, then kissing away the pain.

Her breath came in gasps, her pelvis slapping into his palm where his fingers worked at her core. Moaning his name, she pulled him closer, even as he held her captive, using his teeth to tug the peach material, now wet from his mouth, away from her breast.

Baring all that beautiful skin.

So damned perfect. The breast was heavy and round, her

areole the same peach color as her bra. He licked her from the beautiful underside of her heavy breast, up and over the hard tip, trailing his tongue to the base of her throat where her pulse pounded.

Her release came fast and with enough force that she cried out again, this time with his name on her lips as her spine bowed backward. He milked her orgasm with his fingers, capturing her mouth with his and looking into her lust-fogged eyes as she came apart in his arms. Releasing her wrist, he bound her to him as she peaked, her hips still moving in a frantic rhythm that was erotic as hell to watch.

When she finally stilled, Mitch swung her into his arms and carried her upstairs. She nestled her face into his neck, wrapping her arms around him.

His erection was still so hard, the stairs were a bitch to climb, but he managed to get halfway up before the Labs ran by him, stopping at the top and sitting, tongues out as they panted, tails wagging as if they thought this was a game.

Emma raised her head slightly and ran a hand over the stubble on his jaw. "That was amazing."

"You haven't seen anything yet," he told her, need driving him. "I'm going to rip off the rest of your clothes and fuck you blind, Doc. Hope you're up for it."

Her hand forced his face to turn toward her. She kissed him, her tongue forcing itself into his mouth as her fingers went up the back of his skull and tugged on his hair. "Bring it, on, Agent," she said against his lips. "I'm more than ready for you."

The huskiness of her voice and the way her eyes were steady on his nearly dropped him. His tiny brain—not so tiny at the moment—told him to take her right there on the stairs. "After I fuck you properly in your bed, I'm going to haul you into your office and make you put on those reading glasses. Then I'm going to fuck you on your desk."

"Do you have handcuffs, because I'm thinking of a few things I'd like to do to you as well."

She giggled and her boldness made him chuckle. She always had a comeback. Nothing he said ever shocked her. "I might be able to scrounge up some zip ties from the cab of my truck."

Her smile was mischievous. "Excellent."

His lascivious desire renewed, he had no trouble climbing the last few stairs and throwing Emma on her bed. She rolled to her side and lit a candle on the nightstand. He closed the door on the dogs and stood for a moment, lost in her beauty as she leaned back on her elbows and smiled over at him.

Her hair was undone and messy, her shirt gone, her jeans open at the waist, and one breast on full display. The nipple was still puckered tight from his earlier ministrations.

"Take off your bra," he told her.

"Take off your pants," she countered.

He stalked to the bed, let the pants fall. Lifting one brow, he wiggled his fingers at her to ante up.

Staring at his very out-there erection, she licked her lips and unhooked her bra, dangling it in front of him before dropping it to the floor.

He was naked save for his socks. She still had her pants on. "Lose the jeans. And the panties," he added.

"Yes, sir."

She raised her hips to shimmy out of the pants and he grabbed the cuffs, dragging the tight material off her and knocking her off balance. She laughed, nearly tumbling off the bed. The satin panties went next and then she was gloriously naked for him.

Once more on her elbows, she bent her knees and splayed her legs wide, taunting him. "I need you inside me," she said in that husky voice. "Now."

"This is some therapy technique you have, Doc."

"Why, yes, it is. Thanks for noticing. I promise, you're going to enjoy it." Her grin was wicked and sexy and sent his cock bobbing as she came up off her elbows to reach for him. "I'm good at what I do."

Before he could stop her, she leaned forward, her lips touching the end of his cock. She kissed him there, making his legs go weak. "Jesus," he hissed under his breath.

She slid to the edge of the bed and off of it, going to her knees in front of him. Her lips parted and she guided him into her mouth, deeper, deeper, deeper, until his eyes rolled up into the back of his head.

Her mouth stroked him. Her tongue teased. Her teeth scraped against his sensitive flesh. Grabbing her by the arms, he forced himself to draw back. "Another few seconds of that," he huffed, "and I'm not going to make it."

She twisted her lips into a pout. "That's the idea, Mitch. To make you lose control."

Lifting her from the floor, he set her on the bed, pushing her back. Her mound glistened in the candlelight and he wanted to go down on her, taste her on his tongue, but his cock wasn't going to last for any other distractions. Running his hands under her knees, he raised them up and climbed between them, kissing the soft skin of her thighs, the spot above her pubic bone, her ribs. She arched into his kisses, wrapping her legs around his waist as he settled between her thighs.

She was wet and slick and he drove himself home, the sensation of flying overtaking him as she met him with a pelvic thrust that made him nearly come from the ferocity.

His mind went blank, his body taking over, grinding itself into her. Emma's hips made tiny circles in between the thrusts, her inner walls pulling him in tight. Their bodies slapped together, over and over, the primal sound echoing in the room.

The need, the desperation echoed with it as Emma raked her hands across his shoulders to his back. Her eyes locked on his, her lips swollen from his kisses parted, ready for more. He didn't know how it was possible, but she pulled him in closer, as if she couldn't get enough of him.

Another impossibility, but his cock seemed to grow, just from that look, that need of hers to have more of him.

He wanted to give it to her, give her everything she wanted.

Her eyelashes fluttered, about to close as her back lifted her higher. So close. She was so close and he was going to follow her right over that perfect fucking edge of oblivion.

"Open your eyes." He wanted to see her when she came. Look into her soul. "Don't close me off."

"Never," she whispered, meeting his gaze. "I'm all yours."

The words nearly stalled him, his body locking up as his brain kicked in. But then Emma grasped his hips with her hands, her gaze locked on his. "I need this," she added. "Your brand of therapy."

Catching her bottom lip in his teeth again, he bit her, released, kissed the swollen skin. Her tongue licked into his mouth and he increased their rhythm.

The bed springs groaned, the headboard smacking into the wall. Ah, yes. He needed this too. Fucking her hard and deep and loving how she took it all and gave it back to him.

"Come for me," he rasped against her mouth, feeling her milking him as he bore down on her. "I want to make you scream."

Scream she did. She clung to him, eyelashes at half-mast as she convulsed and writhed under him. He continued to move with her, letting her ride out the orgasm as she took him over the sweet edge and into his.

CHAPTER FOURTEEN

The night was dark but, for the first time in a week, Emma could see stars in the sky as she stared out her bedroom window. A strong wind was blowing down from the north, clearing the air. The last weather report Mitch had gleaned before the satellite lost transmission claimed rain was on the way.

Rain on Christmas. A miracle for sure this year.

The clock across the hall ticked softly, nearing midnight. Mitch lay spooned around her body, his soft snores resonating from his chest into her back. Warm, reassuring.

Comforting.

Her baby had died shortly after midnight on Christmas morning. The pain, so fresh last year, now only ached dully in her chest. She'd miscarried so early, she'd never known the sex of the child, but in her heart, she'd known it was a girl.

As she lay in bed with Mitch's arm around her, she looked out at the stars shining over the ranch and focused on one that appeared to twinkle inside the Andromeda Galaxy. Many nights, she'd dragged herself from bed in order to look through her telescope at the Blue Snowball Nebula inside the Andromeda constellation and talk to her daughter. It made no logical sense to associate a star in the heavens with a soul, yet Emma—like many other people in history—found solace in doing so.

Tonight, however, she was content to stay in Mitch's arms

and watch Blue Snowball from bed. The smell of cinnamon drifted through the house from the pie still downstairs on the counter. The normal soft creaks of the house settling in the night air comforted her, much like Mitch's gentle snores. Every once in a while, she heard the dogs shift in their sleep right outside the bedroom door.

Merry Christmas, Skye. Emma had never told anyone—not even Roland—that she had named the baby. When they'd found out they were pregnant, she'd had a list of possibilities, of course. Allison, Michelle, Kathleen. After the miscarriage, none of them seemed…right. None of them fit.

One night after she'd bought the ranch and was making room in the attic for some of her boxes, she'd come across the old telescope. She knew nothing about telescopes or astronomy, but cleaned off the lenses anyway and soon became an amateur astronomer.

One night, looking at the sky and reading through a book on the Andromeda Galaxy she'd bought off the Internet, it came to her. *Skye.* The perfect name for her daughter.

Mitch's breathing grew lighter; he stretched, running a hand down her hip, his lips finding her neck. "You awake?"

They'd made love three times in a couple of hours. His erection pressing into the crease between her legs told her he was ready again.

She'd never felt so wanton in her life. The spot between her legs ached. At the same time, she was wet for him.

He did that to her. Everything about him, from his messy hair to his eyes, to his strong, muscular body, turned her on. She liked his snarky attitude, the way he teased her and didn't seem to feel the least threatened by the degrees and certificates on her office wall. He was the exact opposite of the men who usually tripped her sexiness meter. "Hard to sleep through your snoring," she teased.

Truth was, she hadn't shared a bed with anyone since Roland. She'd grown used to being alone, sleeping alone. It surprised her that Mitch's presence in her house, in her bed, felt so right.

He leaned up on an elbow and followed her gaze to the window. "I don't snore."

"Haha," she said, noticing how his hand had made its way to her lower belly. "And I don't eat M&Ms when I'm stressed."

He nuzzled her behind her ear. "I hate to bring this up and ruin the moment, but..."

Oh, crud. Here it came. "You're married, aren't you?"

His fingers trailed over her ribs up to her breast where he cupped it. "You wish. That would make it easy, wouldn't it? For you to kick me out of this bed."

Sarcasm. His go-to when things might get serious. It did, however, ease her mind a tad. "Let me guess. You have a librarian fetish."

"Wow, you *are* good. How'd you guess?"

"Earlier you promised to take me on my desk while I wear my reading glasses."

"Ah." His hand moved to her other breast as he nibbled her ear. "Pretty textbook, huh?"

"Classic. But just so you know, I'm happy to enable that fantasy."

He laughed softly in her ear, tweaked her nipple. His erection bobbed against her. "Damn, woman. You make me crazy. And distracted."

"You were about to admit some deep, dark secret, I believe."

He stopped nibbling, sighed. "I'm sorry, but I totally blew it."

"Blew what?"

"I didn't wear a condom. I totally... Well, you made me so freakin' nuts, I didn't even think about it. I screwed up."

A fissure of worry flared to life in her belly. "You have an STD?"

"What?" He leaned up on an elbow and looked down at her. "No. But I possibly just got you pregnant. I'm such an idiot. I used to keep a condom on me at all times, but in the past year or so... Sex wasn't doing it for me, you know? I had no interest in hookups. Just zilch."

Pregnant. If only...

"I'm clean, too." Emma batted back the pressure behind her eyeballs. "Don't worry."

"But what if I just—"

Emma put a finger to his lips. "You didn't. Trust me."

His brows furrowed. "You're on the Pill, then?"

She shook her head, blinked back the tears that suddenly threatened to spill. "I can't have kids. Not after the mis..." She had to stop and take a breath. "Not after I lost Skye."

Everything in his face went flat. His erection no longer poked at her. "Jesus, I'm sorry, Em. I didn't know."

She looked away, slanting her blurry attention to the stars outside again. "Of course, you didn't. Don't be silly."

His fingers worked their way softly into her hair, massaging her scalp. He kissed her cheek, gave her a gentle hug. "Skye, huh? That was her name?"

Emma nodded, causing a hot tear to leak down her cheek. "No one knows that. Her name, I mean. You're the first person I've ever told."

She saw his mouth twitch at the realization that he was the only person she'd told her most intimate secret to. "It's beautiful," he whispered, lying back down and pulling her close. "Just like you."

The office clock struck midnight and Emma let another tear roll down her face into the pillow. Wrapped in Mitch's arms, she gave herself permission to cry, to mourn yet another night, another Christmas, without her daughter and the life she'd imagined she'd be living at this moment.

But no more tears came. Instead, she felt calm, soothed by the presence of the man holding her. He wasn't afraid of tears. Wasn't afraid she would lose her shit talking about her daughter. Her secret, her damaged psyche, as well as her physical body, were all more than safe with him.

"Do you want kids?" she heard herself saying after a few minutes.

And, whoops, that sounded like too much of a leading question. He was going to pull back now, assuming she was asking because she wanted a relationship, and...

"Never really thought about it," he said, still holding her close. His breath was warm on her ear. "I guess I needed the right woman in my life—for marriage, kids, all that normal stuff—and the right one never came along. Then, after Mac died, I was so fuckin' screwed up, it didn't seem like having a family would be a good thing. Like you said earlier, I'd probably end up taking my PTSD out on my family. Hell, I'm already doing that. I can't even talk to my mother."

It pained her, his words. Pained her that she had no easy way to fix him.

Her next words seemed to tumble off her tongue. "I thought I had the right man for all that, but apparently I didn't. He's the only other man I've ever slept with, by the way. My ex. Him and you—you're it."

"Are you kidding me?" Mitch rose up again, a weird grin on his face as he peered down at her. "You were a virgin when you married?"

She rolled her eyes. "Of course not. Roland and I started dating in college. Until then, I was a bookish nerd and made a complete idiot out of myself when a boy so much as looked at me. My freshman year of college, my roommate gave me the clichéd geek to chic makeover." She laughed as she pushed a strand of hair from her eyes. "Roland and I hooked up, and the rest is history."

Mitch was still grinning. "So?"

"So what?"

"How do I compare? Against Roland the Douchebag?"

"Are you serious right now? You want me to grade your performance versus my ex-husband?"

"Damn straight, woman. You're practically a virgin. I wish

I'd known beforehand so I could have really shown you my best moves earlier, but hell. Tell me the truth. I rock compared to that bastard, don't I?"

He did indeed. With Roland, she'd never been allowed to let herself go, ask for what she wanted. She'd sworn she'd never make that mistake again, and with Mitch, she'd felt totally unencumbered. Where Roland had always wanted to please himself, Mitch seemed more concerned with pleasing her. "I believe the dozen or so orgasms I experienced over the three hours of our love-making match speak for themselves."

"Sweet Christmas." He slapped the bed and whooped, his happiness echoing off the ceiling. "I knew it. Roland is a stupid name, by the way, and he's an ass for leaving you. But lucky for me, he did. If you were still with that douchebag, I'd have to steal you away from him."

The thought made her smile. He was always so flippant, she couldn't be sure he was telling the truth. "How would you do that? Work those seductive charms of yours, aka snarkiness and irascibility, to woo me over?"

"I've never gone after a married woman before, but if it was you, I'd have to. You're irresistible. I have to have you."

His erection, now warm and hard against her leg again, confirmed that.

The heat started low in her belly, moved up her chest, her neck. "That may be the nicest compliment anyone's ever paid me."

"Good. You deserve it."

"Merry Christmas," she said. "Is there anything Santa forgot to bring you this year?"

Catching onto her game, he grinned. "I'm still waiting for you to fulfill my sexy, naked librarian fantasy. And I didn't get any pie."

"Pie first. Then I'll fulfill any fantasy you want."

He kissed her quick and hard. "Merry fucking Christmas to me. Let's get that pie."

He chased her down the stairs, both of them naked, the dogs

barking at their heels with glee. Mitch came up behind Emma while she was cutting the pie, his hands running over her hips, down her thighs, around to the inside and back up. She arched back into him, forgetting about the pie as he kissed her neck, massaged her breasts.

When he gently bent her forward, she gripped the edges of the counter and he entered her from behind. She was sore and tight as hell, but it felt good, so damn good, to have him inside her. Holding on tightly to the counter as he stroked her sensitive nub with a thumb, she felt brazen and erotic. He kissed his way down her neck and the vertebra of her back, sending chills over her skin.

A moment later, she cried out her release and felt him tense with his own.

Sagging in his arms, she let him carry her to the half-bath off the mudroom and clean her up. They reheated cups of cold coffee and took the whole pie upstairs to eat in bed.

For the next hour, Mitch fed her apples baked to perfection with just the right amount of cinnamon. He shared a couple of memories of his childhood with his brother Mac, making Emma laugh more than she had in years. While she listened to his stories, she couldn't help but think about her childhood—completely unremarkable compared to his—and realized how much they *didn't* have in common. They were from two different worlds, then and now, and yet they fit together perfectly.

Emma groaned as she waved off another bite of pie. "I'm stuffed." She sipped at her coffee, cold once more. "But I think that was best apple pie I made this year."

"You made it?"

"From the apples in the orchard. The horses love them, and they make a decent pie."

Mitch leaned across the pie plate between them on the bed and kissed her. "I should marry you just for your cooking skills."

Marry. The word hung in the air between them for an awkward moment, then Emma shook it off. "You haven't even seen my porno librarian act yet. You shouldn't commit to anything until you make sure I pass that test."

He purposely ogled her breasts. "True. That could make or break it."

Emma plucked the fork from his hand, dropping it into the empty pie plate and moving the plate aside. "Guess I better get my reading glasses and get to work."

"Will you put your hair up in a bun too?"

She slunk off the bed, giving him a lascivious look as she headed for the bathroom. "You'll have to come to my office if you want your book stamped."

Behind the bathroom door, she blew out a low breath, touched her belly where butterflies churned.

You're irresistible. I have to have you.

The words tumbled over and over in her brain. He thought she was beautiful. He'd been so out of his mind with lust for her, he'd totally forgotten to wear a condom.

He'd just teasingly mentioned marriage.

After Roland, she had sworn off marriage. It had been a moot point. Yet, she'd fallen for Mitch—there was no denying it—in three short days.

Three days!

Marriage wasn't even part of the equation. Were either of them even ready for a relationship? Could it work?

Sweet Christmas is right, I'm foolish for even considering it. Sex—no matter how amazing it was—was not a foundation for a long-term relationship.

We're all wrong for each other.

But sometimes, all wrong felt incredibly right.

––––––––

Mitch leaned against the doorframe, buck naked, as he spoke through the closed door of Emma's office. "Now?"

"Not yet," she said and he heard laughter in her voice. "You're so impatient."

His cock was stiff and ramrod straight, bobbing at the sound of her voice, so sure of herself. She'd expressly denied him access until she was ready. He imagined her pulling her hair up into a bun, setting the glasses on her nose, clearing the top of her desk...

He rested his head against the door. "You're killing me out here, Emma."

Her voice came back, closer to the door. "I know."

Damn woman. "I need to get inside you. Like, now."

He could almost see her licking her lips, biting that full bottom one. "Good things come to those who wait."

She sounded like she was right on the other side of the door. Taunting him. "That's bullshit and you know it. Good things come to those who take them."

She laughed and he heard the sound of the floor creaking as she moved away from the door. "Then you better come take what you want."

Finally. Mitch threw the door open and...

Holy hell. He had to stop and gawk.

In the middle of the candlelit room, Emma sat like a pinup girl on the top of her desk, knees bent, breasts thrusting upward. She wore his shirt, buttoned up to her neck, but her bottom half sat bare-ass on the polished wood, a pair of black high heels on her feet, accentuating her sexy calves. Her reading glasses perched prettily on the end of her nose and she'd twisted her hair up in a messy bun.

She teased a pencil between her lips, a deep red lipstick leaving marks on the wood as she gave him a steely glare.

"Your book is overdue," she said, licking the tip of the pencil as though about to write with it. "I'm going to have to fine you."

The lips, the tongue, the way her gaze dipped to his full cock—it was all perfect. "I can't wait to find out what that involves."

Her knees parted, giving him a view of the sweetness between her legs. "I'm afraid there's a harsh penalty."

Striding across the floor, he grinned at her. "Whatever it is, I'll gladly pay it."

The librarian glare morphed into a sexy pout. She spread her legs wider as she melted back onto her elbows, her tongue sneaking out to lick her lips as she stared at his blatant erection. "Show your librarian some respect."

Grabbing her by the hips, he slid her ass to the edge of the desk. She yelped and he laughed, dropping to his knees and slinging her legs over his shoulders. He lowered his mouth to her, kissing, nibbling, sucking.

Every time he worked on her, she came fast. This time was no exception. With her hands in his hair and her back arching off the desk, she cried out his name and came with a rush in less than a minute.

Easing her down from the orgasm, he kissed his way up her body, unbuttoning the shirt and gently sucking on each of her breasts. His lips climbed to her collarbone, her neck.

"What's your fantasy?" he murmured in her ear.

Her lips parted on a contented sigh. "Anything with you in it."

His ego liked that. "Nothing specific? Maybe a cowboy taking you in the hay? Wait, I bet you're into geeky academics. You probably have some professor fantasy."

"No." Her eyelids fluttered open. She stroked his shoulder. "I don't really have any fantasies."

Seriously? "Everyone has sexual fantasies."

Her eyes were serious, a couple of tiny lines forming between her eyebrows. "I guess I've never met anyone who inspired them."

He traced a finger along her jaw, then removed her glasses and set them aside. "Guess I better change that."

A small smile curved her lips. "Good, because..."

"Because what?"

"I sort of like this role-playing thing."

Yes! He ran a hand down between her legs. "You still haven't stamped my book."

She climbed out from under him and forced him onto his back. His erection stood proud as he lay under her perusal, shadows dancing across her face. Reaching out, she caught him with her hand, then climbed on top of the desk, straddling him.

"I'm going to stamp it right now," she cooed. Leaning over, she ran her tongue up his chest and then settled herself on top of him.

As her slick folds parted to let him in, he grabbed her hips and guided her down. "I can't wait to get you on my motorcycle."

Her body began an erotic rhythm, breasts bouncing as she gyrated on top of him. Her bun had come undone and her hair fell in waves over her shoulders. "Ooh, your motorcycle. I'd almost forgotten about that. I bet I could come up with a fantasy or two involving you and the bike."

Oh, yeah, he was definitely up for those fantasies. His thumb probed her sensitive spot, rubbing her into an even more heated frenzy. "Anything you want, sweetheart."

"Anything?" Her voice was ragged and breathy.

"Anything," he promised.

That was the last word he spoke until he felt her coming with the force of a freight train, her body snapping into an arc that pushed those luscious breasts of hers into an evocative vignette above him.

As his hips bucked under her, he swore under his breath. The flesh-and-blood woman riding him was better than any fantasy. He lasted another couple of thrusts before climaxing himself.

Emma collapsed on top of him, her breasts pressing into his heaving chest, her hair fanning out over him like a protective cocoon. He rubbed her back and closed his eyes, wishing this night would never end.

Funny thing that. The past five Christmas Eves had felt like a never-ending hell on earth, and here he was on the anniversary of his twin's death, wishing it would go on forever.

The desk wasn't made for post-sex cuddling. Mitch helped Emma into the bathroom where they both remained silent as they waited for the water to heat, the deep hour of the night—this night—suddenly seeming to deserve a quiet reverence.

Once he had Emma in the shower, Mitch soaped her up, rinsed her off, and kissed her wet skin from the top of her shoulders to the sensitive spot behind her knees. She swooned, eyes closed, her fingers moving over him languorously. A blind woman learning the planes and valleys of his body.

After drying her off, he started to lead her back to bed, but she wrapped herself in a blanket and tossed a second one at him. "I want to show you something."

Her hair was wet and wild, her face solemn but sanguine. "As long as it isn't in the horse barn," he teased.

She smiled, then led him down the hallway to the pull-down stairs.

He helped her lower them and enjoyed the view as she climbed the narrow steps. Waiting until she was at the top so he could get a could peek at what the blanket couldn't hide, he tossed the one she'd handed him over his shoulder and made his own way up.

A few adjustments and she had the telescope positioned at the window. "I think the smoke has cleared enough we can see it."

"It?"

She nodded, motioning him over.

Earlier, he'd checked his phone, hoping for a text or voicemail from Cooper, but there hadn't been any. Maybe the satellites had been down when he'd tried to call or maybe the SWAT team hadn't breached the house where Goodsman was yet.

And it was Christmas Eve, after all. People had places to go and presents to hide under their trees. Cooper had a young son and a fiancée to take care of. He might have gotten a bit distracted and would try to contact Mitch again as soon as the sun came up.

Dropping his blanket, Mitch came up behind Emma where she stood behind the telescope's lens. Her blanket had fallen off one shoulder as she adjusted a knob on the long, fat tube, and he kissed the soft skin at the curve where her shoulder and neck met.

She shivered under his fingers and he tucked her in close, spooning her as they stood.

"What are we looking at?" he asked.

"Skye." She twisted another knob as she stared through the viewfinder. "There she is."

Not *the* sky. Emma wasn't talking about seeing the swath of heavens stretching out over the hills and valleys here.

Skye. Her daughter.

This woman had lost so much—her child, her husband, her marriage. The potential to have more children. Yet, she had found a way to help other lost souls.

Mitch's hands tightened on her waist. "You named a star after her?"

"The constellation already has a name—Blue Snowball Nebula, but I don't care." Emma shifted her head aside so he could look into the lens. "See the brightest star in this field? That's her."

Her face was an open book, as Bobby Dyer liked to say. Mitch saw an innocence there—a young girl who wished on stars—and behind it a layer of steel grit, forged from great loss.

He lowered his eye to the eyepiece and saw the star she was talking about. "I'll be damn. It does have a slightly bluish disc around it."

"That's the central star. It's a dwarf and it's super hot. Hence the color."

"That's amazing." And it was. Almost as amazing as the

woman showing it to him. Turning his face to look at her, he saw the relief in her eyes. "You're quite the little astronomy buff."

She grinned. "Not really. I've studied Andromeda a bit, and good ol' Blue here, but the sky is vast. There's a lot more to explore."

Mitch had the feeling he had a lot more to explore as well. "Looking at the sky is peaceful."

"It is, isn't it? I wish I could give sky therapy to all of my patients. I think it would give them some perspective about their lives."

"Sky therapy? Is that a thing?"

"Not that I'm aware of, but it should be. Nature, in all its forms, has the ability to heal."

"Maybe you should invent this sky therapy stuff."

Her head dipped so she could look in the eyepiece again. "Maybe I should."

He hugged her from behind again and they lingered in front of the window, taking turns with the telescope. Emma would move the lens a fraction of an inch and then make him look at some random star. He didn't care about the actual constellations so much as her eagerness to share this private love of hers.

No one knows that. Her name, I mean. You're the first person I've ever told.

Why him? Was it this night? Was it the fact he was only the second man she'd ever slept with and that alone perpetuated an unusual intimacy?

Either way, he felt honored and just a little righteous about it.

"You haven't told me about your parents," he mused. "Or your siblings. Do you have any?"

"Parents or siblings?" she joked.

He nuzzled her neck. "Smartass."

"My parents live in Boston. They're both professors who met and married late in life. I came along a few years later. I'm an only child and my parents were nearly old enough to be my grandparents. They're both retired now. Dad lives in the basement, reading biographies and history texts. Mother travels constantly with friends. I see them on occasion, but... Well, we aren't a dysfunctional family by today's standards, just a distant one."

"No wonder you're so damn smart, being raised by a couple of college professors. What in God's name made you decide on psychology? Was one of your parents a psych professor?"

"Literature and economics, I'm afraid. For me, it was always psychology. I find the brain fascinating, and there are people who are truly, clinically, out of their mind when they commit a crime. There are also those who are not fit to stand trial for a crime they committed. They are rare, but it does happen. Allowing people like Chris Goodsman to dissimulate and mislead a judge, jury, and trained therapists—supposed experts in this field—to get acquitted of, or to receive a lighter sentence for, committing murder is an injustice."

"You like to see justice served."

She turned in his arms to face him. "Don't you?"

Of course he did. "That's why I do what I do."

"From a macro viewpoint, my job isn't all that different from yours. You analyze terrorists. I analyze criminals."

When she put it that way... "At the end of the day, we both want justice for the innocent."

She went up on her toes and kissed the tip of his nose. "Thank you for what you do to keep our country safe."

Jesus. He didn't remember ever being thanked by anyone. "Back atcha, Doc."

He wanted to ask her why she'd switched from adult criminals to kids, but deep in his gut, he knew the answer. She was a mother with no child trying to help children living without their mothers.

Taking her hand, Mitch led her out of the attic and tucked her into bed, climbing in beside her and holding her until she fell asleep in his arms.

CHAPTER FIFTEEN

They woke to rain.

Rivulets ran down the bedroom window and Emma nearly laughed. The one, brief blip of the weather report they'd heard the day before had been on the money. Santa Claus, or Jesus, or whoever one attributed miracles to, had come through.

In the yard below, she spotted Will heading to the house in his slicker and wide-brimmed hat. Lady trotted along behind him, both of them wet and kicking up water, and neither seeming to care.

"Oh, crud," Emma swore, seeing the time.

Mitch yawned from the comfort of the bed where he lay on his stomach. "What's up?"

The pie plate sat on the floor, licked clean by two obvious culprits who'd somehow ended up in bed with them. The dirty coffee cups were on the nightstand, Mitch's cell phone next to one.

Wrapping a robe around her, Emma chased the dogs off the bed and smacked Mitch on his butt through the covers. "Danika will be here in an hour if her driver can get here. We need to get moving."

"You're kidding, right? I thought you were going to cancel your appointments."

"I did, but not this one. I recommended to Danika's social worker that she be allowed to come here on Christmas and I couldn't in good conscience take that back once I knew we were staying. The girl is lost, Mitch. She's a decent kid who made a terrible mistake and I truly feel like she's on the edge of making another. It's one day, but an important one emotionally and psychologically for her. If I can get her through today, she stands a fighting chance of turning her life around."

He sat up and swung his legs off the bed. Long, sturdy legs that had put her through her paces all night. "Got it. Save Christmas, save the kid."

His hair was ruffled, his voice husky. Emma dropped to her knees in front of him and looked up at his sexy eyes, still drowsy from lack of sleep. She'd put him through his paces during the night as well. "Last night was amazing. I've never experienced anything like it. Thank you. I'll never be a basket case on Christmas Eve again."

He reached down and stroked her hair, a crooked grin lifting one side of his face. "My pleasure, ma'am. You get dressed and I'll start coffee. I need to check in with Cooper anyway and see what happened with Goodsman."

She rose up on her knees and kissed him. At this point, she didn't care what had happened with Chris and Linda. All she cared about was enjoying every last minute she had with Mitch.

He kissed her back, drawing her in close between his legs and letting her feel his morning erection. A part of her debated whether getting dressed was all that important. Climbing back into bed and helping Mitch out seemed like way more fun.

But then she heard Will knocking on the back door downstairs and the Labs went tearing off, barking like the Second Coming, and Mitch broke the kiss and helped her to her feet.

"Last night meant a lot to me too," he said, holding her hand. His serious tone lightened and he winked at her. "I'm hoping I can get a replay tonight."

Smacking him playfully, Emma went to find clean clothes.

While Mitch threw on the blue flannel and his pants and headed downstairs to let Will in, Emma washed up, dressed, and put a touch of makeup on. Coming out of the bathroom, she paused for a moment to look at the bed.

The comforter was on the floor, the blanket and top sheet askew, pie crumbs and dog hair in the creases. The pillow Mitch had used was dented from his head, and hers was tucked up close to it. The bottom sheet had come off the bottom right corner.

The room hummed from the night's intimate sharings. She and Mitch had shared their bodies, their stories, their secrets. She'd let him into her inner sanctum, a place few people had ever been. The old Emma wanted to straighten the covers and brush off the crumbs. The new Emma smiled and left it all exactly as it was and hoped the two of them would, indeed, replay their night of fun tonight.

The scent of strong coffee and the murmur of male voices hit her at the top of the stairs. A sense of rightness, of belonging, hit her as well. It was good to have purpose with one's life. It was even better to have hope.

As she blew into the kitchen, all three dogs greeted her, and she realized one of the voices she heard came from Mitch's cell phone. Will was putting the coffee carafe back on the burner. When he saw her, he handed her his just-poured coffee and grabbed another cup for himself.

The small TV she kept in the corner on the counter was on, but the volume was muted. Mitch didn't look at her, his arms crossed over his chest, his gaze locked on a spot on the table near the phone. "And you have no other leads?"

"It's Christmas," the man on the other end stated over the speaker. "People are with their families or trying to get back home from the evacuation. They aren't out shopping or grabbing groceries or hanging out at the local bar. Outside of some die-hard paparazzi or a crazy fan, I doubt anyone's looking for our guy."

Emma's stomach dropped. "Chris?" she asked Will softly.

He made a stony face. "He wasn't in the house. They don't know where he is."

Her stomach dropped farther, hitting somewhere around her ankles. As she listened to Mitch end the call with Cooper Harris, she tried to sip her coffee, tried to wrap her brain around the fact that Chris was still out there. The coffee burned like acid down her throat. She set the cup down on the counter.

Mitch pocketed his phone and turned to face her. "The SWAT team went in just before midnight, found two people in the house. Neither was Brown or Goodsman. The couple inside the house claimed they'd never been there, but Cooper found a receipt for clothes, makeup and a couple of wigs that the couple claimed ignorance about. None of the items from their shopping excursion were in the house. Coop and Dupé think Goodsman and Brown might have been there and left wearing disguises before the team arrived."

Emma had to lean against the counter. "So they're still on the loose and no one knows where they're headed?"

"Correct."

She glanced at the TV screen. The rains were a godsend, already helping to tame the fires and the news showed people on the roads, heading back to their houses. On one hand, she still needed a bodyguard and that bodyguard was Mitch. On the other, needing a bodyguard wasn't something to be happy about. "But they were a good ways away, right? So they're probably doing what I said, heading to Mexico."

Mitch interlaced his fingers and wrapped his hands around the back of his neck. He blew out a tired sigh. "You also said it's not Goodsman's normal MO. He likes the limelight. He wouldn't break out of jail and go on the run because then he wouldn't get the attention he needs."

The news now showed a picture of the very actor they were discussing. "And yet, he *is* getting plenty of attention," she said, pointing at the screen.

Will reached over and turned up the volume. What sounded like a recorded voicemail was playing as the picture went full screen with Chris's face—a photo-shoot-perfect smile. *"I am here for you, my resistance fighters. I will not stop in my search for justice. Thanks to those who stepped in to lead you in my absence, I'm now free of the prison system the cyborgs built to hold me. I'm once more ready to take up the fight and lead you to victory."*

Will shook his head and snapped off the television. "He's as wacko as they get."

For a moment, Emma wondered if Chris Goodsman truly was afflicted with a mental disorder. Maybe she'd been wrong all along.

"Doc?"

Mitch's voice cut through her reverie. "What?"

"I think it's time you reconsider the safe house. With the highways clearing out, we can probably get there by lunch time."

At that moment, they heard a vehicle pulling into the drive. Through the kitchen curtain over the sink, Emma saw the van from the juvenile detention center.

Danika.

The poor girl had come all this way to see Twinkie and keep her mind off the holiday. Emma couldn't let her down.

"Chris Goodsman may indeed be certifiable," she admitted as much to herself as the two men in the kitchen with her, "but he's miles away and I promised Danika time with her horse."

"Danika is not my biggest concern at the moment," Mitch argued.

"I respect that, but can't we give the girl an hour at least? The roads will be even clearer by then, I bet."

Mitch squeezed his eyes shut and took a long, slow breath, before he opened them, dropping his hands. "I don't like it."

"I'm not surprised. I don't relish it either, but it's important."

He gave her an exasperated look. "Will can take care of Danika."

"Me?" Will said. "I don't know what to do with that girl."

He did, but he was too much of a curmudgeon to admit it. Emma didn't like the way he always referred to Danika as *that girl*, but understood it was Will's way of keeping his distance emotionally. Like their vet, Danika had gotten on Will's good side months ago but the big dummy was afraid to admit it. He was afraid he'd jinx them.

Emma's fingers itched for a bag of M&Ms. "Danika can't be here without me to supervise."

Mitch looked like he was ready to combust. "Will, would you go get Danika from the van and take her to the horse barn? I'll get Emma packing and bring her out in a few minutes."

It was obvious he wanted her alone for a minute so he could talk her out of staying for even an hour. Fat chance of that.

Will shifted his weight between his feet. "Dude, I can't talk to that girl. She's...well, mental."

"Will," Emma scolded. She shot Mitch a look. "How about if you go get Danika and take her to the horse barn and Will can stay here to guard me? I barely unpacked anything from my bag from the last go-around. All I have to do is throw my toothbrush in and a couple of other things. Once you have Danika in the barn, have her move Twinkie from his stall and start cleaning it. Carla Moses will be with her and can keep an eye on her. While she works on Twinkie's stall, you can come back for me. I'll explain to Danika about the change of plans, and you can fill in Officer Moses. We can all work on the barn for an hour and keep *that girl* from losing her last ounce of sanity on this very emotionally charged day. Seriously, Mitch. She's borderline suicidal. If she were to commit suicide because I denied her a chance to see Twinkie, I couldn't live with myself."

Will looked at the floor. A muscle in Mitch's jaw worked as he stood stock still, sizing up her determination as well as calculating his own. It was easier to read him after their night together. His defenses were up, but they were less solid, more fluid. He wanted what was best for her safety, but he also wanted to make her happy.

"Please, Mitch," she said. "Danika needs this, and there will be three of you here, guarding her and me, all of you armed and quite capable of taking on Chris or whoever else might show up."

Another long pause as he stewed, but her pleading tone must have done the trick.

"Don't let her out of your sight," he said to Will, heading for the back door. To Emma, he said, "One hour. That's it. Then we're out of here."

She reached out, caught his hand on the doorknob. "Thank you."

He leaned over and kissed her on the forehead. "I sure hope I don't regret this."

As he left her standing there with Will and the dogs, she reached for her drawer of M&Ms and let out a sigh.

I hope I don't either.

The state van was a simple white Chevy with no passenger windows and a dented front bumper. *Juvenile Corrections* was printed on both of the front doors.

Officer Moses wasn't in the driver's seat. She was probably unlocking Danika's cuffs.

Mitch waited outside the van, his eyes scanning the area as rain drenched him. The sky overhead was dark with clouds, but these clouds were welcome, relieving the drought for a few minutes and helping quench the wildfires.

Merry fucking Christmas.

People all over the world were celebrating a day of family, friends, and gift giving. Plenty of people weren't as well. But regardless of religious affiliation or personal circumstances, no one could deny that the rain was a miracle.

If there was a God, then He had a pretty shitty personality if He got off on holding out on the rain until today.

Christmas and the rain aside, the day had already set Mitch's teeth on edge. Goodsman and Brown were still loose. No one had any idea where they were.

What if the two of them had put those people up to calling in and reporting they'd seen them in that house? A lark to get the local police, SWAT team, and FBI gathered there, instead of out looking for them. Meanwhile, they'd fled down to Mexico like Emma believed.

Or maybe the people who'd reported seeing them were legit and honestly believed they'd seen the famous actor and his number one fan in that house. Either way, Goodsman and Brown had had plenty of time to get to wherever they were headed.

He just hoped it was miles away from the ranch and Emma.

No one had emerged from the van, so Mitch stepped forward and knocked on the darkly tinted passenger window. "Officer Moses, it's me, Mitch Holden. Dr. Collins asked me to escort you and Danika to the horse barn. She'll join us shortly."

There was no response.

Mitch's gut tightened. He stepped back, looked over his shoulder. Had Carla already taken Danika to the barn?

Walking partway across the yard, he scanned the barn. The front doors were still closed, no one idling around.

Jogging back to the van, he pulled up short when his eyes landed on the side door. Seeping from the bottom edge of the door, bright, red liquid dripped onto the running board.

Blood.

Shit.

Drawing his gun, Mitch closed the distance to the van and put his back against the side, gaze sweeping the drive, the yard, the pasture. He saw nothing moving, only rain drops hitting a few tiny puddles. He heard nothing either, except the same rain.

Danika.

He slid up to the driver side window, cupped his hands around his eyes and peered in.

No Carla, but he saw what looked like blood smeared across the headrest.

"Officer Moses," he called, wiping water from his face. "Are you alright?"

No answer.

Mitch looked back at the house. *God Almighty, don't let Danika have gone off the deep end and killed a police officer. Emma will never forgive herself.*

"Danika? Remember me? I was here the other day when you came to ride Harry. I mean, Twinkie. I know this is a rough day for you—it's a rough one for me, too." Like the girl would believe that if he didn't back it up with the reason. Taking a deep breath, he forced himself to continue. "I lost my twin brother five years ago on this day, Danika. I know how bad the holidays can suck. How about you open up the door and we can talk?"

Silence came from the van. Not even a hint of movement. The blood continued to drip, pooling enough to run off onto the wet ground beneath it.

Mitch felt eyes on him and glanced up to see Will peering out the kitchen window at him. Concern etched the older man's face. Mitch flashed his gun and cocked a head toward the van. Then he gave Will the sign to stay put.

Don't leave Emma.

The kitchen curtain fell, Will's face disappearing.

Grabbing the door handle, Mitch gave a tug. The sliding door was locked.

Great. The only way in was through the front, and he had to hope Danika hadn't locked all the doors.

He also hoped the girl hadn't killed herself in a murder-suicide.

I should have heard gunshots.

Did Danika have a shiv? Had she struck the guard with a heavy object, leaving blood on the headrest?

Mitch eased along the side, still listening for sounds inside the van as he gripped the driver side door handle. This one gave when he tugged.

"Danika?" he said, leaning slowly into the cab, gun ready. "I'm not here to hurt you."

When he didn't hear even the sound of her breathing, Mitch hefted himself up, braced his left hand on the seat, and hooked his gun hand around as he took in the interior of the van.

"Ah, hell."

Danika sat on the bench seat, blank eyes staring up at the ceiling, blood flowing from long, deep wounds running up the insides of her arms. In one hand, she held a knife. Not a shiv, but an honest-to-God three-inch blade.

Officer Moses lay face down on the floor at her feet, her blood mingling with Danika's as the stream ran across the rubber mat over to the side door.

Mitch reached between the bucket seats and felt for a pulse on Carla, found none. Stretching back, he touched Danika's neck, hoping against hope he might find her still alive.

Her eyelids fluttered—for half a heartbeat, he thought he'd imagined it in the dim interior. But they fluttered again and then he found it...the faint throb of her pulse under his fingers.

"Danika, can you hear me?"

Her lips twitched, and damn, he couldn't move fast enough. Whirling around, he found the button to unlock the doors, then he bailed out of the driver's side and threw open the side door.

"Danika, hang in there," he said, moving Carla out of the way as gently, but as quickly as possible. The woman's jugular had been severed on the left side.

Mitch used a hanky to remove the knife from Danika's hands, laying it in the front seat. Finding the keys on Carla's belt, he unlocked Danika's handcuffs.

That's when it hit him.

Her wrists had been cuffed together and then chained to a special reinforced armrest. The chain consisted of two metal links. There was no give to it, no way the girl could have reached forward to slit Carla's throat.

Maybe she'd done it once Carla had left her seat and was about to unhook her. But then, how did blood get on the headrest? Had Carla grabbed at her neck, then grabbed the seat before she'd fallen?

Mitch's head rang with a warning bell.

Shedding his shirt, he ripped it in two, wrapping each of Danika's bleeding arms to staunch the flow as he kept looking out the front windows. Keeping his gun in hand, he jumped out of the van.

There was still no movement, no one in sight. Carefully, he lifted Danika from the seat and started for the house.

The kitchen door flew open and Emma ran out, Will on her heels. "Oh, my God," she cried. "What happened?"

"Get in the house," Mitch said, paranoia swamping him. As Emma met him halfway across the yard, he nearly stumbled. "Emma, get in the goddamn house!"

Hearing the fear in his voice, she met his eyes, then let Will drag her back to the kitchen door. "Oh, Danika," she said, when Mitch jogged into the kitchen with the girl. She brushed Danika's face with a hand. "What did you do?"

"Call 911," Mitch said. It was a long shot with the roads still congested, but worth a try. The van had gotten through. Maybe the cops and an ambulance could as well.

Will swept the cups off the table so Mitch could lay Danika there. "Already did."

The big man had Emma's first aid kit out as well. Mitch locked the kitchen door, then went to work on saving a girl who didn't want to be saved.

CHAPTER SIXTEEN

I have to save her.

"Why would she do this?" Emma said, bringing a bowl of water over to clean Danika's hands. Mitch had told them what he'd found. Officer Moses was dead, Danika nearly so. The girl had used a knife.

Her thin, dark hands were covered with blood and more was coming as Mitch unwound his wet shirt from one of Danika's wrists.

"Don't answer that," Emma said. "I know why she did this, but how the hell did she get a knife?"

Blood was everywhere. It covered Mitch's torso, his arms. Will had brought pillows and they'd propped Danika's elbows on them, lifting her arms above her heart to slow the flow of blood.

Mitch and Will wrapped the girl's arms in bandages and gauze. Mitch grabbed an afghan from Emma's pile in the living room and covered Danika. He touched the girl's forehead, then checked the pulse in her neck. "She's definitely shock-y. Any chance you've got a hot water bottle or heating pad?"

"My heating pad is upstairs," Emma said, heading for the doorway. "I'll grab it."

Will opened the pantry door. "I can make a field IV."

"Do I want to know what that is?" Emma asked.

"Sugar water," was his only reply.

Sugar water. A heating pad. Gauze pads and bandages. Not exactly first-class medical treatment for a girl who'd slit her wrists, but what else could they do until an ambulance arrived?

"Emma," Mitch said, stopping her. His hand left a bloody print on her forearm. "You stay here with Will. I'll get the heating pad."

"Okay." She handed him a dish towel and let him pass her. "Why?"

"Just stay with her."

She didn't argue, seeing the consternation on his face as he worked over the dish towel. Hustling back to Danika, she fiddled with the blanket and noticed that blood was already seeping through the bandages. Danika's face was an ashen gray, her normally pink lips bluish.

Will emerged from the pantry with her sugar and a bottle of water. "Boil some water," he said. "I'm going to the barn for tubing."

Surely he didn't mean... "That tube Mitch used on Second Chance? That's too big for Danika's arm."

Will opened the door, swung out, Lady on his heels. He told the dog to stay. "Lock this behind me," he said to Emma. "I'll knock three times when I come back. Don't open it for anyone but me."

Emma shooed him with her hand. "I know, I know." Danika was growing paler by the moment. "Just hurry."

Mitch returned with the heating pad. He cocked his chin at the door. "Where'd he go?"

"To get tubing for the IV." Emma grabbed the end of the heating pad cord and plugged it in to the wall. "How soon do you think the ambulance will get here?"

"No telling." His phone rang and he answered it while situating the pad under the blanket. "Tell me you found that bastard Goodsman and you have him in custody."

Emma rinsed her hands, then filled a pot with water as Mitch punched the speaker button on his phone and a male voice flooded the kitchen. It was the same one she'd heard earlier.

"Wish I could," Agent Harris said. "Any chance you're on the way to the safe house yet?"

"Not yet." Mitch blew out a frustrated breath, rubbing his forehead. "We have a problem."

Harris's voice was gruff. "What problem?"

"Dr. Collins was scheduled to see a patient from the juvenile detention center twenty miles away. The girl is on the kitchen table right now, bleeding out. We staunched the flow and are waiting for the ambulance and police, but who knows how long that might take."

"What the fuck happened to the kid?"

"It appears she killed her guard and tried to kill herself. Slit her wrists."

Harris paused, then said, "You sound skeptical."

Mitch ran a hand over his face, keeping his gaze on Danika's motionless form. "She had a pocket knife stuck between her cuffed hands. A decent enough knife with six different types of blades. Something a survivalist might use, not some kid in juvie who made a shiv out of a plastic fork. Also, from the way she was secured to the van seat, there's no way she could have reached the guard to slit her throat. I'm not even sure she could have turned the knife on herself, her cuffs were so tight. It doesn't add up, and I didn't have time to thoroughly analyze the scene. I had to administer first aid in order to try and save her. We're attempting to stabilize her now but we've got little to no medical supplies."

"Damn it," Harris swore softly. "Do you think this is somehow tied to Goodsman?"

Emma had to sit down. Her pulse beat in her ear like a freight train.

Mitch's gaze finally met hers. "Who else? I have to go with the assumption that Chris Goodsman, Linda Brown, or one of their cohorts hopped a ride on that van."

"Pack the girl in your truck along with the doctor, and haul ass out of there, Holden."

"I'm seriously onboard with that, Coop, but if I move this girl, she will die."

"There's a hired hand there, right?" Harris countered. "Leave the girl with him to wait for the ambulance. Your job is to get Dr. Collins to the safe house, asap."

Emma forced her knees to lock so she could stand up. "I'm not leaving until I know Danika is safe."

"Dr. Collins." Agent Harris's voice took on a restrained, patient tone. Similar to the one she often used with irrational clients. "There is nothing you can do for the girl at this time."

"Agent Harris, Danika might be dying on my kitchen table because of me. Because I pissed off Chris and Linda and they're looking for revenge."

"I understand you feel responsible, but it's not your fault any more than it is mine. Plus, it is possible this has nothing to do with Goodsman, right? The scene Holden discovered may be exactly how it looks—she slit her wrists."

Mitch was staring at her, waiting, keeping his own opinion buried behind his unfathomable gray eyes.

Emma stared back, reaching out to lay a hand on Danika's shoulder. "If you were in my situation, Agent Harris, and a young girl was bleeding out in front of you, regardless of the reason, would you leave her and run off to a safe house?"

Another pause, this one infinitely longer. The corner of Mitch's lips quirked as if he were suppressing a somber smirk.

"Dr. Collins, your presence at the farmhouse may actually be putting your patient in more danger," Harris reasoned. "Leaving may be the smartest thing you can do."

Three knocks sounded on the door, making Emma jump. Mitch halted her from answering it by lifting a silent hand. "She won't leave, Coop," he said, looking out the window and then letting Will in. "You may as well save your breath."

Will carried a rolled up section of narrow tubing to the sink and checked on the pot of water that was just beginning to steam.

Harris cleared his throat on the other end, sighed. "I'll check the ETA of the ambulance and police backup, see if I can get an extra car to escort you out of the valley. Meantime, stay safe."

"Will do," Mitch answered. "As soon as the EMTs get here, we'll take off."

"By the time you land, Cruz and Heaton should be there. I sent them your way earlier. I figured one way or another, we're getting you two out of there, even if it takes a few more taskforce members to help out."

"Sophie's going to kill me for taking Nels away from her on Christmas," Mitch said. "Who's Heaton?"

"Brooke Heaton. A gal Dupé sent down from L.A. She's an expert investigator on religious terrorism and ritualistic crimes and symbols. He's letting me try out a few potentials for the team and thought she might be helpful with this Tom Monahan shit."

"Assigning her to me on Christmas Day." There was the slightest drollness to Mitch's statement. "Breaking her in properly, huh?"

"Well, if you'd start working for me fulltime, I wouldn't need a bunch of unknowns to fill in."

Mitch again met Emma's gaze full on. "I'm giving it serious consideration."

"Look at the bright side." Harris's tone held a hint of teasing. "You can visit your mother more."

Mitch's expression soured. "Right."

The two disconnected. Without realizing it, Emma had switched her touch from Danika to Mitch. He stared down at her while Will boiled the tubing.

"You should call your mom," Emma said softly, "and wish her a Merry Christmas."

Mitch half smiled and touched her back, skimming his fingers across the top of her shoulder. "Maybe later."

"You think we have a visitor, then?" she asked. "Someone who hitched a ride in the van?"

"What's that?" Will whirled around to face them. "A visitor?"

Mitch filled him in as the two men worked to set up the IV.

"Shit," Will said as he poked at the inside of Danika's elbow. The sugar had been added to the water bottle, the tubing duct-taped to the bottle's opening. Emma wasn't sure if he swore because of the news or because he couldn't hit a vein. "Might be more than one who hitched a ride, goddamn lowlifes. I didn't see anyone skulking around when I went to the barn."

Mitch fiddled with the bottle, tapping on it with his fingers. "You feel like doing some recon for me once you get that inserted?"

"Absolutely," Will muttered. "Those sons-of-a-bitches better hope I don't find them."

Emma bit her bottom lip. "I don't like it. We should all stay inside the house and wait for the police to arrive."

Will's eyes came up to lock with hers. "You told me I'm not bad luck."

What did that have to do with anything? "You're not."

He grabbed her hand, gave it a squeeze. "Then let me prove it, Doc. You've taken care of me for the past sixteen months. Let me return the favor."

Mitch watched Will leave by the back door. Within seconds, he disappeared behind the horse barn.

"It's too dangerous," Emma said, holding Danika's hand. "We don't know for sure that someone did this—Danika was borderline suicidal over the holidays—but if there is a murderer on the loose, Will's out there all alone."

"I'm sure this isn't Danika's doing," Mitch said. "Someone either hitched a ride on that van or they entered it, killed Officer Moses, and tried to kill Danika once the van arrived. Could be either. I suspect that's how our visitor got here two days ago to deliver that army guy to your nightstand—he hitched a ride, only Carla never noticed. So either he was out there waiting to do something like this to continue trying to terrorize you, or this is someone new who used the same mode of transportation to get here and terrorize you. And Will is a trained Spec Ops guy. He'll be fine."

"This is all my fault." Her voice was too quiet, her gaze centered on the girl. "She was depressed and I thought I was doing the right thing, staying here and allowing her to get out of the detention center to visit the horses."

It gutted him seeing her like this, hearing the self-loathing in her voice. He wanted to tell her it wasn't her fault, he would have done the same thing in her shoes, but he knew those empty words made no difference. "No point in second guessing yourself. As soon as the police and ambulance get here, we're bugging out. Danika will live."

Her voice was strained, challenging. "You're going to leave Will here with a murderer on the loose?"

"I'll do what I can to convince Will to let the police handle it and come with us, okay?"

"And what about the horses?"

Mitch had to count down from ten to keep from losing his patience. "You heard Cooper. Some of my taskforce teammates are on the way to help out. Once they arrive, I'll leave them with you at the safe house and I'll come back to take care of the horses. Okay?"

"So *you'll* be here alone with a murderer?"

Jesus, she wouldn't give up. "One of two things will happen, Emma. The guy will leave once you're gone or between me, Will, and the cops, we'll nab his ass and put him behind bars. I will make him pay for this."

He pointed at Danika's lifeless body. At least the ashiness of the girl's skin had receded some, thanks to Will's homemade IV. That wouldn't last, though. She needed blood and antibiotics and actual medical treatment.

Tears clouded Emma's eyes. "I'm so stubborn. If I'd just left when you showed up, none of this would have happened."

Mitch couldn't take it anymore. He gently drew her out of the chair and hugged her to him. "I don't know Danika, but I saw the way she changed the other day while she was here. She came in sullen and withdrawn and by the time she left, she was happy. You were doing what you thought was right to save the girl's life. You didn't slit her wrists; our visitor did."

She melted into him, gripping him around the waist. "You think it's Chris?"

"Do you? Does this seem like something he might do to get your attention and scare you?"

She was quiet for a long moment. "No, but neither does stalking or any of the other stuff he's done so far, if you buy that the reason he killed his fiancée a couple of years ago was because he had a break with reality. If, on the other hand, you believe my analysis that he's actually a sociopathic narcissist, his MO would be to manipulate other people—his resistance fighters, let's say—into doing the dirty work."

She broke free from his arms and he could see the psychologist in her was back as she paced the kitchen floor. "That's it. He's having others do his dirty work so if he gets caught, he can claim innocence."

"He's on the run with Brown. He's not getting off of that charge."

Her eyes lit up with insight. "Unless he's going to claim he was kidnapped."

"Wha…" Mitch shook his head. "No way. No one's going to believe he was kidnapped and held against his will."

"Of course they will. That's what his fans will want to believe, and he's a good actor, remember? If he gets caught, he'll claim he had nothing to do with any of this. That Linda and whoever else is involved, forced him."

"He wrote a threatening message on his wall at the prison before he left."

"You don't think there are prison guards who are fans of his show? If no one saw him write those words, there's no proof he did. He can claim that a guard or another prisoner snuck in and wrote them."

Mitch didn't want to believe it, but he'd seen and heard of far more ludicrous defenses. "You know him better than anyone. How do we get him to show his hand, Doc?"

"I think you know. You were thinking it the other night, then changed your mind about using me as bait, didn't you?"

"It was never a viable option."

"Of course it is. Chris is all ego. He likes to gloat and believes he's superior to all of us, but he's too clever to admit his involvement. He would have to believe he's safe from prosecution and be so full of himself that he couldn't stand not bragging about what he's accomplished." Her gaze came back to his, a newfound determination in her eyes. "He would brag to me. I'm the one person who's never believed him or his insanity plea."

"No. We are not going to give him that chance."

"If I let him catch me, if he thought I was at his mercy, he'd sing his own praises from here to the moon. You could put a wire on me or whatever you need to do to get his confession recorded. I could get him to admit he's been involved all along."

"Catch you? Fuck, no. Not happening."

"You can be nearby and then bust in before he does anything to me."

"He might kill you."

"He might try, but you'd be there to stop him."

"Don't be ridiculous, Emma."

"Do you have a better idea?"

He didn't, but he still wasn't going along with this. "My job is to protect you and keep you in one piece, not throw you into the hands of a psychotic killer."

"I'm still waiting to hear your better idea." She grinned as if this were a game. "Oh, that's right. You already had this idea but didn't act on it."

"Emma, you are undoubtedly the smartest woman I know, and I get that you have a handle on Goodsman's mindset, but being at his mercy, as you put it, is not the same as a clinical environment where your safety is guaranteed."

In the distance, he heard sirens. Finally. A glance out the kitchen window confirmed the ambulance was nearly there, lights flashing as it cruised up the long drive. A lone sheriff's car trailed behind it.

Emma heard the sirens, too. Her shoulders slumped. "I need to do *something*. I feel so helpless! I can't stand waiting around for Chris or one of his fans to hurt someone else."

"I know. It's a sucky situation."

He hugged her before going out to vet the EMTs and sheriff. After letting them inside the house, he spent the next few minutes helping the EMTs get Danika stabilized and into the ambulance. Then another hour explaining everything to the sheriff who had obviously had too many issues to deal with over the past few days and not enough sleep.

"I loved that show," Deputy Korrin said, rubbing a finger over his mustache. "My wife has all the seasons on Blu-ray."

Whatever. This jack wagon was going to be no help at all. Mitch didn't care for the way Korrin looked at Emma, his small, dark eyes roaming over her curves when he thought she wasn't looking. "If we're all done here, I need to get Dr. Collins to a meeting."

Emma raised a brow at him, but he wasn't taking chances. Up until the sheriff had actually confirmed he was a fan of the *Mary Monahan Chronicles*, Mitch had planned to have Korrin escort them to the safe house. Now, he'd decided he wasn't trusting anyone outside of Will with the information that he was moving Emma to a safer location.

"A meeting on Christmas?" the man asked.

Emma gave him *that* smile. The professional, detached one

that Mitch hadn't seen in awhile. "Criminals don't take Christmas off, do they? Like you, Deputy, I end up working a lot of holidays and weekends."

Smooth. As Korrin closed up his notebook and rose from the chair, Emma glanced at Mitch and he nodded at her. *Good girl.*

"I'll need you to come to the station and make a formal statement," Korrin said, sidling over to the back door, "but there's no one there today that has time to take it due to the holiday and the wildfires. Maybe not tomorrow either."

"How about I call you on Monday and set up an appointment," Emma said, opening the door to usher him out.

He handed her a card. "That'll work. You take care, ma'am."

Mitch motioned for her to stay put as he followed the man out to his squad car. The rain had slowed to a drizzle.

At the car, he took a good look around. Will was jogging across the yard, a scowl on his face. Lady loped along behind him. When he saw Mitch with the police officer, he gave the man the once over and shook his head at Mitch. He went to the back door to go inside with Emma.

So he hadn't found anybody or at least nothing he wanted to talk to the sheriff about.

"I'd appreciate it if you keep this off the police scanners," Mitch said to Korrin. "Some of Goodsman's fans may be listening to see if they can find out more info about the doctor."

The sheriff got in his squad car and rolled down the window. "Dr. Collins probably has plenty of former cons angry at her. You might look into other possibilities besides Chris Goodsman."

Mitch's blood pressure went straight into the red zone. "Just keep it off the scanners, alright?"

Korrin didn't respond other than to put the car in reverse. "Don't touch the van. The CS techs will be out as soon as they can to gather evidence."

Mitch had the feeling that *as soon as they can* translated to tomorrow or even later. The sheriff didn't care about a juvenile delinquent or Emma. He didn't even seem to care much about Carla's murder. "The body's going to get ripe fast in this heat."

Korrin waved off Mitch's concern. "The techs will probably be here before you and Dr. Collins get back from your meeting."

As Korrin drove off, Mitch pulled out his phone and dialed Cooper. "I need FBI crime scene investigators, ASAP."

"Figured you would. They're already on their way, and the forensic photographer is my fiancée, so I guarantee you'll be in good hands."

Shit. "You told Celina what was going down?"

"It's fucking Christmas, Holden, and it's not like I could ignore your calls. She wouldn't stop bugging me until I told her why."

Mitch ambled back to the house, seeing Emma's face framed in the kitchen window. "Jesus, I'm sorry. I didn't mean to ruin your day."

"Yeah, well, traffic's a bitch, but we'll be there within the hour."

Mitch froze. "You're coming too?"

"Owen is with his mom and I wasn't about to send Celina by herself as bad as things are in your area. There was a shooting on the highway not fifteen minutes ago. Road rage. Four are dead."

Closing his eyes, Mitch let out a controlled sigh before he opened them again. "I'll make it up to you." He didn't know how, but there would be hell to pay and rightfully so.

"Shut up and go guard that therapist. We'll be there as soon as we can."

Inside, Mitch accepted a towel from Emma to dry his hair. "Ready?" he asked her.

She had her suitcase by the front door.

"Did you see anything?" he asked Will as Emma gathered up the dog bowls and tucked them into a bag.

"Nothing," the man muttered. "These fuckers are pissing me

off. Whoever our killer is, he's got more than survivalist training. If I had a guess, he's former military."

"Maybe when we leave, he'll realize it's a lost cause and leave too," Emma said. "You're welcome to come with us, Will."

"Oh, hell no," he said. "He comes after me or the horses, I'll nail his ass to the wall."

He and Mitch exchanged a fist bump. "Some of my people will be here in an hour or so to go over the van. Agent Cooper Harris is the man in charge and he's bringing some FBI crime scene techs. Once Harris and the FBI are done with the scene, they'll handle the cleanup as well."

Will nodded. "Got it."

Emma touched Will on the shoulder. "Be careful."

He walked them out the door and Mitch froze once more when he saw his truck.

"What is it?" Emma asked, following his line of sight.

Will stopped beside them. "Oh, for fuck sake."

Mitch's blood pressure once more hit the red zone. He had the distinct feeling that wherever Mac was in the afterlife, he was gazing down on Mitch's current situation and laughing his ass off.

Give 'em hell and get your money's worth, little brother.

Mitch glared at the truck, then the area surrounding them. Somewhere out there, someone else was watching this scene as well, probably also laughing at his predicament.

All four of his tires were slashed, leaving his Ford in a sagging heap near the front porch.

As Mitch rounded on Emma and sent her back into the house, he paused and looked over his shoulder at the woods a hundred yards away.

Chickenshit, he mentally taunted whoever was out there. He was tired of playing games and he wasn't about to live like a trapped animal. He had a mind to take Emma's shotgun and go hunting, but he couldn't leave her alone.

Come and get me.

CHAPTER SEVENTEEN

Emma tripped over her feet as Mitch and Will practically threw her back inside. Will caught her arm and kept her upright as Salt and Pepper hovered.

The shades were already drawn, the curtains closed, but Will went to the nearest window and checked the lock. Mitch blew in, slamming the door behind him and locking it.

"Where's your vehicle?" he asked.

His jaw was set. Anger burned in his eyes.

Beside her, Salt whimpered.

Will moved to another window to check its lock. "I have Emma's truck at the cabin. I run most of the errands for Emma and I don't have a vehicle."

"Go get it," Mitch said. He was dialing someone on his phone. "And watch your back. Whoever this is, they obviously aren't afraid to kill. They're amping up their game, and it looks like they're closing in fast."

Emma shivered, not only at his words, but at his tone. He looked ready to murder someone.

Bad choice of words, perhaps, but still accurate.

"Yeah, Coop," he said into his phone as Emma heard Will sneaking out the back door. "Got more trouble."

While he explained what was going on, Emma went to her candy drawer in the kitchen. M&Ms. She needed a handful.

Hell, she needed the whole damn bag at this point.

Salt and Pepper followed, finding their normal spots on the

floor. Their warm, brown eyes watched her, mouths open and panting.

It was silly, but the simple feel of those little candies in her palm calmed her. A tactile crutch. She threw several M&Ms into her mouth, closed her eyes and chewed. Her speeding pulse slowed a tiny bit. She drew a deep breath, went to her kitchen table and bent down.

Blood from Danika had dried in spots on the floor. Ignoring it, she tipped her head to look at the underside of the table. Her backup pistol was there, still duct-taped to the wood. It had been over a year since she'd stuck it under the table, only taking it out once in a blue moon to check it.

She had her trusty S&W in her suitcase, but she wanted—needed more. Ripping off the tape, she palmed the .380 in one hand, the M&Ms in the other. Chocolate and cold, hard steel. Along with the quiet equanimity of the dogs, the combination settled her nerves.

Mitch strode into the kitchen and stopped abruptly when he saw her kneeling beside the table. The Beretta rested in her lap while she pitched candy into her mouth, one after the other, and ground the chocolate shells to bits with her molars.

His gaze lingered on the handgun. "You okay?"

"Do I have a choice?"

After a slight hesitation, he kneeled beside her. "I'm going to get you out of here."

"I know you are." She met his worried gaze. "But I'd be lying if I said I wasn't freaking out."

"You don't have to lie to me. About anything, you hear?"

She bobbed her head, threw another M&M into her mouth. Sweet, sweet chocolate. Sexy, determined Mitch. "I know what you said about Carla and Danika—that it isn't my fault—but it sure feels that way. If anything happens to you or Will, I..."

She couldn't finish the sentence, couldn't even bear to think about it. Everything she cared about was here at the ranch. The dogs, the horses, her house. Add Mitch and Will to that, and she had a lot to lose.

Mitch took the gun from her lap and set it on the table, then drew her to her feet. "Will and I have both been in more dire circumstances than this. We know how to handle ourselves. Instead of worrying about the two of us, I want you to concentrate on the man outside. The one who hurt Danika. We don't know for sure who he is, but we know what he wants. To scare you. Analyze him, Emma. Tell me what motivates him, what kind of person he is. What are the chinks in his armor?"

The feel of his hands holding onto her was as satisfying as the chocolate, but he was right—she needed to do something. Worrying about what *could* happen wouldn't prevent Mitch and Will from getting hurt. What might help was figuring out how to outthink the bastard who was screwing with her world.

Sitting back, she rustled up her conviction, her mind seizing on the productivity of evaluating her stalker. Everyone had telltale methods, approaches, and techniques, especially established criminals. If she took each incident and broke it down...

The couple of M&Ms still in her hand were melting, smears of green, red, and blue on her palm and fingers. "I need a minute to think. Some paper and a pencil too."

Mitch released her and she rinsed her hand in the sink, then took the gun and let him escort her upstairs to her office.

At her desk, she pulled out a yellow tablet—her favorite medium for freeing her brain. Starting in the center of the page, she drew a circle for her attacker, then a line, radiating out from that with a smaller circle attached. She labeled that one with the first incident: *the break-in.*

Another line. Another circle. On and on she went, drawing and writing down everything she could remember. The man in the woods, Linda's phone call, the red words on Chris's cell wall.

After several minutes of analyzing, she sat back and tapped

the pencil on the pad. "First of all, his goal is to terrorize me, not kill me. At least not yet. There are three possibilities as to why." She ticked the options off on her fingers. "Either he's waiting for permission from someone to kill me, he's alone and not able to take on you and Will, or he's playing a cat and mouse game with me."

Mitch stared out the window, his eagle eyes sweeping over everything. "What's your gut say?"

"All three, actually."

He glanced back at her. "All three?"

She stared at her notes. "He's keeping me on tenterhooks, but he's waiting for something. Either for me to be alone or for someone, Chris, perhaps, to give him the go-ahead to kill me. In most cases, the head honcho—such as Chris or Linda— would want to do the killing. At the very least, they'd want to watch."

"Jesus."

The softness of his voice brought her head up. His eyes were troubled, unsettled.

"You wanted an analysis. This is it. My stalker is waiting for Chris, and/or Linda, to get here. We've established that Linda is indeed capable of murder. Chris as well. Meanwhile, whoever is outside is going to terrorize me and try to take out you and Will. He's probably a survivalist like you thought. He obviously knows stealth, knows how to use a knife, knows how to instill fear."

Mitch turned back to the window. "Here comes Will now."

"With my truck?"

A shake of his head dashed the spurt of hope. "On foot."

"So my stalker disabled that vehicle too."

"That would be my guess." He punched the wall. "Dammit."

Abandoning her freestyle circles, she took her gun and followed Mitch down the stairs, her pulse kicking hard.

Her refuge had been turned into a place of fear, of death.

"So what are his weaknesses?" Mitch said as they jogged

down to meet up with Will. "This guy outside. How do I stop him?"

The dogs, having followed the two of them up to her office, barreled down the stairs, pushing by her. Breathing deep to keep her voice from shaking, she resolved not to let whoever her stalker was control her.

Easier said than done.

"A person who likes to instill fear in others is often scared themselves. He wants to be in control so he feels powerful. Take away his power and he ceases to be able to control the situation. Survivalists, too, often feel powerless so they plan for every outcome, including the end of the world. Their name says it all—they'll do anything to survive."

They entered the kitchen and Mitch unlocked the door for Will.

"No go," Will said, shaking his head. He was out of breath from running all the way to his cabin on the outskirts of the property and back. "He stuck a knife in all four of the truck's tires, just like yours. I checked the juvie van. Someone punctured the gas tank. It's going nowhere."

She expected Mitch to swear or punch something again. Instead he smiled. "I'm so going to enjoy making that little weasel pay for this."

Will leaned back on the counter. His hair and clothes were matted to his body from the rain. "You and me, both, brother. I found some tracks. Size 11 and a half boot. Give or take the half."

"Combat boot?"

A nod. "Or someone playing at military. The treads look like desert boots that any idiot can get at the local farm supply store."

"Desert tread isn't ideal in the woods, even when there's been a drought."

Another nod. "By the way, there's a ranger station a couple of miles inside the park on that south entrance you two were checking out. The park service hasn't used it in years, and from what I can gleam from the news, the fires never touched it."

Emma handed him a towel from the stack she had on the dryer. "How do you know about that?"

Will looked sheepish. "I might have stayed there for bit of time before I showed up on your doorstep looking for a job. Hadn't thought of it until now."

He'd been homeless when she took him in, but when he'd come to her that day with nothing but his backpack and his belief in bad luck, he'd been clean and polite. He'd also been honest with her about his PTSD and his need for a quiet environment. He'd wanted to be productive and he had a way with animals. After her own bad experiences with people and situations, her distrust had reared its ugly head. Yet Will had won her over almost instantly when he'd taken Lady under his care.

"You think our unsub might be using it as a landing pad?" Mitch asked.

Unsub. Unknown Subject. Emma knew the term from her days in the courtroom.

Will roughed his hair with the towel. "I think there's more than one of them now. The one that paid us a visit the other day and a second who rode in on the Danika crazy train."

Emma held her tongue over the crazy comment.

"Which might explain why we couldn't find any evidence of the visit from our first unsub," Mitch said, rubbing his chin, "but the second one just left two bodies and some footprints behind."

"Two different stalkers." Emma nodded her head, a rush of excitement taking hold. "One well-versed in subterfuge, the other not. One with violent tendencies, the other not. Why didn't I think of that? It makes total sense."

Mitch pulled his gun from its holster and checked its chamber and clip. His focus jumped to her briefly, then to Will. "My teammates will be here within the hour. All we have to do is keep our visitors at bay. Once backup arrives, we'll get Emma out of here and hunt down these bastards."

Will pushed off the counter. At his feet, Lady whimpered and raised a paw to scratch at his leg. He reached down and rubbed the top of her head. "I'd like to be in on the hunt."

Something passed between Will and Mitch that made Emma shiver. The two men in her kitchen weren't afraid to kill. They'd probably both seen more bloodshed than she could imagine.

She didn't want to imagine it. The horrors that haunted these two would bring most people to their knees.

Mitch nodded at Will. "You stay here, man the entry points. I'll take Emma upstairs where I can keep an eye on the entire sector."

They were trapped. Sitting ducks. A volatile cocktail of fear and anger pushed through her veins. "What about me?" she asked. "What can I do?"

He took her hand and drew her with him to the stairs. "You know that telescope you have in the attic?"

She swallowed, her feet feeling like leaden weights as she climbed after him. "Of course."

He waited until they reached the top of the landing, Salt and Pepper ever their constant companions. "You're the lookout for my team. Train your scope on the southern horizon and look for incoming cars."

Emma felt for her pistol in her waistband at her back. The metal was cool, such a contrast to Mitch's warm hand. There were possibly two men out there who wanted to do her harm. Possibly harm Mitch and Will. The horses, the dogs. No way would she allow that to happen, no matter how scared she was. No matter whether or not help was on the way.

Squeezing his hand, she gave him a quick kiss on the lips. "I'll draw the curtain over the window so only the lens peeks out. The unsubs will never see me."

He kissed her back, a soft, quick kiss that meant as much as the deep, soul-sucking ones he'd given her the night before. He touched her forehead with his. "I swear to you, I will get you out of this."

Her hand brushed his waist. "I know you will."

He wasn't a goddamn bodyguard.

An investigator, an analyzer, an undercover operative—hell, yeah. Mitch had been all of those things. Shortly after Mac's death, he'd donned fake personas and went head-to-head with crime lords and terrorists. His anger and grief had been so acute, pretending to be someone else had been the only way he'd kept himself from blowing out his own brains.

More recently, he'd found his calling working with criminal profiles, predicting outcomes and using statistics and algorithms to stop the bad guys for NI. All from the cool, calm, detached space behind his computer screen.

He protected people on a broad scale, shutting down criminal organizations from the top down. Pulling the plug on terrorist groups, stopping wars from the safety of information, facts, intelligence gathering. He didn't tackle one-on-one projects like this.

Because when you had to look the person counting on you in the eye, keeping them safe made you vulnerable.

Sweat dotted the back of his neck. His face felt flushed, his hands shaky as he made the rounds upstairs, checking out the windows for any sign of their visitors. The place was eerily quiet, soft rain still falling and running down the glass. He'd secured Emma in the attic, giving her the blow-off task of watching for Coop and the others riding to her rescue.

Because he couldn't be her knight in shining armor. If he could somehow conjure up a way to get her off the ranch and into that goddamn safe house, he would do it, but there *was* no way. The vehicles were disabled. He couldn't take the chance of putting her on a horse now and exposing her to whoever was out there, because she was correct—the first visitor might have been a control freak whose assignment was simply to terrorize her, but this latest addition had taken that to a new level and killed a guard in order to make the threat very clear. Regardless, none of the horses were up to the trek out of the valley and into town.

He'd already tried getting the sheriff back out there. A stressed out, overworked, and underpaid secretary had taken the call, assuring him there were officers in the area but all of them were busy assisting highway patrols with the traffic, especially after the road rage incident. While some of the wildfires were now under control, several outliers continued to burn. Christmas morning had started out somewhat peacefully for rest of the world, but here, people were trying to get back to their homes.

"Someone will be with you shortly," she'd said.

Translation: go screw yourself.

Cooper, Celina, Nelson, and the new gal were bound to be there soon. Dupé had ordered an FBI escort to help clear the way, and had sent a curt text that he, himself, would be there within the hour.

All Mitch had to do was keep Emma inside and safe until they arrived.

The only problem was the itch under his skin that reminded him of all the ways this could end badly before his rescue team arrived. As rain dribbled down the window, he tried to stay focused on scanning the yard, the barns, the outlying woods, but his mind kept flashing back to the Christmas five years ago. To the desert and the heat and the look in Mac's eyes right before the building exploded into a hundred jagged pieces of heartbreak and grief.

Not now. He couldn't risk having an episode and ending up with his ass on the floor. Another reason he shouldn't be a bodyguard. He never knew when he was going to have a flashback that incapacitated him.

You know how to bury things deep in order to keep functioning, Agent Holden.

Emma's words throbbed inside his brain. He put his hands up, holding onto his head, feeling the ache there that had come back with a fury. It pulsed with his heartbeat, the same ache of sorrow making his chest tight.

He needed fucking therapy, but he also knew that he wanted it from Emma. She was the only person who could help him, he was sure of it. Would she agree? Probably not, knowing her. She'd already stressed that you couldn't be friends with your therapist. Lovers was definitely out of the question.

His phone rang, sounding distant and indistinct. At first, it didn't even register as his, the sound so far away. He was lost inside his head again, trying to suppress the old, haunting memories, and wrestling with the hope trying to flare to life inside his chest. A state that offered nothing but familiarity, but sometimes the devil you knew and understood was more comforting, safer, than the devil you didn't.

I know Emma. She'll help me.

Brrrring. The phone blared again, sounding louder this time. Mitch lowered his hands from his head and reached for it, hitting the talk button before he even had it to his ear. "Yeah."

"Mitchy?"

Shit. "Hi, mom. I can't talk right now."

"Of course, you can't. You never can, can you? Always working." Her voice was resigned. She knew he was avoiding her. "I know you won't come and see me today, and if you *are* working, you're only doing it to keep the demons at bay. Mac wouldn't want that, Mitchy. He would want you to forgive yourself and move on. Find someone to share the holiday with. It's okay for you to go on with your life."

Mitchy. His mom hadn't called him that since he was eight. He started to give her the usual blow off, but couldn't form the words. Five years was a long time to keep putting one foot in front of the other while his heart was still back there at that bomb site. "I really am working, Mom, but I... I'm not unhappy."

The truth knocked around inside of him like a pinball. Happiness. Such a fleeting, no-good emotion. Yet, here he was, in the middle of a goatfuck and he was happy on some deep, foolish level.

"I'm glad to hear it," his mother responded. She sounded sad, though, rather than relieved. "I'm going to go now. One of these days, stop and see me before I die, okay?"

And there it was. The rub. The thing his mother always did. Act like she wanted to talk to him—that she actually cared about him—and then passively-aggressively turn it around so it was really about her. Adding to his guilt and reminding him how disappointed she was in him.

She was sneaky with it. If you hadn't grown up with her subtle manipulations, they were easy to miss. With him, she'd become less subtle over the past few years and always, always used the threat of dying as a knife jab.

Mac's face swam in front of his eyes. Sweat poured down the back of his neck. He wiped at it and considered hanging up on her.

But that was the old way of dealing with his past. Emma had made him see that he could look at life with fresh perspective. "You know why I don't visit you, Mom?"

His question seemed to surprise her. She stuttered, then fell silent.

Well, that was a first. When had his mother ever been speechless?

"I don't visit you because all you can do is talk about yourself. I could handle talking about Mac, even though it kills me to think about him, but no. I have to listen to how hard your life is without him, your precious son, who would still be here if it wasn't for me. Guess what? I'm here, and I'm your son too.

It's my fault what happened, but there's no changing it. I can't go back and undo it and I've died a thousand times over wishing I could. I can't give Mac back to you, Momma, but I'm here. And I still need my mother sometimes. I need you to forgive me."

The silence on the other end was deafening. His mother said nothing.

He swallowed hard and shook his head at the ceiling, fighting the pressure behind his eyes. His voice came out rough, barely there. "We have nothing to talk about, Mom, until you're ready to forgive me. Have a nice life."

It killed him to hang up, but he did after another pause from his mother's end, heavy with indignation and awkwardness. A simple touch of his thumb to the screen and he severed his connection to her. To that part of his life.

He was still staring at the screen and the words 'Call Ended' when a soft voice spoke from behind him.

"Mitch?"

He whirled around to find Emma in the doorway, a frown on her face. "Is everything okay?" she asked.

His chest hurt but felt strangely lighter. Just seeing her, hearing her voice, soothed the rawness in his chest. "Everything's fine." It was too soon for Cooper and the SCVC cavalry to be there. "What's up? Did you see someone coming down the lane?"

She shook her head. "Not exactly, but... I think you better come see this."

Foreboding cramping his guts, he followed her out of the office and up the attic stairs.

CHAPTER EIGHTEEN

"There," Emma said. "Do you see it?"

Mitch pressed an eye against the lens of her telescope, his body tense. "The gate's closed."

He'd been a million miles away when she'd found him in her office staring out the window. She'd heard the murmur of his voice below her as she'd scanned her property from the attic window, landing on the gate that she never closed. She couldn't hear the contents of his conversation, but it had certainly knocked him sideways.

"Zoom in on the latch."

His long, capable fingers fiddled with the focusing knob as he tweaked the direction of the tube. "Is that a padlock?"

"There were two men, just like we suspected. One tall and thin, the other shorter, but stocky and bald. They closed the gate and locked it; that's not my padlock, by the way." She'd never had one that looked like that.

Mitch straightened, his tenseness now flat-out irritation. "You saw the men who did this? Why didn't you yell at me?"

"I did. You didn't answer. I watched them until they disappeared behind the old outbuilding at the far end, near the creek, then I went to get you. I don't know who you were talking to, but you went dark side for a few minutes. I said your name three times from the doorway before you answered me."

He rocked back on his heels and rubbed his eyes. "Shit. Sorry."

She nodded, seeing the consternation in the pinch of his brows. "Did you have one of your flashbacks?"

He closed his eyes briefly, opened them and shook his head as if shaking off a memory. "No. Yes." Another shake of his head. A lock of his unruly hair fell over his forehead. "Not about Mac. I was talking to my..."

He glanced at the window where the telescope peeked through the curtains. His lips were set in a thin line, his body motionless.

Except for his fingers.

She hadn't noticed it when he was fiddling with the telescope. Now that his hands hung loose by his sides, she noticed the tiny tremor in the fingers of those steady hands.

It hadn't been his boss on the other end of that call. Whenever Mitch spoke to Cooper Harris, he relaxed.

If she had a guess, it hadn't been Victor either. Mitch might fear Victor's disappointment in him, but he respected the man. The emotion she saw in her bodyguard's current posture suggested the person had some kind of control over him in an emotional manner. A very strong, emotional manner.

If his brother were still alive, Emma would have guessed it had been Mac on the other end of that phone.

His mom. It had to be.

Unless he had a girlfriend he hadn't mentioned. A wife—ex, maybe.

Mitch wouldn't lie to you, lead you on.

Would he?

She hated to admit it, but there had been people in her world she'd misjudged. Criminals and other clients who'd fooled her, tricked her into believing in them, and then pulled the trust rug out from under her feet.

Which was why she'd learned not to be suckered by anyone.

"Mitch?" she asked gently. "Who was on the phone?"

He glanced at her, then at the telescope, leaning forward to look through the eyepiece once more. "Did you get a look at the men's faces?"

He didn't want to talk about it. Big surprise. "Yes, actually. Quite clearly."

"Recognize either one of them?"

"One of them, yes; the other no, not personally, but I know of him."

His head came up. "You do?"

She nodded. "They were both wearing camouflage pants and black jackets with a symbol on the back. A gold flaming sword with an all-seeing·eye on the hilt."

His jaw jumped again. "The Reckoners."

"You're familiar with the group?"

"You could say that. How do you know about them?"

"I worked with one of them and evaluated him for a colleague a few years ago. A man by the name of Sean Gordon. Ring any bells?"

Mitch chuckled without humor. "Should have known, Doc."

He took one of her hands and brought her fingers to his lips, where he kissed them as he sent her a heated look. "Our paths were bound to cross one way or another over this wildfire, weren't they?"

Her heart leaped in her chest for a moment, both at the look he was giving her and the synchronicity of the situation. "Sean Gordon is a Reckoner. He's also a fan of *The Mary Monahan Chronicles*. Online, he goes by the avatar, Armagordon."

"I'll be damned." He kept her hand locked in his, his gaze gliding to the window again as his mind worked through the implications. "So, he and his Reckoner brother are working with Goodsman and Brown. Gordon started the fire and Brown was part of that, like we hypothesized."

"She hoped it would spread west and endanger the prison. Sean probably knew the best place to start it and when."

"Exactly. Data about the path of wildfires in this area for the past fifty years isn't hard to come by. Historically, the fires sweep southwest because of the way the valley is situated. The winds sweep down from the north and the fires naturally follow the forest line that spreads west."

Pieces of the puzzle plunked into place for her. "So Sean and Linda snuck out of the park and they followed the creek bed. It took two days after the fires began in the park before they'd spread far enough west to endanger the prison. She had plenty of time to make it back to civilization and join the heist to free Chris."

Mitch nodded. "The man who helped Brown take out the transport van and rescue Chris is probably the same one out there with Gordon now."

"Gordon is an arsonist, but the other man is the murderer. He helped Linda take out the officers on Chris's transport van, killed Carla, and nearly killed Danika. He lives for blood."

Mitch released her to once again use the telescope and scan the area. "Is Gordon's boner for you because of Goodsman, or does he have a personal ax to grind over whatever happened a few years ago when you evaluated him for your colleague?"

"Most likely, both."

"Great." He said it softly, almost like a sigh.

His back was slightly curved over the telescope, the muscles rippling under his shirt. She put a hand there. "There's a bolt cutter in the barn. We can remove the padlock and open the gates for your team members."

He shook his head. "That lock is a high-end, professional, security lock. The shackle is probably armored steel and the base laminated steel, so a hacksaw or bolt cutters won't cut through it. Can't pick it either, because of the tumbler system."

Emma bit her lower lip. "We could remove the hinges on the gates and simply take them down."

"Meanwhile, we're exposed. They could shoot us at any point."

True, and it was a solid half mile down to the gate. Even if Mitch's team got there, it was a long way to walk, run, or ride in the open. "So what do we do?"

Mitch straightened and squeezed her hand. "Stay here. I'll be back."

She watched him until he got to the attic stairs, then dropped her eye to the telescope. What she saw made her hesitate for a moment before she followed the tendril of smoke in front of her to her right.

Her heart sunk, the hair on the back of her neck standing straight up. "Mitch!"

He came hammering back up the stairs. "What?"

Panic building in her chest, she motioned him over and moved back so he could see what she'd spotted.

"Aw, shit," he said under his breath.

"The horses," Emma said, her voice catching. Tears welled in her eyes.

Mitch ran for the stairs, yelling for her to stay inside.

Ignoring him, Emma ran too.

———————

"Barn's on fire," Mitch announced to Will as he entered the kitchen. The man stood at the back door, a rifle in hand. "You stay here with Emma. I'll get the horses out."

"Goddamn SOBs." Will's face was grim. "Not the horses for fuck's sake."

Mitch felt the same way. He stopped, hearing Emma's footsteps on the stairs following. "They know this will flush her out. Flush *us* out. They're baiting us."

"They?"

"We got two for sure."

Will shook his head. "You ain't gonna put out a barn fire by yourself."

Emma was breathing hard and had her S&W in-hand as she stalled in the doorway. "That's why we have to help."

Mitch wheeled on her. "You are not leaving this house. No one is putting out the fire. All I can do is get the horses out."

"You think they'll...?" Will stopped, his gaze saying it all to Mitch, even as he let the words hang in the air because of Emma.

"Think they'll what?" she said.

Mitch grabbed the door handle. *Pick off the horses one by one to draw you out.* "Emma, please, I'm begging you. No matter what happens with the horses, do not come outside. That's what they want and you'll play right into their hands."

Her eyes were floating in unshed tears. Her jaw was clenched. She started to argue, then snapped her mouth closed again. "Just go save my horses."

He nodded, patted her cheek. "I'll do what I can."

"I can't cover you well from inside the house," Will said. "They might be drawing you out just to shoot you. You should let me go."

They were wasting too much time. Mitch swung the door open. "I've got it."

Salt and Pepper tried to rush out with him, but he snapped his fingers for them to stay before he shut the door, sealing them inside.

Slipping along the side of the house, he drew his gun and peered around back. All looked clear, but Will was right. He was a sitting duck if he ran across the yard to the barn.

The horses were neighing, flames shooting from the loft. The rain had stopped and done little to coat the barn's wooden structure that was several years past its last paint job.

A moment of indecision struck him hard in his solar plexus. His job was to keep Emma safe, not the horses.

But damn if he could stomach letting the animals die inside that barn either.

All his training insisted he go back inside. The life of the woman he was protecting was far more valuable than those of Twinkie, Igor, Second Chance and Hope.

And yet, if he let those horses perish, he'd never be able to look Emma in the eye again. The horses, like Danika, meant everything to her. Gave her purpose.

He couldn't let them die.

Racing to the front of the farmhouse, he kept an eye on his surroundings and jumped into his truck.

The cab still smelled like Emma, reassuring and soothing, in direct contrast to his pounding heart. The Ford's wheels might be flat, but it would still run. Two-plus tons of steel and fiberglass was a far better shield than none at all.

Cranking the engine, he eyeballed the barn. A hundred feet or so from the house, but only two exits, neither of which provided him or the horses much cover.

He hit the gas and fought with the steering wheel to guide the truck into the best placement he could get to shield him from whoever might be watching the front barn doors.

The F150 was stubborn, built for heavy payloads and rough terrain, so even though the tires were flat, the engine pulled the truck forward. Mitch kept his head down, only peering over the dash enough to keep the truck headed in the right direction.

Please stay in the house, Emma. The doctor was stubborn and took too many risks. He kept half expecting her to race out and jump in the cab with him.

By the time he finagled the truck into position to provide some cover while allowing the barn doors to open fully, the heat had already busted out several of the windows on the east side and smoke billowed from them.

Get the horses. Protect Emma. The refrain beat in his head in time with his pulse. Grabbing a bandana from the glove compartment, he used it to cover his nose and mouth. Then he climbed out of the truck on the passenger side.

Keeping his body low, he used the truck to hide behind if anyone was watching from across the way in the smattering of trees. He breathed a sigh of relief when there was no padlock placed on the barn doors, and he threw them open.

Flames ate at the peeling paint. Smoke filled the barn, along with the screech of splitting wood. The horses screamed now in their panic and Mitch saw hooves flashing through the smoke as they reared and beat against their stalls with their feet. Overhead, the loft was completely on fire, pieces of burning hay and ash taking wing and fluttering through the air to alight on the stalls beneath.

Filling his lungs with oxygen, he held his breath and plunged inside.

The first stall he came to was Igor's. The old horse quivered and trembled, baring his teeth. Mitch flipped the stall's latch and threw the door open. Igor crashed forward and Mitch whooped at him, raising his arms to send the animal toward the open barn doors.

Igor, the good soldier, ran out.

Across the aisle was Twinkie. Eyes burning from the smoke and sweat running in rivulets all over his body from the heat, Mitch repeated the sequence, opening the stall and sending the horse toward the open doors, ears straining over the noise in the barn, waiting for the sound of gunshots.

He heard none, but didn't dare hope that the men hiding in the woods weren't gearing up for target practice.

Last, at the back of the barn, were Second Chance and her foal. Lungs bursting, fingers clawing at his throat as he suffocated a coughing fit, Mitch waved at the smoke clouding his vision. Three feet from the stall, he saw Second Chance rearing up and kicking at the stall's gate, the whites of her eyes showing, her body covered in ash.

Sprinting forward, Mitch nearly met his end when a flaming board from the loft crashed down in front of him, cutting across his path. He jumped back and sucked in a breath, regretting it the moment his lungs began to burn. Forced to go around the board, he coughed into his elbow and wiped sweat from his eyes as he came at Second Chance's stall from the opposite side.

He reached for the latch and pulled.

The wood had swollen with the heat, pinning the latch to it.

Jerking hard on the metal, he peered over the stall door and felt his hammering heart stutter.

Hope lay on the floor of the stall unmoving as her mother danced around her, kicking and screaming.

Coughing so hard, he could barely stand up, Mitch raised a foot and kicked at the latch. Once, twice, three times. The last kick didn't budge the latch, but ripped the metal completely off the wood.

Grabbing the top of the stall door, Mitch yanked it open.

He sagged back against the stall wall, waiting for Second Chance to run out.

She didn't.

His legs shook, his lungs failing him. Any second, he would be too weak to make it out of the barn, the old thing falling down around him and crushing him before the fire could burn him up.

Get out.

His eyes felt like sandpaper. His lungs were no longer working properly.

Peeling himself off the wall, he dared to peek inside. Second Chance was nuzzling Hope, desperately trying to get the foal to move.

He staggered in beside her, knowing that at any moment, Second Chance could turn wild again and kick him. She could kill him or knock him unconscious.

Fighting through the weakness in his body, he held a hand up and waved her back so he could drop to his knees next to the foal. Hope didn't appear to be breathing and Mitch's brain pleaded with him to leave the horse and get the hell out.

Instead, he shoved his arms under the foal's body, lifting her as he struggled to his feet.

He thought about trying to chase Second Chance out of the

stall ahead of him, but figured the mother horse would most likely follow his lead.

Nearly blinded and barely able to put one foot in front of the other, he staggered around the blazing board, through the smoke, and toward what he hoped was the exit. Good thing his internal compass worked in the middle of a fire, because he could no longer see the barn opening or even a smidgen of light.

As he forced his body forward, the heavy weight of the foal loading him down, he felt Second Chance speed around him. A moment later, in the wake of her breeze, the smoke lifted slightly and he saw the barn opening.

As he neared the doors, he lost his footing, turning his ankle and going down on one knee. He pitched forward, sending Hope flying across the threshold and onto the ground just outside the door.

Body aching, vision dimming, he crawled forward, then grabbed the foal's back legs and pulled her away from the barn.

Fresh oxygen rushed into his lungs and he fell to the ground and rolled over near the flat front wheel of his truck. Before he could wipe his eyes or check to see if the foal was still breathing, a loud crash came from inside the barn.

In slow motion, the right side of the building tilted. The sounds of splintering wood rose over the licking flames. Down, down, down, the side seemed to be curling in on itself, the roof breaking apart. For a moment, it stopped, suspended, then the entire side crashed to the ground.

A new burst of flames shot out from the now crooked barn doors and Mitch backed himself up against the truck, throwing up an arm in front of his face to block the heat and debris.

Ash rained down. He felt heat on his head and knocked a burning chunk of hay from his hair. Once he ascertained nothing else on his body was on fire, he reached over and felt for a pulse in Hope's neck.

The foal's tongue lolled from her mouth, her body lifeless.

Rubbing her chest, her back, her muzzle, he searched again for a pulse.

There! A weak heartbeat. Hope stirred under his hands. Massaging her some more, he spoke to her softly. "Come on, girl. Take a deep breath. You're safe now."

At least, he hoped she was.

The foal blinked her eyes open and twitched. Next thing he knew, she was on her feet, her spindly legs carrying her off, hopefully to her mother.

His own legs and feet were less cooperative and he ended up sitting on his haunches when he tried to rise, his lungs rattling from the smoke inhalation.

And then, *boom!* Just as Mitch was about to climb back inside the truck and hightail it to the house, a gun went off.

CHAPTER NINETEEN

Emma stood in the center of the yard, turning circles, aiming the shotgun at the woods, the collapsing barn, the fenced pasture. "Come out and show yourselves!" she yelled.

As her gaze ventured past the house, she thought she saw the glint of Will's rifle in the upstairs bedroom window. Good. All she had to do was pray Mitch was okay and keep their attackers focused on her.

Second Chance had journeyed to the edge of the drive where she lingered near the juvenile detention van. Hope was by her side, nursing. The other two horses had disappeared into the woods, scared off by the fire, and then Emma's shotgun blast.

The rest of the burning barn collapsed and Emma flinched, praying hard that Mitch was okay. She and Will had seen him stagger out in a swirl of smoke and collapse between his truck and the barn. They'd lost sight of him at that point and that's when Emma had gone from scared to raging angry. The moment Mitch had bailed out the kitchen door, she'd needed more than a chocolate fix.

She'd stuck her S&W in its holster and grabbed her shotgun. When Will asked what she was doing, she'd told him to find a spot where he could train that rifle on the center of the property and be prepared to shoot.

"You know what a terrorist is?" she yelled at the tree line now as she continued to slowly pivot. "A weak SOB. You're not smart or brave or a martyr if you terrorize someone, no matter your beliefs. You're nothing but a sorry excuse. A pussy in my book."

She never used vulgar language, but in her time working with criminals, she'd learned a few from them. Sometimes, in order to get a point across, you had to meet the devil on his own terms.

She just hoped her display of bravado had the intended effect. Mitch had to be suffering from smoke inhalation and burns. Half the barn had crumbled while he was in there; she suspected he might be injured from falling debris as well.

She needed to distract her tormentors, keep them away from Mitch. He'd saved her precious horses; now she needed to do a bit of saving herself.

Will had tried to keep her inside, but she was done waiting for Mitch's teammates to arrive or for someone to catch Chris and Linda and end this ridiculous, dangerous charade.

If Sean Gordon and the man working with him wanted her, they could come out and face her like real men.

She could feel eyes on her as she swept the shotgun past Mitch's truck, now covered in dust and ash from the building. Rain began to fall in earnest again, sprinkled her face, but even at this distance, she could feel heat from the burning barn.

Bastards. They'd killed an innocent guard to get to her. Nearly killed Danika and Mitch in their desire to get to her. They'd burned down her barn and nearly killed four horses to get to her.

Well, here I am. What are you waiting for, you worthless scumbags?

She pivoted again, waiting, taunting them. Igor had come back to the tree line and was chewing on some grass.

"You've done all this to get to me." She stopped circling and lowered the gun so it hung at her side. "You succeeded. I give up."

Nothing moved. No one emerged from the trees. Igor didn't

even lift his head. Behind her, all she could hear was the crackling of the fire, the patter and sizzle of rain.

Tears threatened to break free, and really, why the hell was she holding them back? This ranch meant everything to her. The dogs, the horses, Will. She'd built a life here, helped young men and women here, recovered from her own emotional wounds.

And now these men, at the direction of Chris Goodsman and his number one fan, had ripped off the bandages she'd so carefully placed around her heart. They'd made her vulnerable again.

How had that happened?

Danika and Carla had paid the price. The horses had been terrified and nearly died. And Mitch—he hadn't emerged from behind his truck; hadn't even made a sound when the barn collapsed. What if he was over there dying? What if he was already...

No. Do not go there! Mitch was full of life and he had turned her world on its head, made her believe again in happiness, peace...love? Maybe. All she knew was that she couldn't imagine her life now without him.

"What the hell are you doing?"

The low, irritated voice hissed from behind her. Turning, she nearly sagged with relief. Mitch, face covered with dirt and smudged with smoke, glared at her. His gun was drawn, his arms locked into position as he sidled up to her and put his back to hers.

"You trying to get yourself killed, woman?"

"I'm trying to draw them out so Will can shoot them. He's upstairs with a rifle."

"Jesus! Raise that shotgun. We're going to move in tandem back to the house. If I tell you to duck, your ass better hit the dirt, you understand?"

The relief swirling inside her made her giddy, lightheaded. "I like it when you get all bossy."

Her levity was lost on him. "Move," he growled.

She did, liking the way his bigger body tag-teamed hers, shielding her, protecting her.

Putting him in their enemies' line of sight wasn't what she wanted, however, and it sort of pissed her off that she wasn't going to get to shoot someone.

"If you dare hurt my horses," she threatened the invisible men, "I will personally shove this shotgun up your ass and blow you away!"

She meant it too. She was tired of placating people, not letting them see how they upset her, provoked her. She was done taking other people's shit, especially anyone connected to Chris Goodsman.

Yelling at them was cathartic. It seemed to release the valve inside her where she kept everything pushed down and contained. "I'm going to make sure they fry your ass, Goodsman," she added as Mitch prodded her toward the porch, his back against hers. "If you're out there having a laugh about this, or planning even more fanatical activities, you should know I'm ready for you."

Mitch knocked his shoulder into her. "Will you quit already? Get in the house, for fuck's sake."

But she wasn't done. They hit the porch and Emma whirled around, both hands on her shotgun and the anger inside her boiling. "I don't care what it takes, Chris. I'm going to make sure you go down, one way or— Eeep!"

Before she could finish, Mitch snatched the shotgun from her hand and shoved her inside.

At the same time, a shot rang out, shattering the window next to her.

She fell to the floor, hands landing in glass as a hundred pieces fell around her. More gunshots peppered her front porch, the door, the siding. Curling in a ball, she ignored the stinging cuts in her hands and covered her head, her heart seizing in her chest.

Bang, bang, bang. The gunfire didn't stop.

She peeked through her fingers. Luckily the dogs were nowhere to be seen. She hoped they were safe upstairs with Will.

All around her, bullets flew through the broken window, embedding themselves in her living room, breaking her lamp, exploding a couch cushion, knocking a picture from the wall. She rolled away from the door.

"Mitch!" she yelled over the noise. She couldn't see him, didn't know where he'd gone. He had nowhere to hide in the front of the house since he'd moved his truck. It was just open yard, the steps, and the porch.

Oh God, don't let him be dead.

She was about to risk shifting back toward the door to peek out when he came hauling in from the kitchen.

"Stay down," he commanded, crouched as he ran over to the blown out window and put his back against the wall. He had his handgun in one hand, the shotgun in the other. One booted foot reached out and kicked the door closed.

Blood bloomed on his left shirt sleeve. More streamed from a cut near his temple.

"Are you shot?" she asked, digging her elbows into the old wooden floor and pulling herself across the floor toward him. "You're bleeding."

He stuck his handgun in his waistband and reached out with his free hand. Grabbing hold of the back of her shirt, he hauled her over to the wall next to him. His gaze landed on her hands and he frowned. "You're bleeding too. Are you all right?"

Her body shook with the force of a California earthquake. Her hands stung from the glass and she could see small pieces still embedded in her skin. "I'll live. You didn't answer my question. Are you hurt?"

Will came thundering down the stairs and pressed himself up against the far wall, rifle in hand. He glanced at Emma, then nodded at Mitch. "You done good out there with the horses."

The shooting from outside stopped.

Mitch cocked his chin at Emma and said in a low voice, "Why the hell did you let her out of your sight?"

"Stubborn woman wouldn't listen," Will said at the same time Emma said, "It's not his fault."

Mitch glared between them. His face was covered with soot. His gaze finally came to rest on Emma. "Are you trying to get yourself killed?"

"Look who's talking," she snapped. "You go running into a burning barn by yourself and it nearly collapses on you. I thought you were dead!"

Her voice had risen and without the gunfire to compete with, it sounded shrill and panicky in the confines of her destroyed living room.

"She thought if she could draw them out, I could shoot them," Will added sheepishly.

Mitch banged the back of his head into the wall, once, twice, three times, then sagged against it, resignation at their cross-purposes shadowing his features. "You took ten years off my life, Emma."

His voice was flat, unemotional. She knew he had a clamp on his emotions because he cared for her, but it was still difficult not to fly off again. Couldn't he see she'd done what she had to in order to try and stop these bullies? To stop anyone else from dying?

"Ditto, Agent Holden." She wiped her wet face with her hands. "I'm forever thankful you saved my horses, but I thought I'd lost you."

His jaw worked and his Adam's apple went up and down. "Still only two men?" he said to Will, subtly shifting to eye the yard through the broken window.

Will took ammunition from a pocket, reloaded his rifle. He grinned an evil grin. "Actually, I took one out of commission while you were dancing around the back of the house. The short, bald one."

"Gordon," Mitch said. Emma echoed him. "Sean."

Mitch gave Will a tight smile back. "That only leaves one, then. Between the two of us, we should be able to take out this last POS without too much difficulty."

Except the one left was the brutal killer.

A nod from Will. "You want me to flush him out for you?"

Mitch hesitated a second and Emma reached up to twine her fingers in his. He felt warm; her hands were cold as ice.

She saw him swallow hard, then he took his fingers away from hers and motioned at the stairs. "Go upstairs and lock yourself and the dogs in your bathroom, Emma. Don't let anyone in and don't come out until I tell you to."

What? He was sending her away?

She retorted but the rapid, *ping, ping, ping* of bullets peppering the front of her house again drowned out her words.

As if this day could get any worse, Will's body snapped back and down he went too.

"Shit!" Lucky shot or skilled killer? Mitch didn't have time to figure it out. The man shooting at the house went silent, probably reloading, so Mitch dropped to his knees and grabbed Emma's bleeding hands, pulling her to her feet.

Glass crunched under his boots. He tried to be gentle, but the adrenaline blasting though his system and the memory of Mac caught in that building five years ago made him want to throw her over his shoulder and run.

He gripped her too hard, spots dancing at the edge of his vision. His body swayed. Mac's face flashed across his mind.

Not now. A flashback now could kill him and Emma both. "Stay low but get to the stairs, Doc. Now!"

He sent her scurrying but she pulled up short two steps later when she realized Will was down, the big man swearing and swiping at his upper arm where blood flowed.

His right arm.

Mitch's sharp shooter was out of commission.

"Go!" Will yelled at Emma. "I'm fine."

He wasn't, and she knew it, but she set her mouth in a firm line and crab-crawled to the stairs. Mitch could tell even from this distance and seeing her only in profile she was scared but also pissed. Good. Being pissed might keep her alive if she didn't do something stupid again.

Will scooted on his butt so his back was to the wall between the door and the window, the rifle lying on the floor at his feet. He tore a strip off his shirt and started winding it around his arm, his left hand shaking. "Just let me wrap this up and I'm good to go. Our guy is on the northeast side. I'll head around back and come at him from the south. Flush him out for you."

Wounded or not, Mitch needed him. He withdrew his handgun and held it out. "Trade?"

The rifle wasn't going to work for Will, but he accepted the Glock with his left hand and used his foot to slide the rifle toward Mitch. "Better than nothing, right?" he said, rising to his feet.

A grimace stole over his features and his face went gray. Pain could do that to you. "Watch your back," Mitch said.

Will nodded, then ducked and made his way to the kitchen, his gait slightly unsteady as he held his injured arm close to his body.

Upstairs, Mitch heard a door shut.

How about that? Emma had listened to him for once.

All was quiet out front. Too quiet. Had their shooter run out of bullets? Was he moving to a new location?

Will's fresh blood spotted the floor near the door. Emma's blood was intermixed with glass near his boots.

Have to keep her alive.

If he did one goddamn thing right in his life, it had to be that.

Rain plunked in the puddles, oozed over the landscape. His

gaze kept going back to the blood on the floor. Mac's blood was on his hands. Emma and Will were both injured because he'd chosen to save a couple of horses.

He kicked the wall, huffing, then yelled out the broken window. "Come on, you sack of shit. What are you waiting for?"

Nothing happened.

There was no good answer, no easy solution. Creeping under the window, he locked the door. Not much good that would do since their bad guy could still get in, but he wasn't about to let the asshole just walk in through the door. If he tried to come in, he'd have to crawl through the jagged glass of the broken window.

Mitch crouched and ran to the kitchen.

Once there, he went to the window, checking the area. No Will and no one else either. Second Chance and Hope had moved away from the juvie center van and Mitch could no longer see them either.

He checked the lock on the back door, then went by the mudroom and pantry, circling back out to the living room. The window on the other side of the room was curtained and he peeked out, scanning the area toward the pasture and woods.

A flash of black caught his eye, but it was only Igor among the trees.

Where was Will? Had he lost too much blood and passed out? Had their assailant moved positions? Mitch went back to the front window, every nerve on edge as he carefully eyed the area from the frame.

A noise over the falling rain met his ears and he tipped his head, listening closer but still not seeing anything out of place. As the sound became louder, he recognized the familiar *clomp, clomp, clomp* of a horse's hooves. The horse was moving toward him at a fairly fast clip.

Second Chance. Their assailant was making a break for it.

Mitch tried to calm the sudden rage inside him, flaring to life like a flash fire. But it wouldn't be calmed. This asshole wasn't going anywhere.

Snatching the rifle from the floor and tuning his ears to carefully listen to the cadence of the hooves, he went to his knees and used the gun to clear the jagged glass from the sill. Propping the gun on the ledge, he steadied his pounding pulse.

Before he could blink, a man riding Second Chance came into view, his body hunkered down over the horse's mane as he dug his heels into her side, urging her to go faster toward the gate.

Mitch lined up the scope, following the fleeing form. If he missed and hit the horse...

Not happening.

But hitting the man atop the horse going at that speed would be challenging for a sharp shooter like Will. Mitch was good, but he wasn't a sniper and his military days were long behind him. He'd always been better with a handgun; he wasn't a marksman with a rifle.

No choice. Do it.

God and Emma forgive me if I miss.

The horse and rider had already passed the front of the house. He lined up the man's back, put his finger on the trigger and let the weight of it press the trigger the slightest amount.

Then he took a deep breath, let it out halfway, and...

Boom!

The rifle kicked, the blast echoing in the room. His ears buzzed, a fine match to his gritty eyes and the taste of ash in his mouth. He heard a scream—horse or man?

He was almost scared to look.

Taking his eye away from the scope, he saw Second Chance continuing toward the gate at a much slower pace, red blood running down her side.

But it wasn't her blood.

At least he didn't think so.

The man riding her bareback slumped over her neck, a clear

bullet wound in his upper left side spurting blood. As Mitch watched, the man slid off the horse and hit the ground.

From nowhere, Will came running. "Hot damn," he yelled, sending a look toward the house where Mitch was emerging. "Bulls-eye!"

Mitch joined him, walking across the grounds to the spot where the man lay face down. Will handed Mitch back his Glock and rolled the body over.

The man blinked up at them, rain dotting his face and plastering his hair to his head. The man's lips worked, but nothing came out. He lost his struggle with consciousness, and Mitch fought the urge to kick the son-of-a-bitch.

"What do you want to do with him?" Will said.

Mitch's pulse still beat erratically, tiny dots dancing in his peripheral vision again. What the hell was wrong with him?

"Bind his hands first," he said, wiping rain from his eyes. "Then we'll see about stopping the bleeding."

Will nodded and Mitch's phone rang. He pulled it out, relieved to see his boss's name on the screen. Absentmindedly, he glanced to his left toward the lane and the gate at the far end. "Please tell me you're close," he said upon answering.

"Five minutes out," Cooper said. "You all right? You sound funny."

"I'm fine. Hope you brought your cuffs."

Cooper's voice took on urgency. "Did you catch him?"

"Not Goodsman, but two men who were working for him. One is Sean Gordon, our arsonist. Gordon's dead, but his accomplice is alive, so maybe he can tell us where that prick is."

"Nice work, Holden. We'll be there shortly."

Mitch hung up and let his shoulders slump. "Any chance you have a chainsaw?" he asked Will.

Will's gaze went between Mitch and the man at his feet. "You want to cut him up?"

Don't tempt me. "Gotta get the gate open and the only way I can see to do that is to cut it down."

Will held his injured arm. "I'll be back in a minute with something."

He had no choice but to trust the man. "I'll tie this asshole up and let Emma know the coast is clear."

As Will took off for his cabin, Mitch let out a long, slow breath. He'd kept his shit together and took out the immediate threat. A feeling of relief seeped into his body.

Merry fucking Christmas to me.

CHAPTER TWENTY

The coast was clear.

Emma flew out the kitchen door, the dogs following.

"Mitch!" she yelled as she ran past the juvenile detention van and out toward the driveway. Mitch was cinching a plastic tie around the man's wrists. Her rifle lay nearby.

As she got close, Mitch stood and faced her. He was a total mess—blood, rain, dirt and ash. It didn't matter. She threw herself into his arms.

"You did it," she said, hugging him tight with her bandaged hands. She'd gotten most of the glass fragments out of her palms and wrapped them in gauze.

The dogs were happy to see him, too, Salt and Pepper jumping on him and dancing around. Lady sat in a mud puddle, panting. "You were supposed to wait in the bathroom until I came and got you."

He smelled like smoke and rain and *Mitch*. "You saved me and the horses," she said, nuzzling her face into his wet neck and ignoring his chastising. "Thank you. Thank you so much."

His body was solid and he held her close. Close enough she could hear the wheeze coming from his lungs.

"You need a doctor," she said.

One hand stroked her back. "I have you."

Yes, he did. "A medical doctor, Mitch. You have smoke inhalation symptoms."

She tried to break their embrace and step back so she could

look him over properly, but he didn't let her. He just kept hanging on to her and she didn't resist. It felt too damn good to be inside his arms, to know he was alive.

Will appeared in her peripheral vision, carrying a blowtorch and some large, insulated gloves. Welder's protective goggles rested on his forehead. He'd wrapped his injured arm with burlap.

He was grinning.

Grinning? Emma shook her head as she and Mitch disengaged. "What are you doing with that?" she asked, pointing to the contraption in his hands.

"Cutting down the gate," he said, his eyes like a kid's on Christmas morning.

"That should do it," Mitch agreed. He wiped his forehead on one sleeve. "Emma, get back inside until my teammates arrive. They'll be here any minute and then we can get you to the safe house. Grab your bag, and yes, the dogs can go too. I'll snag their food once I'm done here."

He needled the unconscious man with a boot toe. "Once this asshole regains consciousness, I'll interrogate him to find out what he knows about Goodsman's whereabouts."

The man's skin under his beard had a grayish tint. Blood from his wound soaked the ground. "Are you sure he's alive?" she asked.

Mitch let go of a sigh that suggested he wished the man weren't. "I hit him in the shoulder blade and he hit his head when he fell. Probably has a concussion, but he's alive."

Emma wiped wet hair from her face. "Will, are you okay?"

"Actually," he said, "I'm better than okay, Doc. This is the most alive I've felt since I set foot on American soil again."

"Then this must be why you made it back home." She saw understanding light in his eyes. "You're good to have around, I'd say."

"Ditto," Mitch agreed and Will's neck flushed red.

"What about your arm?" Emma asked her hired man.

"This?" He waved the bandaged arm around. "This is nothing. Barely grazed me."

She'd never seen Will smile this much. The psychologist in her wondered if his being so happy at getting shot and taking down a couple of criminals was a good thing, but the other part of her felt pretty darn good herself, so she let it go. "What should we do about the horses?"

The equines in question were slowly making their way toward the pasture. Hope had caught up with her mother and Second Chance was head-butting the foal in a happy hello. None of them seemed too upset anymore about their barn home, now smoldering in the rain.

"I'll get them inside the fenced area in a minute," Will said, flipping down the welding goggles and heading for the gate. "Tomorrow, I'll draw up plans for a new barn. We needed one anyway."

As Lady went to follow Will, Emma glanced back at her house, the front porch and entryway battered from the attack. "I suppose I better find some plywood to cover the window. What a mess."

"Will can handle that once we get you moved." Mitch picked up the rifle. "After we get the gate open for Coop and the gang, I'll go round up Gordon's body and confirm his ID."

He kissed her sweetly and headed after Will, Salt and Pepper loping along beside him.

"Mitch?" she called, seeing the tired slope of his shoulders. It made her feel completely undone. He'd saved her and her ranch. She owed him everything.

He stopped, turning back to give her a weary smile. "Yeah, Doc?"

"I don't know what I would have done without you," she said. "I hope when this is all over, you and I can have a fresh start, but if you decide this isn't for you—this thing between us—I understand."

If anything, his shoulders drooped even more. He stood

there staring at her in the rain, the rifle dangling beside his leg. "This thing between us?" His smile turned wry, almost mischievous. He shook his head. "Jesus, Emma."

"What?" she said, suddenly self-conscious. Had she misunderstood? Had he slept with her and told her all those intimate things but never planned on sticking around after his assignment was done?

"Sounds odd," he said, chuckling, "to hear you use such a piss-poor description for what's going on between us."

She shifted her weight between her feet and worried her hands. "What exactly *is* going on between us?"

She felt stupid asking, but personal relationships—*her* personal relationships—were one area she never felt comfortable talking about. Helping others explore their emotions when it came to those they loved was easy—she had no attachment to the people they talked about. Exploring her own emotions, her own feelings, was sort of foreign soil.

Mitch stood motionless for another moment, studying her, then lumbered back to her, lifted her chin with his wet fingers and stared down into her eyes. "In less than three days, you've turned my world completely upside down, woman. This *thing* between us is the best thing I've ever had. I don't need a fresh start. I need you, with all the chaos, and the dogs, and the horses, and your freaky mind-reading."

This time his kiss was anything but sweet. He held her chin while he ravaged her lips, gave her some tongue, and made her see stars.

When he finally broke away, they were both breathing hard. He turned her around, smacked her ass, and said, "Now get back inside and get ready to go to the safe house."

Grinning, she did as she was told, giving him a wink over her shoulder as she walked away. Maybe she didn't need to analyze her relationship with Mitch. All she had to do was accept it.

When she got to the back door, she looked over her shoulder

again. Will was torching the latches on the gate, melting the old, rusty metal. Mitch, feeling her stare, looked back at her, the dogs milling around his legs in the soft rain.

Emma let out a sigh of relief, her heart full from his words.

Her bag was still in the living room, so she tip-toed through the broken glass and grabbed that first. Then she headed upstairs for dry clothes.

Noise outside brought her into her office to glance out the window. Two vehicles pulled up at the gate, several men and women emerging from them as Mitch held up a hand and Will continued to work on the latches. Emma could see greetings going back and forth between Mitch and his teammates, lots of smiles all around. Emma found herself smiling too, watching him exchange manly clasps through the gate with one of the men she guessed might be Cooper Harris.

She planned to tell Mr. Harris all about Mitch's heroics. Victor too. Did they know what an amazing man he was? Probably, but it wouldn't hurt to remind them. Mitch had problems, but he knew his job and did it well.

If he stayed with her, how would he work for the taskforce? Would he continue with National Intelligence? The thought sat uncomfortably between her ribs. Mitch was an incredible agent, and she had no doubt she wasn't the first person he'd saved during his career. Could she really expect him to leave that world for her?

Turning away from the window, she pushed the thought to the back of her mind. Right now, she needed clothes and to get back downstairs ready to leave.

Because Chris Goodsman was still on the loose. She still hated the idea of leaving the ranch, but there was no telling who else he might send after her if she stayed here.

In the bathroom, she stripped off her wet clothes. Leaving them on the tile floor, she went to her closet to grab jeans and a dry shirt. A sexy red silk blouse caught her eye and she rubbed the fabric between her fingers. Should she wear another flannel over a T-shirt and be comfortable or should she chose something a bit more festive for Christmas Day? Did Mitch like red? Did he like silk?

She had the feeling he would answer yes to both questions.

The red silk won out and she slipped it off the hangar. Back in the bathroom, she realized she needed a different bra, her current cotton one was slightly damp and sticking to her skin, putting her nipples on full display under the red silk.

Off went the shirt before it ended up damp as well. Grabbing a towel to dry her hair, she headed back out of the bathroom for a second trip to her closet, when a voice stopped her dead in her tracks.

"Hello, Dr. Collins," Chris Goodsman said.

Emma stumbled backward, her pulse skyrocketing.

Chris sat on the end of her bed, running his fingers over the pair of panties Mitch had peeled off her the night before.

His long, brown hair fell forward in that messy Hollywood-bad-boy style and his chocolate brown eyes did a slow perusal of her nearly naked self. "Miss me? I sure missed you."

Gun.

She'd left it on the counter while taking off her wet clothes.

Moving backward, her feet slipped and tangled, her elbow crashing into the door frame, knocking her off balance as panic swept through her. The door banged backwards into the wall.

Dropping the towel, she scrambled for the sink and the shiny metal lying on it.

Her hand slapped at the gun, catching the butt. It spun and tumbled to the floor.

She fell to her knees, grabbing it with both hands and flicking off the safety. Raising it to point at the man defiling her panties, her bedroom, with his very presence, she tried to firm her shaking grasp.

He smirked at her attempt to protect herself, his eyes letting her know he wasn't scared of her gun. Wasn't scared of *her*. He had everything under control.

"What are you doing here?" she gasped, still working on keeping the barrel from shaking.

"I came for you." His tone suggested it was a stupid question.

It probably *was* an inane thing to ask. She'd known since the moment Mitch had shown up on her doorstep that Chris might indeed be for real in his hunt for her. "Why?"

"You ruined my life." He pushed off the bed and stood. "Thought I'd repay the favor."

Emma stood too, slowly rising from her knees and keeping the gun on him. "Your men killed a police officer and nearly killed an innocent girl. They burned down my horse barn. They shot up my house! But you know what? It ends here. You and I? We're done."

Chris gave her an odd look. "I could have ordered my lieutenants to kill you, Dr. Collins."

Lieutenants? "So we're playing this game, huh? I'm a cyborg and you're The Chosen One?"

"I don't know why you believe this is a game."

Heart pounding, she licked her lips, trying to decide where exactly to shoot him. Leg? Chest? Should she wound him or shoot to kill?

She wasn't a killer, but she was damned tired of living in fear from this man. "So why didn't you order your lieutenants to kill me, Chris? You and I both know you don't have the guts to kill me yourself."

"Who's Chris?" He snickered, but she saw the slight twitch at the corner of his left eye. Her words had hit home even though the narcissist in him hid it well. "You know who I am and why I'm here. I *am* going to kill you, Dr. Collins, and lead The Resistance to freedom."

"Good luck with that, Chris." She gave him a smile that she hoped conveyed she was really the one in control here because she knew the truth. "You know what you are underneath your fame and manipulation? Nothing but a scared little boy who never felt loved. It doesn't matter if you're really Chris or you're Tom. Bottom line is, you're nothing but a pussy, afraid to act like a man."

It had worked on the other men, she thought it might be worth a try on him.

He went totally still. Not even the tick near his eye moved. "You really think I don't have the guts to kill you, bitch?"

She cocked the gun. He had to know she'd defended herself before against one of his fans, but maybe he needed reminding. "You really think this is the first time I've ever shot someone?"

His gaze flickered to the gun and back to meet her eyes. That same smirk crossed his lips, his body no longer tense. "Guess it comes down to who has the most to win or lose, doesn't it?"

She would only have one chance. One shot. If she didn't make it count, he'd be on her in a second. No telling what he might do.

And not just to her.

Mitch and the others were still down by the gate. While she hadn't seen anyone else, she knew Linda had to be around somewhere, maybe more of the Resistance fighters.

No one was taking anything else from her. She wouldn't let them hurt Mitch, or Will, and not her horses or her dogs or her ranch either. Chris Goodsman had already taken so much from her.

"No, Chris," she said, her hands finally steadying. "What it comes down to is who has the biggest set of balls. And that, you arrogant asshole, would be me."

She fired—*click, click, click.*

Nothing happened. No bullets came speeding out to wipe the smirk off his face. Blood didn't bloom on his chest. Or his stomach. Or anywhere else.

Not because she had poor aim.

Someone removed the bullets from my gun.

Bewildered, she pulled the trigger again.

Click.

Emma's heart clenched, her pulse suddenly loud in her ears.

Linda Brown sauntered in from the hall, sidling up to Chris. She was dressed in typical Resistance gear: brown pants tucked into boots, a brown jacket over a black T-shirt with a picture of Tom Monahan on the front. Her wild hair was in a messy ponytail, her face devoid of makeup. Strapped around one thigh was a knife holder complete with a hunting knife. She held up one hand, fingers closed in a fist.

Neither Linda nor Chris showed signs of having been in the rain. Neither was dirty or appeared to have been roughing it. They both looked clean, well-fed, and enjoying themselves, like cats toying with a mouse.

A light shone in Linda's eyes, one Emma was bone-chillingly familiar with. With a sly smile, the woman tipped her fist sideways and slowly, one finger at a time, opened it.

Bullets fell to the floor, *plunk, plunk, plunk,* spinning in all directions as they hit.

Chris smirked at Emma's shock. "Bad day, Dr. Collins?"

Somehow, Linda, the bitch, had snuck into the bathroom and removed the bullets from Emma's gun while she'd been in the closet. It was the only explanation.

Linda laughed, a brittle sound that scratched against the thrumming in Emma's ears. "It's about to get worse," she croaked and then she launched herself at Emma.

The swing Emma took with the gun was a lucky one—either that, or her primal survival instincts kicked in and came to her rescue. The gun connected with Linda's temple, drawing a sharp grunt from the woman as her body weight smacked Emma down hard onto the tile floor.

Emma also grunted, the breath knocked out of her, but she managed to hold tight to the gun. Linda rolled her to the right, banging both of them into the sink. Emma forced them to roll to the left.

Linda smacked her across the face and somehow managed to knee her in the stomach. Pain exploded in both places.

With the pain came a memory. Christmas lights bobbing on a tree as she wrestled with an attacker. The smell of pine in her nose. A carol playing softly in the background as she struggled for her life.

Beyond fear, beyond pain, rose an anger she had long buried. It erupted with a loud growl from her mouth, the sensations rolling through her veins like boiling lava.

Instinct took hold again and Emma raised her hand and brought the metal down on the back of Linda's head.

And then again.

The woman's body froze for an instant before she went limp.

With another growl, Emma wrestled the body off of her and came up to her knees, then her feet. She tasted blood and wiped at her lip. The back of her hand came away red.

Chris watched her, more curious than scared, in a wide-legged stance with his arms crossed over his chest. "God, I hate cyborgs. You're a bitch to kill."

"Fuck you." There was one bullet lying just across the threshold, but even if she dove for it, Chris would still have plenty of time to knock her out or kill her before she could get it loaded into the gun.

She could scream her lungs out, but Mitch and the others probably wouldn't hear her from so far away, and if they did, they still couldn't get to her in time, could they?

She toyed with the S&W, rubbing a thumb over the stock as she stared Chris down. He didn't appear to have a weapon. Maybe if she jumped him and started swinging, she could knock him out like she had Linda. He only outweighed her by oh, fifty pounds...

Chris clucked his tongue. He didn't seem to care that his cohort was down, that federal agents were only a few hundred yards away. "Why do you believe there is only one reality, Dr. Collins? We can create as many realities as we want. Don't you see? We can be and do anything we want."

Was this part of his delusions or part of his act? Did he actually believe he was Tom Monahan or was he pretending so he could claim insanity again if he was caught?

Emma honestly wasn't sure anymore.

"I have to kill you," Chris continued, "and all the people— and those stupid animals—that you care about."

Pretend. Go along with him. You need that bullet...

Her heart was still tripping over itself, but she forced herself to take a slow, steady breath. She purposely slumped her shoulders, allowed tears to well in her eyes. It wasn't hard, really, when she thought about the people he'd already harmed because of her.

For a long moment, she simply stood and looked dejected, channeling her own inner actress. "You're right, Chris. I mean, Tom. I've been in denial, but I understand now. I'm tired. I don't want to fight anymore."

She took a wary step toward him, felt a small sense of relief when he didn't tense or take on a defense posture. Forcing herself to give him her practiced, professional smile, she let the gun dangle at her side as she crossed the threshold into the bedroom and stopped, her little toe next to the bullet. "No one else needs to get hurt. I give up. What is it you want me to do?"

Nothing in his face changed, but she saw his pupils dilate. He was in exploitation mode—in control once again.

He held out his hand. "Give me the gun, cyborg."

Cyborg. It almost made her laugh. Maybe Mitch was right. Maybe everyone was right and she was wrong. Chris Goodsman was a nutcase.

She had no choice. She was going to have to jump him. If she handed him the weapon, she was done.

Hesitantly, she held out the S&W, not enough for him to reach it, but enough to make him think he'd won. "Don't hurt anyone else, okay? I'll come with you. I'll do whatever you want. You can kill me in front of your Resistance fighters if you want. Show them what a great leader you are."

The words made her want to gag—she was a terrible actress and couldn't believe when Chris took the bait, stepping forward. "I'd hoped you would see the light."

"I do. I see the light now," she lied. *Come on, come on. Closer...*

Just as he touched the gun, ready to take it from her, she let go of an ear-piercing scream and swung it at his head.

He must have anticipated it, because he ducked to the side, the gun barely grazing his ear.

But Emma's body was in motion and she tackled him, knocking him onto the bed. His elbow connected with her temple, pain exploding behind her left eye.

Her arm had its own agenda, like it had with Linda, rising up and pummeling him with the gun again, this time, making contact with his hand as he bought it up to block the attack.

She heard a bone crack, the force of his hand driving hers and the gun back several inches. He didn't seem fazed, grabbing her by the throat and squeezing.

Spots danced in her peripheral vision as she scratched at his vise grip with her free hand. An evil grin split his face as he squeezed tighter, lifting her off his chest. She couldn't breathe, her hand on the gun loosening.

Rage poured through her again, burning in her veins and lighting her up from within. With her free hand, she reached down and clawed at his grin, her already bloody nails digging into his movie-star handsome face.

With a yelp, he threw her off to the side. She hit the edge of the bed, rolled, and belly-flopped onto the floor.

Her ribs cried out in pain and she gasped for air, coaxing her throat to work. Above her, Chris swore loudly, calling her names, the bed bouncing as his weight shifted to come after her.

Move!

That's when she spotted the two bullets. Under the bed.

Knocking part of the draping sheet out of the way, Emma scooted under the box spring and reached for a bullet.

"What the fuck?" she heard Chris say as she flipped open the chamber.

Her fingers shook so bad, she dropped the bullet. Twice. The shadows under the bed made it difficult to see. In her peripheral vision, however, Chris's booted feet weren't.

He dropped onto his knees, throwing the sheet back and bending down to eye her, that awful grin on his face again. The bullet slipped around in her fingers, her throat sucked air, making her wheeze.

The added light from Chris lifting the sheet landed on something under the bed she hadn't noticed until now.

A dozen or so green Tom Monahan Resistance soldiers, some in a line, others fallen over as if a child had just been playing with them, sat like a prop in a movie.

Oh my God, he was here, under my bed. Chris Goodsman had been under her bed playing with toy soldiers.

For how long? The possibilities filled with her revulsion.

A hand slid toward her. "Come here, you little bitch."

Emma's fingers stopped their shaking. The bullet slid home into the chamber with a satisfying *clink*. She flicked the cylinder closed and aimed at Chris the same moment as he lunged and grabbed her leg.

She hollered, her body shifting as he dragged her toward him, her arm flying off target.

She righted her arm, aimed once more as he tugged her legs out from under the bed.

One shot. *Don't blow it!*

Taking a deep breath, Emma imagined the eye of the bird on the can she had shot only a few days ago under Mitch's tutelage. *Let everything else fall away.*

As Chris pulled her the rest of the way out from under the bed, Emma pulled the trigger.

244

CHAPTER TWENTY-ONE

Mitch heard the gunshot and his heart stopped.

Emma.

Not only had Cooper and the others arrived, so had the county sheriff's CSI techs—finally—and a woman claiming she was Emma's veterinarian. Will had vouched for the doctor, and she had started rounding up the horses, saying she would help Will care for them until Emma could come home from the safe house.

Mitch's feet moved on their own accord, sprinting for the house, his heartbeat pounding in his ears.

The dogs barked behind him, people yelled at him. He had the sense that the dogs and several of the men—Cooper, Nelson, and Will—were following.

In the distance, he heard the solid *whap-whap-whap* of a helicopter's blades.

Or maybe that was his heart, a heavy, bass drum pounding out dread.

The long lane was full of mud-filled ruts. Mitch hopped some, ran straight through the larger ones. He tore past the juvie van, catching a whiff of the dead man inside, all of his senses heightened and firing off messages his brain didn't like.

"Emma!" he yelled, hitting the door into the kitchen.

The dogs ran past him as he hesitated and glanced toward the mudroom, the pantry. He kept hauling.

Living room. Nope. No Emma. Broken glass still covered the floor, bullets embedded in the walls.

The other men hit the kitchen as Mitch tore up the stairs. His gun was already in his hand, sweat mixed with rain running down the back of his neck. "Emma!"

"In here," he heard her soft voice calling from her bedroom.

His muddy boots skidded on the wood floor as he tried to stop his forward projection on the landing. He nearly slid right past the bedroom door. Salt and Pepper came to stand on either side of him as Mitch finally righted himself in the doorway.

"Jesus," was all he could say at the sight that met his eyes.

Emma sat in her underwear on the side of her bed, staring down at a man with a bullet hole between his eyebrows. Blood pooled under the man's head as his unseeing eyes stared up at the ceiling.

Chris Goodsman.

She raised her gaze to Mitch, her body teetering uncertainly, her face as white as Salt's fur. She stuck out a hand to balance herself and Mitch saw the gun lying next to her. "He was under the bed, playing with his Tom Monahan figurines."

She shivered hard, her face filled with revulsion.

"Jesus," he said again.

He walked into the room, eager to get to her, but checked Goodsman for weapons first. The man had a camping knife on a belt around his waist, but didn't appear to have anything else.

The dogs stayed in the doorway, noses lifted at the scent of blood. Salt growled low and deep in her throat. The other men clattered up the stairs, and Cooper yelled, "Holden?"

"First room on your left," he called, turning to Emma, the body still between them. "Are you all right?"

Emma reached over and pulled a blanket toward her. "I'm..."

A scream split the air, a banshee cry if Mitch had ever heard one. He jerked toward the bathroom to see a flash of brown clothes, frizzy hair, and a lifted arm coming at Emma full-throttle.

"What have you done?" the banshee screamed.

The glint of light on metal, the arc of the knife slicing through the air.

Everything went into slow motion. Mitch jumped across Goodsman's body, throwing himself toward the bed, but Emma—strong, determined, protective Emma—was already up, gun in hand, as Linda brought the knife down.

For some reason, Emma threw the gun at Brown instead of firing. The gun hit the knife, sending the knife off center, but Brown instantly counterbalanced, whirled in a martial arts circle and drove the knife into Emma's chest.

"No!" Mitch hollered, firing his own weapon and hitting Brown square in the throat.

Two other shots were fired as well, Brown's body jerking from Cooper's and Nelson's bullets.

She was dead before she hit the floor.

"Emma." Mitch fell to his knees beside her.

The knife was lodged deep, up and under her left ribcage. Blood gushed down her stomach, her side.

Her eyes were wide, staring up at him as she tried to say something. He sensed Cooper and Nelson moving into the room, pulling Brown and Goodsman aside, shoving the bed out of the way. From the doorway, Will said, "I'll get Doc Jane."

Heavy footsteps on the stairs. Women's voices down in the kitchen. "What's going on? Who's hurt?"

Nelson moved in beside Mitch. "Don't pull the knife out. Too close to the heart. Might have nicked something."

Above him, Mitch heard the *whomping* noise of the helo again, felt the sound vibrating inside his chest where his heart had stopped beating.

"That's Dupé." Cooper came out of the bathroom with towels and tossed them to Nelson. "Wrap her up and get her on that helo. I'll radio ahead to the hospital and have them on standby."

The voices, the helicopter noise...all of it receded as Mitch stared down into Emma's hazel eyes, fluttering to stay open.

"Hang in there, doc," he murmured as he tucked a towel around the knife wound. His movements were stiff. Once again, the threat of slipping back into the past and the horror of the day he'd lost Mac threatened to take him under.

"I..." she said, then licked her lips and grimaced as she reached for his hand. "Don't leave me, okay?"

Leave her? He would never leave her.

But he wasn't the one dying.

She was.

Her body trembled, probably from shock. "I'm cold."

Mac had left him. Their father had left them. Their mother had left Mitch emotionally a long time ago, his brother's death only making it more pronounced.

He yanked the blanket off the bed. "Help is on the way."

"I did...what you said..." One side of her lips lifted in a tired smile. "I aimed for the eye." And then her face sobered. "I didn't want to kill him, Mitch. I didn't...but..."

"You had to. I know." He brushed a strand of hair away from her face. "You did the right thing, Doc. He wouldn't have stopped until he killed you."

Her eyes closed. Her chest heaved and blood ran from the corner of her mouth. "So tired."

"Emma." Mitch leaned over and gave her a gentle pat on the face. "Stay with me. Keep your eyes open."

"Come on," Nelson said, giving Mitch's shoulder a squeeze. "Cooper went down to tell Dupé we need the helicopter. Let's get the good doctor here to the hospital."

Mitch hadn't realized it but Nelson had stripped the bed sheets and laid them on the floor. Carefully, they worked together to wrap them around Emma.

They heard more heavy footsteps on the stairs and Cooper entered with Dupé and the helicopter pilot, who was carrying a stretcher.

"What the living hell?" Dupé said, taking in the scene, his face tight with anger.

Mitch and Nelson gently loaded Emma onto the stretcher. "She's been knifed in the chest," Mitch said, even though it seemed obvious from the hilt still sticking out from her upper body. "She needs immediate medical attention."

The man's dark eyes cut to his. "You were supposed to keep her safe."

Bile rose in his throat. Anger, hot and potent. "I…failed."

The director shifted aside and motioned at them impatiently. "Get her into my chopper."

The veterinarian appeared in the doorway, her face blanching as she took in Emma's condition. "Oh, dear God. Is she alive? What can I do?"

"If you know anything about knife wounds, you can ride with her in the helicopter to the hospital," Mitch said as she moved aside and he and Nelson swung the stretcher into the hall. "Otherwise, stay here and help Will."

It took careful finagling to get Emma down the stairs and outside. The vet ran alongside confessing to Mitch that she didn't feel qualified to handle this type of emergency, but that she would do her best to stabilize Emma until they got to the hospital.

With the stretcher inside the tight quarters of the helicopter, there was only room for the doctor and Director Dupé. Having secured her in with the help of the pilot, Mitch was about to back out when Emma's hand grabbed hold of his shirt.

He looked over and saw her lips moving, but he couldn't hear what she was saying over the noise of the blades.

Leaning down, he gave her hand a squeeze. "You're going to be okay," he yelled over the noise.

She said something again and he put his ear close to hers. "What?"

"I love…you."

His head snapped up and he met her eyes. *Love*, that one little word making his heart swell and recoil at the same time.

He opened his mouth to respond, saw her eyes go fuzzy and roll up into her head.

Shit. He had to let the chopper go. Get her to decent medical care.

Letting go of her hand, he hung his head for a brief moment. *If she dies...*

Mitch climbed out of the helicopter and faced Dupé who was about to climb in. He stuck his arm out, barring the director from his seat.

"I want to ride with her," he yelled, ignoring a hollowness inside him that made it hard to breathe.

Dupé's brows crashed together as he bent over from the wash of the blades. Behind him, Cooper and the others watched somberly. The CSI techs were half-watching too, as they processed the van's crime scene. Will, standing on the porch with the dogs looked on with a grim countenance.

"Please," Mitch insisted. When was the last time he'd said *that* word to a superior? He didn't even say it to his mother anymore. "Collins is still my responsibility, sir, and I don't intend to let her die."

Dupé brushed his jacket back, a muscle in his jaw jumping.

"We're ready, Director," the pilot called.

Mitch was sure Dupé was going to tell him to get out of the way, when instead, the director's gaze flicked to his chest. "Are you wearing my shirt?" he yelled.

Mitch's blood ran cold. "*Your* shirt?"

Dupé gave him a curt nod and waved him off. "Get in the chopper, son, and don't make me regret this."

He was wearing Victor Dupé's shirt.

Victor Dupé, the man who had helped Emma through Christmas last year. Helped her grieve.

Mitch shut down the jealousy and transplanted the veterinarian, hustling her into the seat next to the pilot as he took up a position next to Emma.

The pilot handed both of them headsets.

"I can't help her from here," the doctor said as she spoke into the microphone.

Mitch clasped Emma's hand between his own. "Tell me what to do. I'll keep her alive."

The vet gave him a pointed look, but she must have seen the determination and downright stubbornness on his face. She nodded, and as she began reeling off instructions, they lifted into the air.

Six hours later, Emma was still in surgery. The injury was serious; she'd lost a lot of blood before they'd gotten her to the ER. If it had happened a few hours earlier, when Dupé was nowhere near and the others hadn't arrived, she would be dead.

That thought churned in Mitch's head as he paced the halls, dead on his feet, but unable to sit still.

He'd sworn he'd never let anyone else die on his watch. He'd finally allowed himself love again and that incredible person had nearly lost her life because he hadn't been paying attention.

He stopped in a dark section of the surgical floor and banged his forehead against the concrete wall. Emma wasn't out of the woods yet and if she *did* die...

Well then, he was going back to the cemetery, laying down next to Mac's grave with his gun in hand, and ending it all. He was done. Done with loving people. Done with living. Because there was no way he could survive the pain of losing her. Emma—the only woman who'd ever looked inside his screwed up brain and not judged him. Not felt sorry for him.

The one woman who hadn't tried to fix him.

Maybe she should have.

But no, there was no fixing him and the good doctor was smart enough to know it.

Mitch spun around and sagged against the wall, his chin falling to his chest. He was too tired, too burned out. His hands had Emma's dried blood on them. Emma's blood covered his shirt too.

Not mine. Dupé's.

"What the hell are you doing?" Cooper Harris growled from the end of the hallway.

The big guy stood with his feet planted and his face screwed up. He looked ready to knock Mitch's head into the wall.

Too late. Already done that. "I'm brooding. Leave me the fuck alone."

"God, you're an idiot." Cooper strode forward and joined Mitch on the wall. "Crime scene's been processed, the proper authorities notified. Goodsman's death will hit the media shortly. Dupé has suppressed the details about Collins in order to keep her from being a target of the actor's fans, but there's no guarantee it won't leak. High-profile case like this? Celebrity involvement? People are going to demand to know what happened and who was involved."

And I can't keep her safe. "She won't leave the ranch."

"You should talk to her about upping her security measures."

"Already did. She thinks her dogs and her shotgun are all she needs."

"Maybe she'll be more inclined to listen after this."

His gut churned. *If she lives.* "I'm sure Dupé can change her mind."

"Yeah, about that. The director wants to speak to you. He's downstairs."

His career was over. *Should have been over the day Mac died.* "I'm not leaving the surgical floor until Emma does. If Dupé wants to talk to me, he'll have to come up here."

"I thought you'd say that, Agent Holden."

Mitch and Cooper both looked left. The director stood in almost the same spot Coop had, his hands on his waist. His dark hair was combed back, his suit freshly pressed, his cheeks shiny from a recent shave.

Mitch pushed off the wall, a sudden hot rebellion propelling its way up from his gut into his chest. He faced the director. "I put her here and I'm staying until I know she's okay."

"She's a unique woman, isn't she?"

The words bloomed in his mouth. "I think I'm in love with her."

If Dupé was surprised, he hid it well. "She sent me an email earlier. I didn't get it until a minute ago. Apparently, she seems to think highly of you as well."

A thick lump formed in his throat. "I never wanted this to happen. I thought Goodsman and Brown were long gone. Will and I took out the other two and I was set to get her to the safe house, and then..."

Dupé came forward, closing the distance. Mitch saw the condemnation in the man's eyes. "I hear you saved her horses."

Really? That was what he was going to pick a bone about? "Yeah, I saved the goddamn horses because Emma was going to risk her own life if I didn't."

Cooper left off the wall and came to stand beside Mitch. "Holden never signed on to play bodyguard, sir, and I take responsibility for not backing him up sooner. Regardless, I'm keeping him on my team."

Regardless. The word seemed to hang in the air. Regardless of what Dupé wanted? The taskforce was the director's puppy. His pride and joy. He only wanted the best of the best on it.

Mitch was definitely not that.

Mitch turned to glare at Cooper. "You're not to blame, and you shouldn't want me on your team after this fuck-up. I'm a screwed up SOB and I'm no good to anyone."

Cooper started to respond and Dupé interrupted. "Neither of you are to blame." He rubbed his forehead and looked exasperated. "And if you'd shut up and stop throwing yourselves on your swords, I might be able to get a word in edgewise."

Mitch and Cooper exchanged a look, both of them zipping it.

"Good," Dupé said. "Even though I'm keeping her name out

of the media, it won't be hard for some of Goodsman's fans to figure it out. The doctor is going to need extra protection for a while."

Silence hung. Mitch looked at Cooper again, but the man shrugged. He had no idea what Dupé was suggesting either.

The director put an arm around Mitch's shoulders. "Let's take a walk, Agent Holden. I have a proposition for you."

CHAPTER TWENTY-TWO

Click, click, click…

Emma woke with the taste of blood in her mouth. Metallic, bitter. Her jaw tightened. She wanted to spit.

But her head felt too heavy to turn, her lips too dry to purse. Her brain floated inside her skull, unfocused, fuzzy—an abnormal feeling that scared her on some primitive level. She wasn't the floaty, unfocused type.

Click, click, click… the sound reverberated inside her skull, adrenaline firing somewhere in her solar plexus. But the rest of her weighed 200 pounds. Her chest didn't want to inflate, and when she forced it to, pain radiated from her ribcage, pulsing with every beat of her heart. Her ribs seemed to have a band around them. When she tried to open her eyes, her eyelids felt leaden and unresponsive.

The clicking gave way to a distant beeping sound. The sound triggered a memory of white sheets, nurses.

Sedatives sending her into a free-float.

A hollow ache in her lower abdomen.

Agony clawing at her heart.

The baby.

Her chest hiccupped, hands digging into the bed. The action sent a spike of adrenaline through her system and another memory clicked into place.

She was in the hospital again, but her heart didn't feel like it had been ripped to shreds. She didn't feel empty inside...if anything, she felt...satisfied.

That couldn't be right.

Something had ended, but not the life of an innocent, unborn child. Whatever that something was, it gave her peace.

For a moment, she gave herself over to the floaty feeling. Letting go felt good. She didn't want to think, didn't want to be stuck in the past, remembering Skye's death.

The darkness tugged at her, promising peaceful sleep. Her body longed for it, reminding her of her post Mitch-induced orgasms—a buoyant sensation as if she were defying gravity.

Mitch.

Her chest hitched again, and it took three tries, but she managed to pry her eyelids open. Everything was blurry and she shut her eyes against the light coming through the window, the monitor beeping along with her pulse rate as anxiety tripped under her skin.

"Hey, beautiful."

The voice sounded far away, but happiness filled her. The owner of that reassuring voice took her hand and gave it a squeeze.

Biting her lip, she forced her eyes open. Forced them to stay that way as Mitch's face swam into view, hovering above her. "MMM—Mitch?"

Her voice cracked, his name only a whisper.

He brought her hand up to his lips, kissed her knuckles. "Boy, am I glad to see those crazy eyes of yours."

"Crazy..."—she had to swallow—"eyes?"

He chuckled. "The first time I saw you, I couldn't decide if your eyes were green or brown. You were standing in the light of your porch light and those eyes totally mesmerized me, Emma. I fell for them first, then the rest of you in quick succession."

Her brain tried to follow his words, but the connections were a mess of gossamer threads that stretched, tangled, and broke apart the more she forced her brain to function. The only thing that popped into her mind was a fact. "They're hazel."

Her voice was scratchy, like she hadn't used it in eons. He released his grip on her and disappeared from view for a moment, then came back with a paper cup filled with water.

He maneuvered the straw to her lips. "Have a drink, but go easy. You've been heavily sedated and your stomach's empty."

Even the slight movement of lifting her head made her flinch, but the water tasted so much better than the metallic tang in her mouth. She sipped greedily.

"Not too much, Doc."

Mitch pulled back and got rid of the cup, coming back to sit on the edge of her hospital bed. Her hand instinctively found his again, some of the heaviness leaving her as she tried on a smile.

He smiled back and they stayed that way for a few moments. Behind his smile, she sensed sadness, regret. There were dark circles under his eyes. His jawline was covered with several days' worth of beard.

How long had she been out? Why did Mitch look so sad?

"What happened?" she finally asked, dread threading its way around her heart.

His thumb rubbed the sensitive flesh of her palm. "You tell me. You were upstairs getting ready to go to the safe house. Next thing I know, I heard a gunshot. I found you sitting on your bed, Chris Goodsman at your feet with a bullet in his forehead."

A sinking feeling filled her stomach. "I killed him?"

"You don't remember?"

Closing her eyes, she willed her brain to work. *Click, click, click*...the sound echoed in her ears. In flashes, the scene came back to her. "I was in the bathroom. I came out and Chris was sitting on my bed. Linda took the bullets out of my gun."

Her breath hitched, sending fresh pain through her system.

Mitch touched her arm. "Hey, it's okay. We can talk about it later. You need to rest."

"No." Her voice came out firmer. She opened her eyes. "I need to remember."

He nodded and waited patiently, letting her think it through. In her mind's eye, she let the scene play out. "The bullets fell all over the floor. The gun was worthless."

"How did you manage to shoot him, then?" Mitch asked softly.

"I jumped him. We wrestled. I ended up on the floor and I crawled under the bed and found a bullet. That's where..." She swallowed hard. "That's where I saw the army men. The Tom Monahan fighters. Like he'd been under there playing with them."

Tears flooded her eyes. She felt violated all over again.

The same disgust she felt rolled through Mitch's eyes. "Are you sure it was him? Might have been Brown."

"I managed to get the bullet in the gun. Chris bent down and grabbed me by the foot and pulled me out, so I..."

She couldn't finish the statement.

"You did what you had to do, Emma." He squeezed her hand, letting her process her conflicted feelings, a sentiment he knew all too well, and continued. "Will found Goodsman's hideout. He and Brown were camped in that abandoned ranger site. Coop said that must have been where Sean Gordon squatted as well. As we suspected, Gordon and Brown probably set the fire—there were dozens of files there, meteorology reports, past forest fire analyses, and detailed park security measures so they could figure out how and where to get in and out without getting spotted, and the best place to start the fires in order to send them in the direction of the public. Our guess is, that if your ranch got caught in the crossfire—no pun intended—Brown would have been quite happy about it."

Her head hurt remembering. "Are the horses okay? Did Will get them rounded up?"

"The horses and the dogs are fine. Doc Jane is helping Will at the ranch. At least she's trying to help him. They seemed to rub each other the wrong way a lot."

"They're perfect for each other." The thought made Emma smile. "They just haven't figured it out yet. I'm working on it—or at least I will be once I'm up and out of here."

"Let's not rush anything. Brown nearly killed you, Emma."

The knife. Another flood of memories wiped the smile from her face. "How bad is it?" she asked, placing a hand on her ribcage.

"She sliced through your inferior vena cava. You were in surgery for fourteen hours."

No wonder he looked tired and she felt like road kill. "You stayed here the whole time, didn't you?"

His face was all hard lines. "It's my fault Brown and Goodsman got to you."

It wasn't just sadness behind his eyes. Guilt lingered there as well. "Don't do that to yourself. This is no more your fault than it is Will's or mine or the man on the moon's."

He looked down, a muscle in his jaw flexing. "The other man has been identified as Roger Colfax. He's the one who killed Carla and injured Danika. You might know him as—"

"Punisher." The instant Mitch had said Roger's name, Emma stiffened. The Punisher, a Marvel comic moniker that the *Mary Monahan Chronicles* had borrowed. A character whom thousands of fans had embraced because of his vigilante tendencies. "I'm quite familiar with him."

Her tone made Mitch give her a questioning look. "Did you analyze Colfax somewhere along the line?"

Ice encased her heart. Her teeth chattered and she ground them together for a moment before she could speak. "I had a very *personal* run-in with him once."

Understanding creased Mitch's features. "Ah, jeez, Emma. Colfax is the guy who broke into your house two years ago, isn't he? The guy you shot?"

She nodded, her head cold now too. Every part of her

was covered in ice. Soon, she wouldn't be able to breathe.

"Hey." Mitch rubbed her arm, touched her cheek. "He's in jail for a good long time. He can't hurt you."

Except in her dreams. The Punisher would keep returning in those. Skye would keep dying.

Fiddling with the sheet, she blinked back the deluge of tears threatening to fall. "This isn't your fault, Mitch. None of it. I brought all this on. Me and my crusade to prove Chris Goodsman was a sociopath. Skye should be alive. Danika shouldn't be fighting for her life."

"Danika's fine." Mitch shifted his hand over to the opposite railing. He hovered over her again, a frown deepening the crease in his forehead. "I saw her not two hours ago and she was eating ice cream and pretending she had a concussion so she didn't have to go back to juvie. She asked about you and Twinkie. Wanted to know when she could come out to the ranch for her next session."

It was Emma's turn to frown. "She still wants to come for therapy?"

Mitch nodded. "She loves you, Doc, in case you didn't realize it. You and Will and the horses."

"Did you tell her about the barn?"

"Nah. By the time you get home and she's allowed to come back, you'll have a new one, anyway."

"What?"

"Cooper and the gang are hanging out for a week. Because of the holidays, our caseload is light and Director Dupé gave his okay to help you out. They've already cleared the site and the supplies for a new barn are being delivered today. I don't guarantee the quality of workmanship—we're talking about a bunch of federal agents, here, not carpenters, but Will says he's got it under control. Apparently, his father was in construction, so he knows a thing or two about buildings."

Emma's heart felt light. "A new barn. What do you know? The horses are going to love that."

"Doc Jane says she has a lead on another horse for you, too. A rescue a few miles north. She's not that old, but she has special needs because of neglect."

Emma scooted herself up a bit in the bed, ignoring the pain cutting through her chest. "How soon is the doctor going to release me?"

"Hold on there, tiger." Mitch put his hands on her arms, forcing her back down. "You're not going anywhere for a while."

"But I need to get that horse."

"I figured you'd say that. Victor and I've already taken care of it."

"Victor?"

"Yeah, we're on first name basis now, thanks to you. I gave him back his shirt by the way."

"Oh. He told you?"

Mitch smirked and something sparked low in Emma's belly. "He told me. Like you said, he's a friend. Someone who cares a lot about you. I get that, believe me. I care about you, too."

"You do?"

He leaned over and kissed her softly. "Of course, I do. You know that."

She touched the side of his face. The sadness in his eyes was back and she suddenly understood why. "You're going back to work for him, aren't you?"

"He and I are picking up the horse tonight. Dr. Jane made the arrangements. Will's already got a spot for her fenced off in the pasture."

Her heart loved him so much. "You answered my question by omission. How very Mitch of you."

He grinned and sat back. "Yes, Emma, I'm going to continue working for the taskforce. At least for now."

"So you'll be going to San Diego or wherever your next undercover operation takes you." She swallowed hard, forcing nonchalance into her voice. "That's great. Victor needs agents like you."

"I'm not so sure about that. I failed big time at protecting you."

"You tried repeatedly to get me off the ranch, and I refused almost as many. The fires shut down the roads, but I suppose in your warped way of thinking, you should have forced me to leave and somehow magically transported me to that safe house. Is that correct, Agent Holden?"

"Are we back to last names?"

A protection mechanism. "You saved me and my horses and Danika. I'll never forget that."

His grin faded. "You may not like my new assignment."

She was sure she wouldn't. "You'll handle it with flying colors, but honestly, Mitch, I think you should get counseling to deal with your PTSD surrounding your brother's death before you take on undercover work."

"Victor agrees."

Her brows went up. "You told him about the flashbacks?"

"Yeah, after he offered me to stay on as your bodyguard. He thought we might both benefit from a few sessions."

"Bodyguard? I don't understand."

"He's kept your name out of the media for the time being, but it won't take much for it to leak out or for some other Tom Monahan superfan to go Linda Brown on us and come after you. So unless you're willing to sell the ranch and go into hiding, you're going to need to increase your personal security. For the next few months at least, part of that security is me."

A grin broke over her face. "I'm your new assignment?"

"Yes, ma'am."

Words escaped her and her eyes finally let go of the tears she'd been suppressing.

"If you're that upset about it, I can get you a different one," Mitch teased.

Emma found the strength to swat his arm. Then she dashed her hands at the tears on her cheeks. "I can't be your therapist."

"To hell with that. I've already got about five fantasies I

want to act out." He reached over to the side table and brought back a bag of M&Ms and set it on her stomach. "One of them involves these."

Her mouth watered. "Fantasies are not therapy."

"They are if they involve you. Everything about you is therapy for me."

"I guess you can help with the horses," she teased, eyeing the candy, "in exchange for room and board."

"I can cook, too, remember?"

For a moment, they simply smiled at each other. Then Emma reached out and drew him in close. "I love you, Mitch Holden. I hope I'm going to need your bodyguard services for a long time."

"I love you, too, Doc." He kissed her gently, deeply. "And I'm pretty sure I'm going to need therapy for the rest of my life."

"I'll look at my schedule and see if I can fit you in."

He chuckled. "Good, because every Christmas from here on out, I'm going to be in your bed, making you a happy woman."

"I think I might actually like the holidays again."

He gently coaxed her body to the side and climbed into the bed next to her, the bag of candies rattling as he fit his big body around hers. "Me, too, Doc. Me too."

Emma snuggled into him and let the floaty, happy feeling take her away.

CHAPTER TWENTY-THREE

Three months later

The timer went off and Emma and Mitch exchanged a look. Outside the dogs were playing Frisbee with Will and Jane. Danika was due for her normal Wednesday session any minute. Second Chance and Hope were running in the pasture as Zig Zag, the new horse, chased them playfully.

"I can't look," Emma said, covering her eyes with her hands. Her stomach was tied in knots. This couldn't be happening. "You do it."

Mitch peeled one of her hands away from her face. "We'll do it together."

He drew her off the bed and toward the bathroom where the little white stick sat on the vanity. He stopped, bent forward and squinted. "Oh boy."

Emma snuck a peek over his shoulder. "Or girl."

Mitch picked her up, twirling her in his arms and making her squeal. "Congratulations, Doc. Looks like we're adding to your menagerie."

Miracles really did happen, because that's what this was. After miscarrying Skye, the doctor had told her she'd never have another child, and yet, here she was with a very clear plus sign on the pregnancy stick. "I can't believe it."

Mitch kissed her, set her down, and said, "A plus sign means positive. I read that to you six times. Guess my considerable skills extend even farther than I realized."

"Not sure you should list impregnating the barren on your resume, Holden."

"Seriously? I mean, you have to admit, that's pretty impressive shit."

She laughed, enjoying the teasing light in his eyes. She saw that a lot more these days, the past having less hold on him. He was focused on the future now. So was she.

"We should call your mom."

Mitch grimaced. "She'll be here next week. I'd rather break the news in person, if you don't mind. She's going to freak and ask a million questions, and well, you know how she is."

The mother and son were on the road to reconciling, and Emma had learned a lot about what made each of them tick. Their mutual love for Mac had initially torn them apart; now, it was forging a bond between them. The baby would no doubt strengthen that.

"How about we call your parents?" Mitch said.

"Later." Emma grabbed his hand and tugged him along after her. "I think Will and Jane should be the first to know."

The spring had been a wet one so far, the wildfires already a distant memory as the hills and valleys bloomed with new life.

As she and Mitch stood on the front porch, the dogs came running, all except Lady, who stayed by Will's side.

Jane looked over, face flushed with fun. She put a hand up to shade her face from the sun. "What's up? You coming out to play?"

Will stalked toward them, a frown on his face. "Everything okay?"

He was always on alert, much like Mitch. So far, Emma's name hadn't made it into the papers or onto the Internet in connection with Chris's death. Victor had spun the story, and the world believed Linda Brown had killed Chris. Fans of their series were devastated, both that their hero was dead and that a woman who claimed to be his number one fan and believed she was the legitimate mother of Tom Monahan, had been the killer.

Cyborgs. They were everywhere.

While she had no doubt Linda had been a stone-cold murderer, there were times when Emma wondered if she'd misdiagnosed Chris. She'd been so sure he was fooling her colleagues, but after finding those toy soldiers under her bed, she now had doubts.

If it hadn't been Chris, it had been Linda playing with those action figurines. Either way, she knew between the two of them, they had planned to kill her. Because of their actions, several good men had died. Danika had almost died as well.

Sociopath or just a damn good actor? She would never know for sure, but a part of her stuck to her original diagnosis. She knew criminals and she trusted her training and her gut instincts. Like Mitch had said to her a dozen times before, some people were just fuckin' crazy.

Standing there on the porch, she grinned as Mitch wrapped his arms around her waist. "We have an announcement."

Jane caught up to Will and the two of them stopped at the bottom of the steps. Lady laid down at Will's feet and the veteran and veterinarian both stared at them. Jane clapped her hands together. "Wait, let me guess. You're getting married!"

Mitch made a face and looked at Emma. "Are we getting married? We probably should, shouldn't we?"

Emma rolled her eyes. "It's not a bad idea. Children who grow up with loving parents don't care about a marriage certificate in most cases, but research has found that it does lend a level of security to them."

"Wait," Will said, frowning. "Children?"

Emma beamed. "We're pregnant."

Jane squealed and ran up the steps to hug Emma. Will climbed the steps, too, and shook Mitch's hand.

"Congrats," the man said. He patted Emma on the shoulder, but he didn't meet her eyes. "I'm happy for you, Doc."

She grabbed his hand before he could pull away. "You've brought me a lot of luck, Will Longram. I hope you're up for babysitting."

One of his eyebrows disappeared under his hat. "I don't know anything about kids."

Jane squeezed his arm and leaned into him. "You didn't know anything about horses, either, when you first came to work for Emma. Now, look at you. You're running this place. Emma's right, you've brought a lot of good here with you."

He peeled her hand off his arm and slipped down the steps. "That girl will be here in a minute. I better get Twinkie ready."

"Harry," Mitch called after him. "How many times do I have to say it? His name is Harry."

Emma and Jane laughed. "Don't let him name your kid," Jane said to her.

Mitch looked indignant. "What's wrong with Harry?"

Jane rolled her eyes and left them on the porch. "Time for me to get back to my real job. I'll see you kids later for dinner."

The four of them had plans that night to take a trip into town for a quick bite and a movie. Emma now had the urge to do some baby shopping as well. "We'll meet you at the restaurant. I want to go into town early for a couple of errands."

Jane waved. "See you there."

As her truck pulled away down the drive, Mitch gave Emma a quizzical look. "What errands? Or is this another undercover run to the lingerie store for me, Dr. Collins?"

He did love his lingerie and their little fantasy sessions. She had one scheduled for them that afternoon. "I still have a stack of sexy stuff to show you. I want to get some things for the baby."

"We don't even know if we're having a boy or a girl."

"Does it matter?"

Mitch drew her into his arms for a kiss. "Anything you want, Emma. I'm up for all of it."

She was too. "Good. Let's get married next week when your mom is here."

He laughed long and deep. "You sure you want to marry a mixed up, crazy-assed guy like me?"

"Oh, yes," Emma said, kissing him back. "You're my kind of crazy."

In case you missed the first book in the
SCVC Taskforce Series...

DEADLY PURSUIT

by Misty Evans

"Take your gun, Davenport." Chief Forester's voice was low and ominous, rising out of the back seat of the car where he was hiding. Not an easy thing to do, Celina figured, with so much body mass.

Bending down, she motioned at her partner Ronni in the passenger seat and shucked off her mittens. "Give me your bag."

Celina rarely carried handbags to work. She hung her badge on her belt like her male counterparts and carried her ID in her back pocket. Her gun was always in a shoulder holster. Now her gun, ID and badge were lying on the Fairmont's floor. "Avon ladies don't carry guns," she murmured to her boss. "At least not in Iowa."

Ronni handed Celina her brown leather purse and the Avon catalog. "Right behind you," she said, giving her a wink.

"Take. Your. Gun," the chief ground out again. His voice carried as much threat in its low volume setting as it did at its ear-piercing level. "You want to end up a goddamned hostage?"

That was her plan. Celina knew when she approached the door, Annie would immediately sense something was up. Something in Annie's world always involved police. Celina could see no other outcome but a dangerous hostage situation. She doubted Annie would even open the door, but if she did, Celina was going to offer herself as a trade for Annie's kids. Any mother, even an outlaw one, would look for a way to save her children. Celina was prepared to give it to her.

Slinging the strap of Ronni's bag over her shoulder, she shut the car door, defying the chief's direct orders. Not the best idea, but he'd stuck her in a no-win situation and therefore, Celina decided, she was calling the shots. For a split-second she wondered if he and Quarters would transfer her like Cooper had after the Londano case. Where would she end up this time? South Dakota?

Probably.

Not the end of the world. If I can get the kids out safely, she thought, that will be enough.

Shifting her shoulders, Celina forced her feet to walk up the cracked sidewalk toward the steps of the duplex. She loved her job, wanted to serve her country, but if there was anything she'd learned in the past year, it was that she didn't always get what she wanted.

Ronni's car door slammed and Celina glanced at her partner. Her hair was a bright apricot color, her skin darker than Celina's but no less smooth. As they walked down the sidewalk, the sun popped out, glaring off the new fallen snow. Celina started up the stairs, shielding her eyes against the glare and trying to keep her breathing even. There were fifteen of her counterparts hidden around the block, watching the apprehension and scrutinizing every move she made.

Annie was one honest to God bad girl. Having been on the run for more years than Celina had been legal, Annie was an experienced fugitive. The woman had once shot her partner in his nether region in the middle of a bank robbery because he wouldn't let her carry the bag of money.

Clearing her mind, Celina tried to think positive. Ronni was by her side and definitely carrying. Chief Forester was right behind her in the car for immediate backup with his Remington, and the other guys were scattered up and down the block. All had extensive training in marksmanship and deadly-force decisions.

Voices from a television filtered through the door. Muffled laughter drifted down from upstairs. Little girl laughter. She had to do this right, not to prove that she was as good as any of the men in the unit, but to keep those little girls safe.

Glancing at Ronni, Celina mouthed Ready? Ronni gave her a

nod. Do it.

Celina knocked sharply on the door. "Avon calling," she said, trying to mimic the singsong voice Ronni had used earlier when they'd decided to approach the house under this outdated guise.

At first nothing noticeable changed inside the house. Then the TV went silent and Celina heard a man's voice, low but commanding. A man? No one had reported a man being inside the duplex.

Before she could consider who or what she was now up against, Celina saw a drapery move in the window to her right. Instinctively, she shifted her weight and her hand went for her gun.

And came up empty.

Before she could curse her poor judgment, the door handle turned and her eyes dropped to it. Watch their hands, the words of her Quantico instructor echoed in her head. Not their eyes. No one could shoot you with their eyes.

"Don't want no Avon," a man's voice said as the door opened a notch.

A fragment of sun bounced off metal. Instinct had Celina moving before she could think. "Gun!" she yelled, pushing Ronni to the side.

The sawed-off shotgun boomed in her ears and the iron railing gave out as Ronni and Celina toppled off the porch and into the dead evergreens by the house. They landed with a thud on hard ground next to the concrete foundation. A thousand prickly evergreen needles showered down on them as they rolled in unison away from the porch.

Before the spent shells hit the concrete, Celina was hauling Ronni up by her jacket. "Run!" she yelled, hearing the distinctive click of the shotgun snapping back into place.

BOOM!

The sound sent her to her knees, but adrenaline had her back up in the blink of an eye, her legs moving like a runner taking off out of the blocks. More gunshots cracked through the air.

Celina heard the Fairmont's windshield explode.

Crouching with her arms thrown over her head, she ran for the edge of the house where Ronni had disappeared. She rounded the corner at full speed.

And ran smack dab into a wall.

Bouncing back as her feet scrambled for purchase on the late season ice and snow, she grunted when her butt hit the ground. Glancing up, black Magnum boots were in her line of vision. Big boots, laced military tight.

She hadn't run into a wall. She'd run into a man.

A hulk of a man with very broad shoulders. Celina followed the line of his body up to his face. The sun was reflecting off the house and snow and blinding her. She could make out a few things: a black baseball cap with the letters DEA across the front pulled down low on his forehead, a mean-looking semi-automatic gun in his left hand. His scowl made her already-racing heart shift into warp speed.

When did the Terminator arrive in Iowa?

He shifted his gaze down to her and the look of disgust in it made her, if only briefly, entertain the idea of taking her chances with the sawed-off shotgun.

"Get up," he ordered, and the sound of his voice and the impatient tone clicked in her brain, but her ears were ringing from the shotgun blasts and she wasn't sure she'd heard him correctly. He reached down and grabbed her by the knot in her knitted scarf. Hauling her to her feet, he pulled her with him as he backed up against the side of the house. Her legs wobbled and her feet skimmed on the ice. She lost her balance and fell face first into his chest.

His bullet-proof vest was hard, but under it, she sensed a wall of pure, solid muscle. Just like his arms and his legs and everything else hidden under his DEA-approved wardrobe. Celina knew once her adrenaline slowed down, she was going to ache all over, not from falling off the porch but from hitting the Terminator at full speed.

The machine-like DEA agent pulled her closer. "You all right?"

"Cooper?"

There was a spurt of gunfire from the street and then the sound of more glass breaking. Cooper drew her in tighter. She flinched at the sound of the shotgun booming again. It sounded like a small explosion.

But then Cooper pushed her away, pushed her against the house. She mimicked his position, wishing she could have stayed in the protective embrace of his arms and knowing why she couldn't. Ronni was a few feet away, sitting on the ground, back against the house with her gun out. Leaning her head back against the siding, Celina let out a breath. They were both a little shook up, but otherwise unscathed.

The gunfire stopped and total silence descended on the street. No birdsong. No traffic noise. Cooper had his eyes on her, sizing her up from top to bottom. "What the hell did you think you were doing?"

On one hand, she was excited to see him. On the other, the tone of his voice and his general man-handling pissed her off. Celina knew the silence around them meant her FBI counterparts were regrouping, while they tried to figure out their next move.

"I was doing my job," she said to him. She let her eyes run over him in the same sizing-up he'd given her. He looked good. Solid and handsome, and serious as ever. "What are you doing here?"

"Where's your gun? Or do female Feds in Des Moines carry Avon books as weapons these days?"

Celina shut her eyes for a moment. She had fantasized relentlessly about her reunion with Cooper. Never had her fantasy involved the current scene. Ronni cleared her throat and Celina glanced at her. Her partner was watching the exchange and had a questioning look on her face. Celina mouthed Cooper, and Ronni raised her brows and nodded her nice, very nice look

273

of approval.

"Dickie Jagger is mine, Celina."

"Dickie Jagger? Annie's ex-boyfriend?" Celina scanned her memory. Richardson and Jagger had been tight in the late 90's, pulling off more than their fair share of petty crimes together before Jagger had joined a gang in L.A. It was probably Jagger who'd fathered at least one of Annie's kids. "That's who answered the door?"

"You were expecting the Great and Powerful Oz?"

"I was expecting Annie Richardson or her mother."

Cooper grunted. "You can have Richardson, but Jagger's mine."

Turf war coming up. The FBI and the DEA often overlapped each other's jurisdictions with criminals, which is why taskforces like Cooper's SCVC were created. But even though they were supposed to be working together, they were more interested in trying to one-up each other.

Think Big Picture, Dominic Quarters always preached. His Big Picture was now clearer to Celina. Her boss and her boss's boss wanted jurisdiction over everything and they'd do whatever it took to keep all other agencies in the dark.

She wondered what Forester was doing in the Fairmont, and if he was okay. If he was, she was going to give him and Quarters a piece of her mind when this operation was over. They had sacrificed children and two agents in a hurry to beat the DEA to the house.

"I'm sure Chief Forester would like to talk to you about that," she said, when what she really wanted to say was, "Where have you been? Why didn't you call me?"

For months after her transfer, Celina had analyzed Cooper's behavior out loud while on stakeouts with her partner. Ronni had put it in six easy to understand words: he's just not that into you.

Cooper did a quick scan of the area again. "Where is he, your chief?"

"In the car."

His eyes snapped back to hers and the brim of his cap rose with his eyebrows. "The car in the driveway?" He shook his head. "What kind of half-assed FBI unit is this?"

"You should know," Celina retorted, mad all over again. "You sent me here."

"I didn't send you here," Cooper corrected her. "That was Quantico's orders after your face was splashed all over Time magazine as the New Face of the FBI."

"But you kicked me off—"

"This is not the time, Celina."

Before Celina could reply, Cooper cocked his head, picking up noise inside the house. His hand came up to silence her. For several seconds he stilled; a freeze frame of anticipation. Not even a breath escaped his body, only a prevenient energy radiating from every inch of him. A cat preparing to pounce on a mouse.

Another noise inside the house—this time Celina heard it too—voices and the sharp snap of a shotgun locking into position. Cooper pulled a mouthpiece out of his cap and spoke into it. "Assume take down positions," he announced quietly to whoever was listening. "We're going in."

"There are three innocent people in that house. Kids." Celina's voice sounded too loud in her ears. "You can't just bust in there. Someone could get hurt."

Cooper pointed one of his fingers at a spot next to Ronni. "Have a seat, Agent Davenport. This take-down no longer concerns you. You shouldn't be here and if you and your buddies hadn't screwed this up to begin with, we wouldn't have this problem."

"Now, wait a minute," she started, but Cooper grabbed her shoulder, twirled her around and pushed her down hard on her butt. She gasped from the impact and his incivility.

"Everybody move on my count," he said into his radio.

Walking to the corner of the house, he locked his gun into

firing position under his arm. "One, two, three." His voice rose. "Go! Go! Go!"

And then he was gone.

Celina looked at Ronni, whose eyes were still on the spot where Cooper had disappeared. "So that's The Beast, huh?" A silly grin split her face. "That gun powder and Wheaties diet is working for him."

"Yeah," Celina huffed, sarcasm blowing out with her breath, "and he definitely wants me. Did you notice how he was practically falling all over himself to see if I was okay?" She pushed herself off the ground to follow him. "Asshole."

ABOUT THE AUTHOR

USA TODAY Bestselling Author Misty Evans has published nearly forty novels and writes romantic suspense, urban fantasy, and paranormal romance. She got her start writing in 4th grade when she won second place in a school writing contest with an essay about her dad. Since then, she's written nonfiction magazine articles, started her own coaching business, become a yoga teacher, and raised twin boys on top of enjoying her fiction career.

Misty likes her coffee black, her conspiracy stories juicy, and her supernatural characters dressed in couture. When not reading or writing, she enjoys music, movies, and hanging out with her husband, twin sons, and two spoiled puppies. A registered yoga teacher, she shares her love of chakra yoga and energy healing, but still hasn't mastered levitating.

Learn more and sign up for her newsletter at
www.readmistyevans.com.